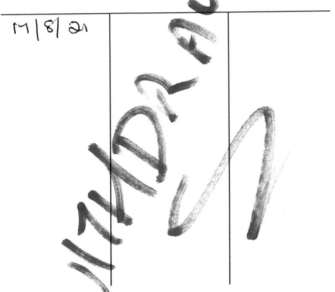

By Peter May

FICTION

The Lewis Trilogy

The Blackhouse
The Lewis Man
The Chessmen

The **China** Thrillers

The Firemaker
The Fourth Sacrifice
The Killing Room
Snakehead
The Runner
Chinese Whispers
The Ghost Marriage: A China Novella

The Enzo Files

Extraordinary People
The Critic
Blacklight Blue
Freeze Frame
Blowback
Cast Iron

Stand-alone Novels

The Man With No Face
Entry Island
Runaway
Coffin Road
I'll Keep You Safe
The Noble Path
A Silent Death

NON-FICTION

Hebrides (with David Wilson)

PETER MAY

LOCKDOWN

riverrun

First published in Great Britain in 2020 by

riverrun

an imprint of

Quercus Editions Ltd
Carmelite House
50 Victoria Embankment
London EC4Y 0DZ

An Hachette UK company

A CIP catalogue record for this book is available
from the British Library.

PB ISBN 978 1 52941 169 0
EBOOK ISBN 978 1 52941 168 3

14

Typeset by CC Book Production
Printed and bound in Great Britain by Clays Ltd, Elcograf S.p.A.

Papers used by Quercus are from well-managed forests and other responsible sources.

For Susie

'This is the worst flu virus I have ever seen . . .
there will be no place for any of us to hide.'

Robert Webster
Virologist
St. Jude Children's Research Hospital
Memphis, Tennessee, USA

FOREWORD

In 2005 when I was finding it impossible to secure a publisher for either *The Blackhouse* or my first Enzo book, *Extraordinary People*, I started researching a crime novel set against the backdrop of a bird flu pandemic.

Bird flu, or H5N1, was being predicted by scientists at the time as the likely next flu pandemic. In 1918, the Spanish Flu had killed anywhere between twenty and fifty million people worldwide, and bird flu – with a mortality rate of sixty per cent or higher – was being forecast to exceed that by a wide margin.

Having done a considerable amount of research into the Spanish Flu for *Snakehead*, one of my China Thrillers, it was a topic in which I was already well versed. But none of that prepared me for what my research on H5N1 would turn up, and the horrors that a bird flu pandemic could unleash on the world.

I began looking into the chaos it would inflict, and how society as we know it could rapidly start to disintegrate. I chose London as my setting, the epicentre of the pandemic, and a city in total lockdown. Against this background, the rendered bones of a murdered child are uncovered on a building site where workmen are feverishly constructing an emergency hospital. My detective, Jack MacNeil, is told to investigate, even as his own family is touched by the virus.

During a six-week spell of burning the midnight oil I wrote *Lockdown*. It was never published. British editors at the time thought my portrayal of London under siege by the invisible enemy of H5N1 was unrealistic and could never happen – in spite of the fact that all my research showed that, really, it could. Then an American publisher bought the Enzo series, and my China Thrillers were published for the first time in the States. My focus shifted to the other side of the Atlantic, and *Lockdown* was consigned to a folder in my Dropbox, where it has remained. Until now.

As I write this, I am hunkered down at home in France, forbidden to leave my house except in exceptional circumstances. A new coronavirus, Covid-19, is ravaging the world, and society as we know it is rapidly disintegrating. Even with its mortality rate being just a fraction of bird flu, politicians are having to fight to control the chaos and panic that Covid-19 is spreading worldwide. The parallels with *Lockdown* are terrifying. So this seemed like the moment to open up that dusty Dropbox folder and dig out that old manuscript to share with my readers – if only to make us all realise just how much worse things could actually be.

Peter May
France 2020

PROLOGUE

Her scream echoes through the dark, squeezed through a throat constricted by fear. It quivers with the terror she feels, and would make the hairs stand up on the arms and shoulders and neck of any caring mortal. But the thick walls of this old house wrap themselves around the horror of the night, to ensure that the only ears to hear her are deaf to her plight.

He curses and hisses and spits in the dark, angry and frustrated. She can hear him on the stairs, and knows that he means her harm. The man she has known and trusted, even loved. She is drowning in her own incomprehension. How is it possible? She remembers the cool touch of his hand on her fevered brow during those long, tortured days of sickness. The pity in his eyes. Eyes which burn now with anger and malice.

She holds her breath. He has gone up another flight. He thinks she is on the top floor, and she slips from the study and sees his shadow on the stairs as he heads up to the attic rooms. And she turns and hurries down, small feet padding on thick carpet, to the light that falls through stained glass windows on to the floor of the hall. Desperate fingers grasp and pull the handle. But the door is locked. There is no way out.

She freezes as she hears him bellow at the top of the house. He knows he has missed her. For a moment she hesitates. The steps to the cellar lead from the bathroom below the staircase. But she understands that if she goes down there she will be trapped. There is only the old coal chute leading up to the alley between the houses, and tiny though she is, she is not small enough to squeeze through the gap.

The house shakes with his footsteps on the stairs and she turns in panic only to find herself confronted by a little girl. A ghost in a white nightshirt, short-cropped black hair, almond eyes wide and black, face etched in chalk. The sight of the child sends fear spiking through her like the stabbing blades of the knives that await her, before she realises she is recoiling from her own reflection. Unrecognisable, distorted by fear.

'Choy!' she hears him bellow in the stairwell, and remembers suddenly the woman who had first shown them around the house all those months ago. The false panel in the wall of the big dining room at the front. A room they have never used. A room which has

simmered always in a sweltering darkness, daylight and lamplight shining in turns through the cracks around the edges of the blinds. The estate agent had shifted a small table to remove the panel and reveal the door behind it. An old, white-painted door with a round handle which she had opened into the darkness beyond. The damp, cold, fusty darkness of a tiny brick room where a family of six had cowered in the blackout to hide from the bombs.

Choy had no idea what the lady had meant by 'the Blitz', but she had said that when the German bombers had finished over London they swung south again, and dropped their unused cargo on this hapless borough. And when the sirens went, people scurried like rats into their brick rat-traps to listen and wait and pray in the dark. Choy hears him scream her name again, and like the sirens of more than half a century before, it sends her scurrying for the front room.

Quickly she slides the table aside and fumbles to release the catches on the dark blue panel. It is heavy, and her tiny hands struggle to pry it loose. She can hear him on the first landing, then his footfall in the master bedroom above. She leans the panel to one side and pushes the door. It opens into blackness, and the cold, damp air wraps itself around her. She steps inside, and drags the panel back into place. She is unable to fasten it from the inside and can only pray that he will not see that. She shuts the door, and all light is extinguished. She hunkers down and wraps her arms around herself for warmth. It is so cold in here, so dark, so final.

There is no way out. She cannot think how six people could squeeze themselves into this space. It is beyond her wildest imagination to know how it must have felt to hear the bombs falling all around and wonder if you might be next. But she needs no imagination to picture the man she hears now on the stairs, or the light catching the blade she knows he carries. The orphanage in Guangdong is a distant memory, the child she had been, another person in another life. So much has changed in only six months, yet still it has seemed an eternity, and that other life just the shadow of a dream.

Her breathing is shallow and rapid, and seems inordinately loud. But above it she can hear him in the front hall. Heavy footsteps on parquet flooring. The anger in his voice as he calls her name again. And then silence. A silence which stretches from moments to what seems like hours. She holds her breath now, for as long as she can, for she is sure he must hear it. Still the silence. And then she gasps as she hears the scraping of the panel on the other side of the door. Her heart beats so hard it feels like someone is punching her chest.

The handle turns, and she presses herself back against the wall as slowly the door opens. He is silhouetted against the light from the hall in the doorway behind him. She can see her own breath misting in the cold air, caught by the same light. He crouches slowly and reaches a hand towards her. She cannot see his face, but she can hear him smile.

'Come to Daddy,' he says softly.

CHAPTER ONE

I.

The Friends of Archbishop's Park – those who were still alive – were spitting blood. Those who were not, were certain to be turning in their graves. Years of careful planning, aimed at preserving this tiny patch of green and pleasant land for the people of Lambeth, had been brushed aside by a single emergency Act of Parliament. A flag was hanging limply in the dark above the crenellated turrets of the palace. The Archbishop was in residence. But since the bulldozers had started up at five, after only six short hours of silence, it seemed unlikely that he was still asleep. Neither did it seem likely that those of his predecessors who had gifted the park to the borough were resting in anything like peace.

Arc lights illuminated the site. Caterpillar tracks had churned and macerated the earth where once children had played, the echo of their tiny voices drowned out now by the roar of the machines. The railings around the football pitch and basketball court had been ripped up and cast aside. The mangled remains of swings and climbing frames were piled up against the derelict buildings on the west side of the park awaiting removal. The old toilet block, destined to have become a café, had been demolished. Time was of the essence. Hundreds of men had been assigned to this task. Shifts were eighteen hours. No one complained. The money was good, although there was nowhere to spend it.

They moved around under the lights without speaking. Figures in orange overalls and hard hats, and white masks. Each one kept his own counsel – and his distance from the others. Cigarettes were smoked through the fine fibres of the masks, leaving round, nicotine-stained patches, and a brazier was kept burning for the cigarette ends. Infection was too easily spread.

Yesterday they had dug the holes for the foundations. Today, the mixer lorries were arriving in fleets to fill them with concrete. A giant crane was already on site, ready to hoist and swing steel girders into place. A delegation from the emergency committee had taken the short walk from

Westminster the previous afternoon to watch with hope, and fear, the vandalism they had sanctioned in desperation. White cotton masked their faces, but could not hide the anxiety in their eyes. They, too, had watched in silence.

Now a voice rose above the churning of cement and the growl of the diggers. A single figure raising his hand in the dark, calling for a halt. He was a tall man, lean and fit, perching on the edge of a ten-foot crater in the north-west corner. The concrete chute swung wide and shuddered to a halt. It was only moments away from spewing its thick grey sludge into the earth. The man crouched on the edge of the hole and peered into its darkness. 'There's something in there,' he shouted, and the foreman strode angrily through the mud towards him.

'We've got no time for this. Come on!' He waved a thickly gloved hand towards the man whose levers controlled the concrete. 'Move it!'

'No, wait.' The tall man swung himself over the edge and dropped into the hole, disappearing from view.

The foreman raised his eyes to the heavens. 'God save us. Get a light over here.'

A group of men crowded around the lip of the hole as a tripod rattled and a light was tilted downwards. The tall man was crouched over something small and dark. He looked up at the faces peering down at him and shaded his eyes against the glare of the light. 'It's a fucking holdall,' he said. 'A leather fucking holdall. Some bastard thinks we dug this hole just so's he'd have somewhere to dump his crap.'

'Come on, get out of there,' the foreman shouted. 'We can't afford any delays.'

'What's in it?' someone else called.

The tall man dragged a sleeve across his forehead and removed a glove to unzip the bag. They all leaned closer to try to see for themselves. And then he jumped back, as if he had touched live electric wires. 'Jesus!'

'What is it?'

They could see something white, something catching the light. The tall man looked up. He was panting, short, shallow breaths, and all colour was washed from a face already pale from lack of sleep. 'Jesus Christ!'

'What the hell is it?' The foreman was losing patience.

Carefully the man in the hole leaned over the bag again. 'It's bones,' he said in a hushed voice which was, nonetheless, audible to them all. 'Human bones.'

'How do you know they're human?' The question came from one of the others. His voice seemed somehow shockingly loud.

'Because there's a fucking skull looking up at me.' The tall man turned his own skull upwards, and his skin seemed to be stretched very tightly across it. 'But it's small. Too small for an adult. It's got to be a kid.'

II.

MacNeil was somewhere far away. Somewhere he shouldn't have been. Somewhere warm and comfortable and safe. But there was a strange nagging at the back of his mind, an uncomfortable sense of something forgotten, something missed. And then he remembered, with a sickening start, that he hadn't been to work for months. How could he have forgotten? But he'd done it before, he knew. He had this vague recollection. Oh, Jesus, how was he going to explain it? How could he tell them where he'd been, or why? Oh, God. He felt sick.

He heard the phone ringing and knew it was them. He didn't want to answer it. What could he say? They'd been paying him all this time, and he hadn't even bothered to show up. Others must have had to cover for him. To fill in his shifts. They would be angry, accusing. And still the phone rang, and still he didn't want to answer it. 'Shut up!' he shouted at the phone. It ignored him, each ring a stab to his heart. It was going to carry on stabbing him until he picked it up. Sweat broke out all across his forehead. Something was sticking to him. And the more he tried to free himself the more it stuck. He turned and pulled and kicked and woke up gasping, staring at the ceiling with wide, frightened eyes, his short, cropped hair damp on the pillow beneath his head. The figures 06:57 stretched in digital fragments towards the light rose. It was the only thing he'd taken with him from the house. A gift from Sean. An alarm clock that projected infrared figures on to the ceiling. No need to turn your head to look at the clock during all those insomniac hours. There was always that big clock in the sky to remind you how slowly time could pass.

Of course, he knew that it wasn't really Sean who'd bought it. Martha knew how he liked his gadgets. But it was Sean who'd had the pleasure of giving it to him. The innocent pleasure that only a child seems to derive from the act of giving, as real as the joy of receiving.

MacNeil disentangled himself from his sweat-soaked bed sheets and swung his legs over the edge of the bed. Cold air embraced him. Wake up! The phone was still ringing. And, like in his dream, he knew that it was not going to go away. He reached for the bedside cabinet and lifted the receiver. His lips stuck to his teeth. 'Yeah?'

'I hope you're sober, MacNeil.'

MacNeil unstuck his tongue from the roof of his mouth, and smelled stale whisky on his own breath. He rubbed grit and matter from his eyes. 'I'm not on for another twelve hours.'

'You're on now, boy. Double shift. I figured since it's your last day you could hack it. I'm another two men down.'

'Shit.'

'Shit's right. Someone's dumped in our backyard and I've got no one else to send.'

MacNeil tipped his head back and looked blearily at the great clock in the sky. He had no idea how else he would have filled the next twelve hours anyway. He could never sleep when it was light. 'What's the deal?'

'Bones. Bunch of workmen on the site at Archbishop's Park found them at the bottom of a hole.'

'Sounds like they need an archaeologist, not a cop.'

'They were in a leather holdall, and they weren't there yesterday.'

'Ah.'

'Better go straight down. The ministry's shouting blue fucking murder because they've had to stop work. Wrap it up fast, eh? I don't need this shit.'

MacNeil winced as the phone crackled in his ear. Laing had hung up.

In the bathroom across the landing, MacNeil stared back at his vacant reflection as he brushed his teeth. Other people's brushes crowded together in a cloudy tooth mug. He kept all his things in his room, and touched nothing in the bathroom. He even sprayed and washed the taps before touching them. He needed a shave. And a few more hours of sleep might have helped ameliorate the penumbrous shadows beneath his eyes. Nothing, however, was going to undo the damage of the last few months. The mask that stress had etched on a face not yet forty. It was not an image he cared to dwell on.

He scraped his razor across dark stubble and heard someone stirring in the room next door. The car salesman. When MacNeil had first taken a room here, the landlord, who still lived on the ground floor, had taken him through a roll-call of his fellow inmates. A divorced doctor, barred from practice, who could usually rustle up a medication for most ills. A handy person to have around the house, especially these days. The car salesman. Gay, the landlord thought, but not ready to accept it. There were two officials of the railworkers' union, only it wasn't called that any more and he couldn't remember what they called it now.

One was from Manchester, another from Leeds, and they were serving their time on the union's executive committee in London. The union had a long-standing arrangement in Baalbec Road. There was only one woman in the house. She smelled a bit, and looked like death, and the landlord was sure she was on drugs. But she paid like clockwork, so who was he to judge her.

It was a strange collection of misplaced humanity, living on the edge of society, in a kind of twilight zone where you neither lived nor died. Just existed. When he had first moved in – was it really only five months ago? – MacNeil had felt like an outsider. Someone looking in. An observer. He didn't belong, and he wouldn't be staying. But they must all have thought that once. And now, like them, he couldn't see a way out. He was no longer on the outside looking in, but on the inside looking out.

He had chosen this area because he felt it was somewhere he could bring Sean. It was no slum. There existed here, still, a sense of faded gentility. Highbury Field was at the end of the road. Somewhere he and Sean could kick a ball, walk a dog – if they'd had one. Some of the street names, too, had a ring of home about them. Aberdeen, Kelvin, Seaforth, Fergus. There was something familiar, and comforting, in the echoes of a Scotland he had left long ago. There was a swimming pool just up from Highbury Corner. The landlord told him it had once been open to the elements. But a less hardy generation had built walls around it and put a roof on top. Somewhere else he and Sean could spend – what was it they called it? – quality time. And MacNeil figured he would get them season tickets to go and see the Gunners at the Emirates Stadium.

But Sean's mother had refused to let him cross the city to Islington. It was too dangerous, she said. Maybe when the emergency was over.

MacNeil pulled on his coat and turned up the collar. His suit needed pressing, and his white shirt was fraying just a little around the top of the collar. The top button was missing, and his tie was tied tight to hide it. He pulled on his gloves and hurried down the stairs to the narrow hallway at the bottom. There was a time, even just a month ago, when the landlord would have poked his head around the door to say good morning. But now none of them spoke. They were all too afraid.

III.

As he pulled the door shut, he could hear his phone ringing at the top of the house. He didn't want to speak to Laing again, and so he quickly fished his mobile from his pocket and turned it off.

The air in his car was icy cold as he slipped behind the wheel. There had been no frost, but condensation clouded the windscreen. He set the blowers going and turned down Calabria Road. The radio was playing a selection of hits from last year. No one had released anything new in the last two months. The music segued from one song to another, and MacNeil was glad of the absence of the mindless, prattling DJs who used to fill the early morning airwaves. He had missed the seven-thirty newscast.

As always, his route into the city was determined by the army checkpoints. Certain areas were simply off-limits, even to him. There were demarcation lines that would require special permission to cross. He drove south to Pentonville, turning west along Pentonville Road into Euston Road. It was nearly seven forty-five, and the air was suffused with a grey light that forced its way through low pewtery cloud that seemed to graze the tops of distant

15

skyscrapers. In another life, taxis and buses and commuter traffic would have choked the city's arteries, like cholesterol. MacNeil still could not get used to the empty streets. There was a chilling quiet in this early morning light. He passed the occasional troop carrier, soldiers with gas masks and goggles staring from beneath khaki canvas covers, like faceless troopers from a Star Wars movie, nursing rifles they had been forced all too frequently to use.

Now that there was daylight, there was a limited traffic of private and commercial vehicles with the requisite clearance to move around designated areas of the city, tracked by cameras and satellite. Controls were most stringent around the city centre, where much of the looting had taken place. The government had used the old congestion charging infrastructure to monitor and control all vehicles moving in and out of the area. MacNeil cruised along its northern limit, passing a deserted Euston Station, before turning south into Tottenham Court Road, where a camera recorded his number plate and fed it directly into the central computer. Without clearance he could expect to be stopped within minutes.

The city's shopping streets were like a battlefield. Those shops which hadn't already had their windows smashed had boarded them up. The burned-out carcasses of stolen vehicles smouldered at the roadside, the debris and detritus of a once civilised society scattered across ruined streets. The wreckage of another night of violence. The Dominion Theatre, opposite the Tottenham Court Road Underground station, was a blackened, burned-out shell. Every time it rained, the air still filled up with the charred smell from *The Death of a Salesman* – the last piece to be performed there. McDonald's too, in Oxford Street, had been gutted. Flame-grilled burgers overcooked. The Harmony Sex Shop had been broken into so many times, the owners no longer bothered to board it up, and a scantily clad siren in black leather pouted defiantly at MacNeil as he drove past.

Further south, *The MouseTrap* had finally ended its record-breaking run, and St. Martin's Theatre, with all its neon lights smashed and ripped from the walls, looked sad and neglected.

He was stopped at an army checkpoint at Cambridge Circus. He should have been used to it by now, but he could never feel comfortable with half a dozen semi-automatic rifles pointed at his head. A sullen soldier glowered at him from behind his mask, keeping his distance and reaching for his papers with latex-gloved hands. He handed them back quickly, anxious to be rid of them, as if somehow they might be contaminated – which well they might.

MacNeil drove on down Charing Cross Road, through Trafalgar Square and into Whitehall. There was more activity here, a Civil Service still functioning after a fashion, government seeking to deal with a disintegrating society. Men and women with masks leaving and entering the corridors of power with the same sense of bleak despair that gripped most of those who lived in the capital.

As he neared the river, he saw black smoke rising into the heavy morning sky from the four chimneys of the old Battersea Power Station. A more potent symbol of human helplessness in the face of an unforgiving Nature he could not imagine. How many dead was it now? Five hundred thousand? Six? More? No one believed the figures anyhow. There was no way to verify them. But even at their most optimistic, those the government put out were barely conceivable.

The eight o'clock news carried the story which had been running all night. But it was MacNeil's first time hearing it, and it hit him hard. Shortly after midnight, doctors at St. Thomas' Hospital had announced the death of the Prime Minister. Two of his children were already dead, and his wife was still critically ill. It had been no secret that his condition was serious. But if the most powerful person in the country could be taken so easily, what chance did the rest of them have?

In sonorous tones, the newsreader reported that there was now expected to be a power struggle between the Deputy Prime Minister and the Chancellor of the Exchequer for control of the party. The Deputy Prime Minister, a toad of a man whom MacNeil had never liked, had the upper hand, since he would automatically fill the Prime Minister's shoes – at least temporarily. Although MacNeil could not understand why anyone would want to, given the circumstances. The allure of power, it seemed, was irresistible to some. Quietly MacNeil hoped that the Chancellor would win the power struggle. The present incumbent of number 11 Downing Street was, it seemed to him, eminently more sensible, a man of intelligence and conscience.

As he drove across Westminster Bridge, through yet another army checkpoint, he glanced west to see the eleven-storey facade of St. Thomas' Hospital rising up from the South Bank of the Thames. Somewhere, behind the concrete and glass, the man who had once run the country lay dead. Cold and powerless, infected by his own children. Beyond, the three remaining original wings of the hospital,

Friday, Saturday and Sunday, were filled, he knew, with yet more stricken patients. Perhaps if the four other wings had not been destroyed by the Germans during the Blitz, it would not have been necessary to construct emergency overspill in the park across the road.

CHAPTER TWO

I.

MacNeil pulled his Ford Focus into the bus stop opposite the accident and emergency department in Lambeth Palace Road, confident in the knowledge that none of the four buses which used to traverse this route would be inconvenienced.

The gates and railings at the entrance to Archbishop's Park had been torn down to create access for the heavy equipment brought in by the contractors. He recognised the unmarked vans of the Scenes of Crime officers from the FSS laboratories, although they might have been quicker on foot, since the lab was just a short walk away along a narrow path at the south end of the park.

The Forensic Science Service had been forced to draw its resources into one central facility following the lockdown of the Capital, and had established the former Metropolitan Police Forensic Science laboratory in Lambeth Road as the centre for most of the medical and scientific services required by the police. Right now, the officers they had sent were standing around waiting for MacNeil.

MacNeil surveyed the wreck of the park, monstrous machinery standing idle amongst the ripped-up remains of what had once been a tiny oasis of green in a sea of concrete and glass. Hundreds of workers in their distinctive orange jumpsuits stood around in groups, talking and smoking. In the misty early morning light, a group of ghostly figures in white Tyvek suits and masks clustered around a hole in the ground which should by now have been filled with cement. A man in a suit, wearing a calf-length camel coat and a white hard hat, picked his way delicately through the mud as MacNeil approached. He wore a standard-issue white cotton mask, as did MacNeil, but stopped well short of him. 'DI MacNeil?'

MacNeil kept his distance and eyed him cautiously. 'Aye. Who's asking?'

'Derek James. I'm from the office of the Deputy Prime Minister. You'll understand if I don't shake your hand.'

'What do you want?' MacNeil had never been slow in getting to the point.

'I want,' said James, with a certain edge, 'to get this site back to work.'

'Then the sooner we stop talking about it, the sooner I'll do what I have to do and get out of your hair.' MacNeil walked past him towards the gathering of ghosts.

James went after him, still concerned to keep his shoes mud-free. 'I don't think you understand, Mr MacNeil. This work is being carried out under an emergency decree of Parliament. Millions of pounds are being poured into this project. There is a strict timetable. A delay could cost lives.'

'Someone's already dead, Mr James.'

'Which means they're beyond help. Others are not.'

MacNeil stopped in his tracks and turned to face the man from the ministry who immediately recoiled, as if afraid MacNeil might breathe on him. 'Look. Everyone in this country's entitled to justice. Alive or dead. That's my job. To see that justice is done. And when I've done it, you can do yours. Until then, stay out of my face.' He turned again and trudged through the mud to the men in Tyvek. 'What's the score here?'

'Bag of bones, Jack,' one of them said, his voice muffled by his mask. 'They only excavated yesterday. Someone must have dumped it overnight.' He glanced around the hundreds of faces that watched them from a distance. 'And these guys want us out of here toot sweet.'

'All in good time.'

Another of the Tyvek suits handed MacNeil a pair of plastic shoe covers. 'Here, you better put these on, mate.'

MacNeil pulled on the plastic and peered into the hole. There was a figure crouched in the bottom of it. 'Who's down there?'

'Your old pal.'

MacNeil rolled his eyes. 'Aw, shit,' he said under his breath. 'Tom Bennet!'

The forensics man grinned behind his mask, stretching it tight across his face.

MacNeil snapped on latex gloves and reached out a hand. 'Help me down.'

It was an expensive sports holdall with a PUMA logo on the side. Tom was holding it open with gloved hands and looked up as MacNeil dropped down beside him. 'Don't come too close to me,' he said. 'You never know what you might catch.'

MacNeil ignored him. 'What's in it?' he asked.

'The bones of a child.'

MacNeil leaned over to peer in. The bones looked very

white, as if they'd been left out in the sun, a sad collection of the bits and pieces of what had once been a human being. He recoiled from a stink like meat left in the refrigerator a month past its sell-by. 'What the hell's that smell?'

'The bones.' A crinkle around the young pathologist's eyes betrayed his amusement at MacNeil's disgust.

'I didn't know bones smelled.'

'Oh, yeah. Two, even three months after death.'

'So this kid was alive quite recently?'

'Very recently, I'd say, from how much they stink.'

'So what's happened to the flesh?'

'Someone's stripped it off the bones. Using some pretty sharp cutting gear.' Tom lifted out a long shanked bone, laying it delicately across both hands. 'The femur. Thigh bone to you. You can see the scores left in the bone by the knife, or whatever it was he used. They're quite deep, and broad, so it was a heavy instrument.'

MacNeil looked at the cuts and grooves in the bone, most running parallel, and cut in at an angle, as if from a repeated sideways chopping motion. 'Not an expert, then?'

'I don't know who I'd describe as an expert in cutting flesh from bone, but it's a pretty crude job.' Tom ran a long, delicate finger around the bulb of the joint. 'You can see the hash they've made of the disarticulation, and these dried-out remnants of tissue and ligament that they couldn't get off.'

MacNeil looked into the bag again and carefully lifted out what looked like the curve of a small rib. He cocked his head and looked at it curiously, running his fingers along the smooth white bow of it. 'How did they manage to get the bones so clean?'

Tom shrugged. 'Washed them, likely. I've done it myself from time to time, when I've wanted to clean up a skull. Boiled it up with a little bleach and laundry detergent.'

'Wouldn't that kill the smell?'

Tom crinkled with amusement again. 'The marrow's still going to rot, whether you've cooked it or not.'

MacNeil slipped the rib back into the bag and stood. He peered up at the faces leaning over to try to catch their conversation, then looked down at Tom. 'Can you tell what sex?'

'Not right now. But I'd put the age at somewhere between nine and eleven.'

MacNeil nodded thoughtfully, and wondered how you performed an autopsy on a disarticulated skeleton.

Almost as if he'd read his thoughts, Tom stood up beside him and said, 'Naturally, I can't do any kind of real autopsy. All I can do is lay out the bones and look for clues.' A stray strand of blond hair was caught in the elastic of his plastic shower cap, and his corn-blue eyes held MacNeil in a gaze so direct that the older man had to look away. 'Of course,' he said, 'I'm not much of an expert on what goes where. I can sort out the ribs, but not in the correct order. I can separate the finger bones, but not necessarily which goes to which hand. We really need an anthropologist for that.'

MacNeil forced himself to meet the pathologist's eye. 'Is that a problem?'

'She's sick.'

'Oh.'

'But I can make a general assessment, spot any major bone injuries and missing parts, recover tissue from the marrow and order up some toxicology.' He paused. 'I'd suggest we get Amy in. She's good with skulls, and she's done a lot of work on human ID.'

MacNeil felt his heart skip a beat at the mention of her name, and he wondered if it showed in his face. A slight blush, perhaps. He sensed Tom watching him closely, as if looking for some sign, but if he was it did not betray itself in his eyes. 'Sure, if that's what you think,' MacNeil said. He turned and reached up a hand to be helped out.

'Careful,' Tom said quickly. 'Some people think it's dangerous to turn their back on me.'

MacNeil turned his head slowly to look at him. It was a dark, dangerous look that needed no words.

Tom smiled. 'You're so butch.'

Silence hung over the site, like a low-lying fog. It was extraordinary, really, here in the very heart of the Capital. No traffic noise, no voices raised in casual communication or amusement, no overhead roar of jet engines as planes circled towards Gatwick or Heathrow. Just the plaintive cries of the seagulls which had flown up the estuary to escape the stormy weather in the North Sea, fragments of white wheeling overhead, for all the world like vultures waiting for death.

Death had already come, but there was nothing left on the bones to pick.

MacNeil was aware of all the faces watching him. The man from the ministry stood off, arms folded across his chest. 'Well?'

'I want everyone off the site,' MacNeil said. 'We're going to seal it off and make a search.'

The man from the ministry tilted his head to one side. Only his eyes betrayed his anger. 'There'll be trouble,' he said.

'There'll be trouble if anyone doesn't do as they're told.' MacNeil raised his voice so that everyone on the site could hear him. 'This is a murder scene.'

II.

'What the fuck did you say to him?'

'I told him it was a murder scene and we were going to search the site.'

Laing looked at him sceptically. 'Well, whatever you said, he's pretty pissed off. You any idea what kind of shite's coming down on me right now?'

'I can imagine.'

'Can you?' Laing glanced at his watch, then picked up the remote to turn on the TV on the filing cabinet. 'You know, when I came down to the Met from Glasgow thirty years ago, I thought I'd left cowboys like you behind. People are better mannered down here, know what I mean?'

'Yeah, they threaten you more politely.'

Laing glared at him. 'I never imagined for a minute I'd be haunted by some Highland hard case just as I'm looking forward to retirement.' He turned up the sound on the television. They were reporting again on the death of the Prime Minister, and Laing clearly wanted to hear it.

MacNeil glanced at the framed photograph of the DCI and his wife which sat on the bookcase behind his desk. They were an odd couple. Laing came from the old school of working-class Glasgow cop. He swore, he made crude jokes, he was physically aggressive. He wore Brylcreem in his hair, and slapped Old Spice freely on to shiny, shaved, drink-veined cheeks. You smelled him before you saw him. His wife, on the other hand, was a genteel lady, a doctor's daughter from Chelsea who liked opera and theatre and lectured in English and drama at the Queen Mary University of London. They lived somewhere out west, in a large, terraced town house. Laing was a different man in her company. MacNeil had no idea what she saw in him, but whatever it was, she brought out the best in him. Some people did that to you. MacNeil reflected that while Martha might not have brought out the worst in him, she certainly hadn't brought out the best. He envied Laing his relationship.

He glanced through the open door into the detectives' room. There were only a couple of DCs on duty, and a handful of uniform and administrative staff. The pandemic had taken its toll here, too.

Something on the news caught his attention, and he

turned to see a line-up of dark-suited men sitting at a table groaning with microphones. They all wore masks, as did the journalists firing the questions. Centre table was a man whose face had become familiar during these last few months, even behind the mask. He had large, dark eyes, beneath thick black eyebrows that contrasted with blond, crew-cut hair, and wore distinctive silver-rimmed oval spectacles. He had a creamy, smooth voice which spoke English with just the hint of a foreign accent whose origin was impossible to define. His name was Roger Blume, and he was the doctor in charge of Stein-Francks' FluKill Pandemic Task Force.

'Fucking leeches!' Laing's expletive echoed MacNeil's unspoken thought. 'I see their share price is up again.'

Stein-Francks was the French-based pharmaceutical company whose antivirus drug, FluKill, had been singled out by the World Health Organisation during the run-up to the pandemic as the remedy most likely to be effective against the bird flu, should it ever become transmissible from human to human. The WHO had also warned that such an eventuality was inevitable. As a result, those countries around the world who could afford it had placed more than three-and-a-half billion euros' worth of orders. Britain alone had bought nearly fifteen million courses of the drug to treat a quarter of the population. Health and law enforcement workers were to be the first in line to receive it. Not that it was a cure. The best that could be hoped for was an amelioration of symptoms, and a shortening of the course of the flu, making survival more likely. And with a mortality rate of nearly eighty per cent, anything that could improve your odds was in huge demand.

The Stein-Francks press conference was to announce a further stepping up of FluKill production to meet the increased requirements. A cynical journalist amongst the press pack asked Dr Blume if the increase in production might have anything to do with the announcement by several developing countries that they intended to produce their own generic form of the drug. Blume easily shrugged off the clear implication that his company was only interested in maintaining its monopoly.

'We have a brand-new facility in France, custom-made to produce FluKill,' he said. 'It comes on-line next week. It has been a long time in the planning. So this is no rush move to fight off the competition. We can produce the drug faster and more efficiently than anyone else. And we have all the quality controls in place to ensure its effectiveness.'

'Your vaccine didn't prove very effective.' The journalist's tone reflected the general feeling of resentment around the country that anyone should profit from the disaster.

'A matter of great regret,' said Blume. 'Not for any crass, commercial reason, but because of the lives it might have saved.'

'And why didn't it work?' Another voice fired off its accusation.

'Because we guessed wrong,' Blume said simply. 'Bird flu has been around for a long time, but it was only in 1997 that we confirmed the first human case of it. On that occasion, the virus was transmitted from bird to human. But from that moment on, it was only a matter of time before the bird virus combined with a human flu virus, making it transmissible from human to human. We knew when that happened, the human race would be in big trouble. A pandemic was inevitable, and would almost certainly be worse than the Spanish Flu of 1918. That killed fifty million people. So the race was on to find a way of beating it this time before it began.' He ran a hand back across his bristly skull. 'We, along with many others, tried to create in the laboratory something that would look to the immune system like a humanly transmissible avian flu. And so create a vaccine. That involved mixing and matching genes from the H5N1 bird flu virus with a common human flu virus. For that purpose we chose the H3N2 strain, which has been behind most recent human flu outbreaks.' The doctor shook his head. 'The goal was to substitute the eight genes of each virus, one by one, with the eight genes from the other, to see which combinations would create versions easily spread amongst humans. The trouble was, that with more than two hundred and fifty possible combinations, hitting on the right one was a bit like winning the lottery.'

'But you thought you'd done it.'

'Yes. Because when the real virus actually emerged, we found we had created something almost identical. The trouble was, it was just different enough that the immune system wasn't fooled, and we knew it was going to take anything up to six months to put that right.'

'So has anyone at Stein-Francks come up with a reasonable explanation of why the pandemic started in London rather than Asia?'

'That's not our job,' said Blume smoothly. If he detected the hostility coming from his questioners, he was ignoring it. 'It's something you'll need to ask the Health Protection Agency.' He paused. 'But you don't have to be very smart to figure that it only takes one infected individual from Vietnam, or Thailand, or Cambodia, to fly into London, New York or Paris, and you've sown the seed. In this modern age of air travel, we really do live in a global village. And we've created the perfect incubators for breeding and passing on infection, in the buses and planes and underground trains we travel on. We were a human disaster waiting to happen.'

The newscast cut back to the studio and breaking news of a development in the race to fill the power vacuum left by the death of the PM. But by now Laing had lost interest and turned it off. He swivelled in his chair and looked speculatively at MacNeil. 'You're a fucking idiot, man. Quitting now. You're a good cop . . .' He hesitated. The compliment had been grudging. Something he was loathe to admit. 'You could have been sitting in my seat in a few years.'

'By which time Sean would nearly have finished school.' MacNeil shook his head. 'There's no second chances with kids. You can't turn the clock back on childhood.' He looked beyond Laing, out of the window to Kennington Road below. The shops and restaurants opposite the police station. Trafalgar Lock and Key, Perdoni's Restaurant, Peter's Gents Hair Stylist, the Imperial Tandoori. All more familiar to him than his own son. He'd spent more time in the company of Laing, for God's sake!

Laing said, 'I'll need to ask for your FluKill back before you clock off tomorrow.' MacNeil looked at him. 'I'm sorry,

Jack. You're no longer on the front line. Or at least, you won't be.'

'Fine.'

Laing slapped his palms on his desk. 'You've got two hours to get that site searched before I send the diggers back in.'

CHAPTER THREE

I.

It was a little like a jigsaw puzzle, putting a person back together. Amy sat breathing into the claustrophobic cotton of her mask and smelled the decay rising from the table in front of her. She remembered her first real facial reconstruction. It had been in Manchester. She had travelled up by train and stayed with relatives. The lady had been dead for nearly three months. Her skull had been boiled slowly in water and detergent, with some bleach, and still it stank so much that the FSS had rented her a hotel room to work in. They didn't want Amy stinking up a lab, or someone's office.

The hotel management had been suspicious of all the plain-clothes cops popping in and out, parking unmarked cars out front, visiting the young Chinese woman in room 305. They probably suspected some kind of prostitution. In any event, the chambermaid had complained about the smell, and Amy had been asked to leave.

Tom had laid out a body bag on the table, draped it with a clean sheet and assembled the bones in their rough anatomic position. The hands and feet he had left in small piles. The spine he had divided into its cervical, thoracic and lumber sections, but the pieces were not in their correct order. Neither were the ribs. Amy smiled when she saw the skeleton diagram that he had pinned to the wall. Bones had never been his forte. From day one at med school he had been more interested in the organs, the cardiovascular system, the brain. But something about the human frame had attracted Amy. It was, after all, the structure around which everything else was built. Which was what had led her improbably, in the end, to teeth.

She started carefully rebuilding the hands. The small hands of a child. There were 206 bones in the adult human, more than half of them in the hands and feet. But there were 350 in an infant. Some bones fused as they grew. Amy was uncertain how many bones there would be in this particular child, but she was sure she would spot any that might be missing.

She looked up, along with half a dozen others, as the door swung open and Zoe came in. They all knew she'd been standing out on the front steps even before they smelled the smoke off her.

'Mask!' someone called. She'd forgotten to put it back on.

'Oops, sorry.' She pulled it up over her mouth and nose. 'You know you're just as likely to catch it from touching something an infected person's been touching,' she said. 'As long as no one's sneezing in your face.' She was a post-graduate microbiologist training in forensics at the FSS, and she liked to show off. But the contagious qualities of the flu virus were known to everyone these days. It was why the government had introduced emergency measures to prevent the printing and distribution of newspapers. Paper was a perfect carrier. Newsprint handled by an infected person would pass the disease on to another reader. Once the virus was on your hands, it could pass into your system via food, or even by rubbing your eyes. News was only disseminated now by radio, television and the internet.

Zoe wandered over to Amy's table to look at the skeleton. 'Just a kid, huh?'

'Yes.' Amy was annoyed by the interruption, but held her peace. She could smell the cigarette smoke now. It was better than the stale body odour which had hung around

Zoe in a faint cloud while she was still living with her boyfriend. She had admitted once to searching through the laundry basket for something to wear when her blouse drawer was empty. Apparently, she thought this was an amusing anecdote. For everyone else it just explained the smell. But things had improved since she had moved back in with her parents. Her mother, it seemed, was doing her laundry now.

Zoe said, 'You know, they're gearing up for mass production of a new mask that'll actually sterilise pathogens when an infected person sneezes or coughs. It's got thousands of tiny perforations allowing it to breathe, so that it doesn't blow back into your face. But here's the clever bit – the perforations are medicated with an antiseptic that'll sterilise any emissions passing through. Clever, huh?'

'Very.' Amy was trying to sort through the metatarsals of the right foot.

'Have you any idea how many droplets there are in a sneeze?'

'Millions.'

'Yeah, and every one carrying the virus. Like an infected aerosol. Jesus, aren't you glad they've given us a course of FluKill?'

'Let's just hope we never have to take it.' Amy wanted to

tell her to piss off, but it wasn't in her nature to be rude. Her rescue came unexpectedly.

'Isn't there something you should be doing, Zoe?' Tom threw Zoe one of his supercilious looks as he stepped up behind Amy, and she tutted a little huffily.

'Yes, doctor.' She flounced off across the lab.

Amy smiled at him gratefully. 'Hi.'

He lowered his voice. 'She's a pain in the arse, that one.'

Amy raised an eyebrow. 'You would know.'

He pursed his lips. 'Not that kind of a pain.' He looked at the skeleton. 'How are you getting on with our unknown child?'

'Getting to know her a little better,' Amy said.

'Her?'

'Yes. She's a little girl. But she wouldn't have survived as long as she did if her bones had been in the order you laid them out.'

He grinned lasciviously. 'Much more into the flesh, me.'

Amy completed the jigsaw of the right foot. 'Speaking of which, how *is* Harry?'

Tom raised his eyes to the ceiling and sighed theatrically. 'You know, I spend my life falling for straight guys, and the first gay who fancies me back turns out to be the most promiscuous creature on God's earth. And you know me. A one-man man.'

'What I know,' Amy said with some certainty, 'is that you and Harry are not a match made in heaven.'

'Yes . . . there's always some dick coming between us.'

Amy couldn't resist a smile. Tom had made her laugh from the moment they had met at med school nearly twelve years ago. Oddly enough, their first encounter had been in anatomy, and Tom had made some crude comment about having a boner for the prof. Even though they had gone on to quite different specialities, they had remained friends throughout their training, and beyond. She had no idea how she would have survived those dreadful months following the accident without him. He had been, literally, the best friend a girl could have. And so she put up with all his foibles and moods and let him sleep on the settee in her apartment when he and Harry fell out. Which was regularly.

She waved a hand vaguely towards the next table. 'Could you get me that dental chart over there?'

'Get it yourself, girl.'

She gave him a look, and he tipped his head and cocked an eyebrow at her, and she thought how good-looking he was. And what a waste. That shock of straw yellow hair, and pale blue eyes. It was his way never to pander to her. He had always insisted she do things herself. He wasn't her slave, and she wasn't an invalid. It was his forcing the issue that had made her as independent as she was now. She grabbed the controller on the right armrest and spun the chair around, propelling herself towards the next table to get her chart.

Across the room there was a loud sneeze and all heads turned towards Zoe. Everyone was hypersensitive these days to the slightest sniffle. A sneeze was enough to cause cardiac arrest. Zoe raised a hand of apology and grinned. 'It's okay. Honestly. I'm not coming down with anything. It's my parents' cat. I'm really allergic to it.'

II.

The area between the road and the hole where the bag had been found was divided up into squares. Fine white plastic lines stretched between short stakes, a little like the lines of latitude and longitude on a map. Yellow and black crime scene tape fluttered around the perimeter in a chill breeze blowing down from the direction of the river. A six-man team in Tyvek and bootees and plastic caps moved from square to square, each allocated his own area to search, each tiny item recovered from the mud carefully placed in its own plastic evidence bag.

The workforce stood around in the park in small orange clusters. The cement trucks had gone, and the heavy machinery stood cold and silent, waiting with the rest of them.

The man from the ministry sat in the back of a black BMW parked up on the pavement by the hospital, smoking cigarette after cigarette, the window down, watching them through clouds of escaping smoke. MacNeil could feel his anger from where he sat on an upturned wheely bin next to the old basketball court. The foreman was pacing restlessly next to him. 'It's our bonuses, mate,' he said. 'The only reason we're here, risking life and fucking limb, is 'cos of the money. And that's dependent on meeting the targets.'

'What is the target?' MacNeil turned disinterested eyes towards him.

'Seven days.' The foreman shook his head. 'It was tight before. But now . . .'

MacNeil shrugged. 'What's the point in setting unrealistic targets?'

'Not me that sets them, mate. The Chinese built a whole hospital in a week during the SARS outbreak. So our lot figured, why couldn't we do the same? We're not even building a hospital here. Just an overspill facility. A space they can heat, a space that can take beds. A place for people to die in.'

'And is it really worth the money?'

'Well, we're not making it any other way right now. And they're treating us good, aren't they? A lot of the lads come from outside the M25. And ever since they declared the ring road the outer limit, we knew that if we came inside we wouldn't be allowed out again. It's fucking creepy, you know, like something out of a movie. Seeing all those soldiers with guns on the bridges and flyovers.'

'So where are you staying?'

The foreman chuckled. 'That's part of the deal. All the big tourist hotels are empty. So we get our own rooms, meals cooked for us at all hours. Me and some of the boys are at the Ritz. There's others at the Savoy. And we get to stay there till the emergency's over.' A cloud cast a shadow on his smile and he remembered to glower at MacNeil. 'Assuming we meet our targets, that is.'

In the distance, an ambulance siren pierced the cold January air. Another victim. Another bed required. Every hospital in the city was full, but at least the high mortality rate meant that beds were constantly becoming available.

Illness had reduced staffing by nearly thirty per cent. Health workers were at greatest risk, and suffering the highest casualties. In spite of FluKill. Nobody went to work any more. Only a handful of shops were open for a few hours a day. There was no public transport. The airports had been closed indefinitely. The economy of the capital was in free fall, and the rest of the world was ready to do anything it could to help the city contain its sickness. Primarily by banning all traffic in and out of the UK. It was, of course, only a matter of time before the virus swept the world. But if it could be contained long enough to produce a vaccine . . .

MacNeil sighed and felt the first spots of rain on his face as he turned it up towards the bruised blue and black of the low cloud overhead.

'Jack.'

He turned his head towards a Tyvek figure trudging across tyre tracks cut deep in the mud.

'That's us done.'

MacNeil checked the time. They'd taken less than the allotted two hours. 'Find anything?'

The forensics man held up a clear plastic bag, and MacNeil saw a scrap of something faintly pink in it. 'Might be something. Might be nothing.'

'What is it?'

The officer handed it to him. 'Remains of an Underground ticket. Off-peak, one-day pass. Can't read the date on it, but we might just be able to retrieve something from the magnetic strip.'

MacNeil took the bag and held it up to the light. The printing on the ticket was blurred and smudged by the rain and all but obliterated by mud. One corner of it was torn away. It was nearly eight weeks since they'd closed the Underground. If this was all they had to go on, they weren't going to get very far. He handed it back to the forensics man and jumped down from his wheely bin. He turned to the foreman. 'Go build your hospital.'

III.

Amy ran her hand back over the smooth surface of the skull and felt a peculiar empathy for this little girl. There was no sign of damage. Except for the trauma inflicted by Nature on the maxilla. There was no way to determine cause of death, unless the tissue recovered by Tom revealed poison of some kind. Amy suspected that was unlikely. Why would you poison a child? A tiny, frail-boned creature like this?

She would have been utterly vulnerable to the strength of an adult, defenceless against it.

That someone had killed her was beyond doubt. Why else would they have gone to the trouble of stripping all the flesh from her bones and removing the evidence? And yet, to have gone to all that bother, and then simply dumped the bones on a building site, was strangely careless. But that was for others to worry about. All of Amy's focus and expertise would go into trying to identify her. To bring her back to life in a way that might lead them to her killer.

She looked at the empty eye sockets and knew that once they had held dark, liquid brown eyes. She knew that once this scalp had grown thick, blue-black hair. What length it might have been was impossible now to know. Amy ran her fingers along the high line of the left cheek and down to the jaw, distinguished by its deformity and the disfigured smile which would once have characterised it.

She was aware of Tom stooping down beside her. His face close to hers. 'Don't look now, but here comes the *ape man*.'

Amy raised her eyes and saw MacNeil making his way across the lab. She looked at him dispassionately, and wondered how she might view him if she didn't know him. He was very tall – his most distinguishing feature. But not skinny. He was built in proportion. Which made him a big man. He certainly wasn't conventionally good-looking, but there was extraordinary warmth in his green eyes flecked with orange. He didn't suit his hair cut so short, but there was something distinguished in the touch of grey at either temple. His suit was too tight, and his coat too big, and there was a generally dishevelled air about him. One of his shoelaces was undone, she noticed. And then saw that his shoes were covered in dirt, and that he was leaving a little trail of dried mud in his wake. The *ape man*, Tom called him. Of course, Tom didn't like him because he thought MacNeil was homophobic.

Amy couldn't remember the first time she'd laid eyes on MacNeil, so it was impossible now for her to imagine that first impression. There were still odd little gaps in her memory from before the accident. Little things that frustrated her, sometimes to the point of tears. Though only when she was on her own. Tom would have no truck with self pity. But he stood beside her now, arms folded across his chest, like her guardian protector, jaw thrust towards the approaching MacNeil, almost daring him to be rude to his poor, crippled little friend. After all, it was he who had got her the work here after she had been unable to carry on as before.

MacNeil stopped in front of the table, ignoring him, and

looked at the child's skeleton. Then he looked at Amy and made a vague nod of acknowledgement. 'So what can you tell me?'

'Quite a lot, actually.' Amy focused her attention on the child again. She ran the backs of her fingers across the forehead, almost as if she were still alive. 'She was a poor soul, really.'

'How do you know it's a she?'

'How do I know *she* is a she,' Amy corrected him, as if the child might be offended by being described as *it*. 'There is no single, conclusive factor,' she said. 'Rather, an accumulation of pointers, and a little instinct.'

'Let's leave your instinct out of it,' MacNeil said, 'and stick to the facts.'

Amy was unruffled. 'Okay. The facts. Females generally have smaller, less developed muscle attachments than the male.' She ran a fingertip along one femur. 'You can quite clearly see the ridges here which provided attachments for the muscles and tendons.' She moved up to the pelvic area. 'The female pelvis is constructed to meet the needs of child-bearing and has several features which distinguish it from the male. Notably wider hips.'

MacNeil allowed a tiny smile of recollection to stretch his lips. He remembered his mother describing the girl next door – when contemplating her as a possible future wife for her son – as having good childbearing hips.

Amy glanced up and caught the shadow of his smile. 'Do you find this amusing, DI MacNeil?'

'No, Miss Wu.'

She gave him a long look before returning to the bones on the table. 'Apart from general appearance, a number of measurements can be made of the pelvic bones to help establish sex. Primarily the difference in ratio between the lengths of the pubis and ischium, commonly known as the ischium-pubis index.'

'Of course, you'll be familiar with the ischium-pubis index,' Tom said, an irritating little smile turning up the corners of his mask.

'Of course,' MacNeil said. And to Amy, 'And you took those measurements?'

'I did.'

'And?'

'In themselves, not conclusive. She is just a child, after all, and at her age, sexual characteristics have not yet fully developed. But the index does tend to suggest female rather than male.' She picked up the child's head and cupped it gently in her palms. 'The skull is often a better indicator. For a start, it's smaller than you would expect of a male.

The mastoid processes and orbital ridges are less promi-
nent in the female, and the eye sockets and forehead are
more rounded.' She traced those curvatures to illustrate
her point. Then she looked MacNeil square in the eye. 'I'm
around ninety-five per cent certain this is a female.'

'And the other five per cent?'

'Instinct. But then, you told me to leave that out of the
equation.'

MacNeil smiled. 'So I did. What else can you tell me?'

'I can tell you that this child probably came from one of
the poorer developing countries, and that she had two very
distinctive visual characteristics.'

MacNeil was taken aback. 'How the hell can you tell all
that from a bunch of bones?'

'Because she's good at what she does, Mr MacNeil,' Tom
said, taking obvious pride in her expertise. 'Amy was one
of the best forensic odontologists in London before . . .' He'd
started down the road before he could stop himself, and
his hesitation only drew attention to itself. 'Before the accident,' he added quickly. 'You don't ever lose those skills.'

Amy blushed and kept her focus on the skull. 'It's
Mongoloid, you see. I know that's not very PC, but none
of these terms are. Skulls are either Negroid, Caucasoid or
Mongoloid.'

Tom said, 'I've always thought that *Caucasoid* sounded like a sanitation robot from Star Wars.'

MacNeil didn't smile. 'And Mongoloid is what, Asian?'

'Yes, that's right,' Amy said. 'Eskimo, Japanese, Chinese . . . all Mongoloid. It's how I'd describe myself.'

MacNeil looked at her slanted almond eyes and high cheekbones, her fine jaw and shallow brow, and thought that he would be more likely to describe her as beautiful. Her long, shiny black hair was drawn loosely back and tied at the nape of her neck, and her fringe came down almost to her eyelashes. She glanced up to find him staring at her, and her eyes flickered quickly back to the child.

'But it's really the teeth that tell us most about her. The Mongoloid characteristics of the skull are more muted in one so young, but Mongoloids typically have shovel-shaped upper incisors.' She pointed to each of them in turn. 'Also, the tooth crowns are more bulbous, and again the incisors tend to have shorter roots.'

'So how do you know she wasn't like you? Chinese, or Asian, in origin but born and raised in the UK?'

Amy smiled. 'Because her teeth are perfect,' she said. 'She's had no dental treatment. None whatsoever. Didn't need it. No sugar in the diet, a decay-free mouth. Which would be very unusual in a ten-year-old British kid.'

'She was ten?'

Amy nodded. 'Yes.'

'Margin of error?'

'Plus or minus three or four months. The development of the teeth is a very accurate indicator.'

MacNeil mulled over for a moment everything she had told him. 'You said she had *two* very distinctive visual characteristics.'

'She was Asian, of course. And by that I don't mean Indian or Pakistani. More like Chinese. I know you think we all look alike, so to your eye she probably wouldn't have looked dissimilar to me at the same age. Except for one particularly compelling feature.' She paused, leaving MacNeil impatiently waiting to hear what that might be. 'She had a very marked harelip,' Amy said. 'At least, that's what you would know it as. We would call it a cleft palate.' She turned the skull towards him and tilted it back so that he could see it better. 'A serious defect in the maxilla – the bone which holds the upper teeth. The cleft can be minor, or severe, as in this case. It can be unilateral, or bilateral. This one is unilateral. You can see the severe displacement of the upper anterior teeth.' Amy looked at MacNeil. 'I'm afraid this was a very distinctive-looking little girl. She would have turned heads. And she probably got a really hard time from the other kids at school.'

An electronic rendition of 'Scotland the Brave' burbled inappropriately somewhere deep within the folds of MacNeil's coat. He fumbled to pull his mobile phone from his pocket and expose the lab to the full, unmuffled performance of his ringtone. When he had switched it back on earlier, he had seen that there were two missed calls. Both from Martha. She had left messages, but he had not picked them up. The display told him it was her again. He cut off the call without answering it, and thrust the phone back in his pocket.

'An important call, then,' Tom said.

MacNeil shrugged off his embarrassment. 'My wife.'

'Ah,' said Tom. 'She who must be obeyed.' He paused. 'Or not.'

MacNeil said to Amy, 'You'll write me up a report before you go?'

'Of course.'

He nodded. 'Thanks.' And he pushed his hands in his pockets and headed for the door. Tom watched him leave with clear contempt. 'You were pure genius,' he said to Amy, 'and all he could say was *thanks*.'

'I was just doing my job, Tom. When he does his job, there's probably not many people who even say that.'

Tom humphed. 'He's a cretin. God knows what any woman sees in him.'

'You mean his wife?'

'She's probably got a white stick.'

'They're separated.'

Tom looked at her, surprised. 'Well, aren't you just a fund of interesting information. How the hell do you know that?'

Amy blushed and shrugged and turned back to the bones to hide her discomfort. 'I don't know. It's just something I heard, that's all.'

CHAPTER FOUR

Pinkie often dreamt of his mother. He knew she was his mother, because in his dreams that's what he called her. But she didn't really look anything like the woman he remembered from his childhood. Which was always disappointing when he woke up. Pinkie usually found reality disappointing. He liked to think that his waking hours were really dreams, and that his dreams were real. That way he could do anything he liked, and when he fell asleep, well, none of it had happened. It was a neat way of dealing with the strange things that pleased him. Things that others might not understand.

Right now he was back in his grandparents' house. This was real. He remembered it so clearly. All those nights spent sleeping on the sofa in the front room. Icy cold in the winter. Hot and stuffy in the summer. And the bookcase that stood against the far wall, at the end of the sofa where his pillow went. He had lost count of the mornings he had woken before anyone else, and lain looking at those books lined up along the shelf at his eye level. Books with weird and wonderful titles – *Eyeless in Gaza*, *Cloud Howe*, *For Whom the Bell Tolls*. Written by people with the oddest names – *Aldous Huxley*, *Lewis Grassic Gibbon*, *Ernest Hemingway*. Who in God's name was called *Aldous*?

It had taken him a long time, two years maybe, before he had ventured to slide one of the books from the shelf and gingerly open its yellowed pages. His grandfather had taught English at the local grammar school, and so there were all kinds of books on that shelf. This one was called *Brighton Rock* by someone called *Graham Greene*. He had only meant to read the first sentence. Which stretched to a paragraph, and then a page. And then another. In a year, he had read every book on the shelf. But that first one had always stayed with him. A strange darkness about it, set in an era before his time, beyond his ken. And a hero, or rather, anti-hero, with whom he had found instant empathy. The teenage gangster, Pinkie. Ruthless, heartless, manipulative. Quite compelling. Flawed, of course, but then weren't we all?

He immediately adopted the nickname for himself. Pinkie. And insisted that's what the other kids at school call him. It never struck him how risible it might seem to them, or how ridiculous it sounded. Because for him the name was synonymous with the character. And that's who he wanted to be. It caused a great deal of hilarity at first, but that soon stopped. No one laughed at Pinkie a second time.

Now his mother was stooping over his bed. He could smell her perfume, feel the warmth of her cheek next to his. Then the softness of her lips and her sweet breath whispering *goodnight, little man, sleep tight, little man*. And then the phone rang, and to his annoyance she said, *I'll have to get that*, and she was gone. Who the hell was phoning at this hour anyway? Why couldn't she just let it ring? And yet, it did. On and on, until with a whispered curse under his breath, Pinkie rolled over and snatched the phone from the bedside table. The dream was gone. He was back in the waking world.

'What the fuck do you want?'

'Good morning, Pinkie. I hope I didn't wake you.'

Pinkie took a deep breath to calm himself. This was business. He recognised the voice immediately. The smooth, strangely monotonous tones of Mr Smith. He had thought they were all done. 'No,' he said. 'Sorry, I was busy with something.'

'Pinkie, I have a problem.'

Pinkie could not imagine what possible problem there could be. 'What problem?'

'That young man you found for me . . . he didn't follow through.'

'What do you mean?'

'I mean he didn't dispose of the bones. He dumped them on a building site. And now the police have them.'

'Shit!' Pinkie felt anger tighten the muscles of his neck and shoulders. That little bastard! 'You want me to off him?'

'I want you to keep a watching brief, Pinkie. Make sure the bones don't lead them anywhere. You know what I mean? Take whatever action you need to tidy things up.' Mr Smith sounded very calm, but Pinkie knew that he wasn't. He'd witnessed his temper, knew he was capable of things Pinkie could never have contemplated. In truth, Pinkie was a little scared of Mr Smith.

'How am I going to get around?'

'You can take my car. It has clearance to go just about anywhere.' There was a pause at the end of the line. 'I think I have found a way to monitor whatever progress the police might be making. That way we'll know exactly what it is you might have to do.'

'Why don't we just take out the cops?'

'No, no,' Mr Smith said quickly. 'If anything were to happen to the investigating officer that would only draw attention. And that's the last thing we want.'

CHAPTER FIVE

I.

Amy drove east on Tooley Street in her little yellow Toyota. It was the Japanese motor manufacturer's concept *welfare* vehicle, especially adapted to take her wheelchair. A clever arrangement with a backward-sliding driver's door and an extending ramp with a short rise and fall that slid her neatly in behind the wheel. It had not come cheap – none of the accoutrements of disability did – but the compensation money had enabled her to equip herself for a life as normal as she could make it.

It was easier getting around now that the streets were mostly deserted. Not that she ventured out much these days.

She passed a convoy of military vehicles speeding west

and glanced north towards the river and the tilting curves of the glass and steel edifice that was City Hall. All that glass, the Mayor had once said, should be seen as a metaphor for the transparency of government. Now you could see right through it. Because it was empty. Hollow promises which had come to nothing. For all their planning, they had never envisaged anything on this scale.

She turned north on Three Oak Lane, where presumably three oaks had once grown. But they were long gone. In Gainsford Street she turned into the multi-storey car park and drove up the ramp to her parking place on the second floor. It had been the only spot she could get at the time, and it left her always at the mercy of the lift. If it was working, there was no problem. If it was not, then she was in trouble. Today it rumbled down to the ground floor without a hitch, and she steered herself across the cobbles to the gated entrance of Butlers and Colonial Wharf, a collection of new-build and warehouse conversions around an open concourse. The whine of her electric motor seemed very loud in the quiet of this still grey day, a strange blue light leeching all colour out of the honeyed brick. There was not a soul to be seen. Once, in a bygone age, these streets and alleys and buildings would have heaved with life. Dockers and warehousemen and stevedores. Ships sailing up the estuary to the Pool of London to unload exotic foodstuffs and spices from the far reaches of the British Empire. Girdered metal bridges ran at peculiar angles overhead between towering warehouses. A huge, arched gateway gave on to the Thames, where workers had queued daily in the hope of picking up a few hours' work. Now these were the homes of those renaissance city dwellers who could afford them, serviced by the wine bars and gourmet restaurants which animated the cobbled lanes. The silence was eerie. Not a single echo of the past remaining.

Amy tilted up the ramp to her front door and unlocked it to let herself in. This had once been a warehouse for the storage of spices. The old lady who sold it to her told her she had toured the building in a hardhat before the conversion work began. 'It was heavenly, my dear,' she'd said. 'The whole place smelled of cloves.'

It was on three floors and Amy had the top two. Quite impractical for someone in a wheelchair, but she had been determined not to sacrifice anything to her disability. If she'd had the money before the accident, she would have loved to live in a place like this. Now that she could afford it, she was determined not to make any compromises. So she had installed stair lifts on both flights of stairs and a wheelchair on each floor. She slept on the first floor and lived on the second – in a huge open space up amongst the rafters which she had subdivided with furniture and book-shelves. In the far corner she had an open-plan kitchen, and on the back wall, French windows led out on to a square metal balcony where, in summer, she could sit and read and soak up the sun.

Amy transferred from her wheelchair to the bottom stair lift. She had developed strength in her arms to heave herself about, although there was not much weight in her slight frame. Sometimes she found the lift frustratingly slow. Today she simply closed her eyes and drifted up with it, cradling the small package in her lap. It had been a traumatic morning. To find herself identifying with a murder victim was a unique experience. But something about this poor little girl had touched her in a way she had not believed possible. She thought of all the corpses she had handled, the heads she had brought home to work on, and how she had always been able to separate herself from the unpleasant reality of her job. Until now. There was something about that collection of small bones which somehow still contained the spirit of the child. Amy found it disturbing, and when she held the skull in her hands, she could almost have sworn she felt the child's fear, passing through bone into her very own flesh.

All the doors on the first floor landing were closed, and only the light filtering up from the front door permeated the darkness. There was a faintly unusual smell hanging in the air, but Amy was distracted, putting down her package to enable the move to the wheelchair at the top of the stairs, and it didn't really register. She didn't mind the dark. Sometimes she would sit for hours with the lights out and pretend that none of this had ever happened. That she would simply decide to turn on the light and get up and do it.

She steered herself along to the foot of the second staircase and stopped in sudden confusion, unaware of the shadow moving through the darkness behind her. The stair lift was not there. She craned her neck to peer up and saw that it was at the top of the stairs. How was that possible? She had left it on the landing when she went out this morning. And in that moment she registered the faintly lingering scent which had eluded her just seconds earlier, and her heart seized. Just as a hand came around from behind and clamped itself over her mouth. She tried to scream, but she couldn't open her lips, and the strength in the arm from behind held her firmly in place. She put both hands up and grabbed the sleeve as her attacker moved silently around to scoop her up and out of her chair.

Amy was helpless, legs dangling uselessly. All she could do was hold on to him as he moved across the landing and kicked open the door to her bedroom. In three strides he reached the bed and laid her down amongst the quilt and cushions. He took his hand from her mouth. 'You bastard!' she screamed, and she reached up and grabbed him by the neck, pulling with all her strength until he tipped towards her and she found his lips with hers.

When they broke apart she was breathless, and he was grinning at her. 'You were brilliant,' he said.

She couldn't resist a smile. 'Just doing my job, Detective Inspector.'

He kissed her again, lightly this time, then brushed her hair from her eyes. Such lovely, dark eyes. He gazed at her, full of admiration and desire. 'What would Dr Bennet say if he could see us now?'

A shadow passed over her face. 'He'd hate it. He thinks you're the kind of cop who would beat someone up just because they were gay.'

'I wouldn't mind taking a pop at him sometime. But not because he's gay. Because he's such an obnoxious little shit.'

She pushed him away. 'He's my friend, Jack. My best friend in the whole world. I'd never have survived the last two-and-a-half years without him.'

MacNeil drew a deep breath and held his tongue. 'I know. But you've got me now.'

'For how long? As long as it takes the novelty to wear off?'

'Don't be silly. You know how I feel about you.'

'I know how I'd like you to feel about me. I'm not sure you've ever really told me.'

'Let me show you, then. I've never been good with words.' He leaned over to kiss her again. At first she resisted. She hated it that the two men in her life were so at odds that she had to keep one secret from the other. It wasn't even as if they were in competition. MacNeil forced her lips apart with his tongue, and finally she succumbed, passion rising in a sudden flood tide.

When they had told her that she was unlikely ever to walk again, she had thought her sex life was over. The spinal cord had not been severed, just damaged. And she had always kept control of her bladder and bowels. But she just didn't know if she would ever have any feelings down there again. Until that first time with MacNeil. And it had been like the first time ever. Full of pain and pleasure and tears. And until that moment, she had never quite trusted his motives. Why would a healthy strapping man like MacNeil be interested in a little Chinese girl who couldn't walk. But he had been so gentle with her that she had known immediately there was much more to him than met the eye. A complex, shy, caring man full of the hang-ups instilled in him by his Presbyterian upbringing. It wasn't that he was homophobic, he was just embarrassed by any overt display of sexuality. And Tom wore his homosexuality like a badge.

MacNeil stripped off his shirt and slipped off each of her boots, before removing her blouse and her long black skirt. Then he paused suddenly. 'We shouldn't do this,' he said. 'I might give you the flu. I'm more exposed than you are.'

'Then we might as well stop living now, because we'll die anyway.' Amy gazed up at him. 'And if we don't live life while we can, then we'll die without ever having lived.'

II.

The white Mercedes truck rattled east on Aspen Way. The dual carriageway was deserted. The truck passed under the Docklands Light Railway, and the lead grey waters of West India Quay slopped against the concrete berths all along the south side of the road. There was the merest thinning of the cloud overhead, and the cold morning air was suffused with a watery glimpse of insipid yellow light.

Pinkie felt uncomfortable in his ill-fitting uniform, but

secure in the anonymity afforded him by the gas mask and goggles that covered most of his face. The peak of his baseball cap was pulled down low over his eyes, and he kept a careful watch on the soldiers who approached as he turned right and swung his vehicle into the opening that led to the North Bridge beside Billingsgate Fish Market. There were twenty or more troopers based here in what had become a semi-permanent camp, a Mexican stand-off with the snipers on the far side of the water. There were armoured vehicles and a barbed wire barrier. He pulled up and rolled down his window. He smelled fish on the breeze, even though the fleets had not been out for weeks now. The stink had been absorbed into the fabric of the place.

The lead soldier approached cautiously, pointing his weapon up at the driver's window. He held his hand up for Pinkie's papers, gave them a cursory glance and then handed them back. He flicked his rifle through the air. 'Take the mask off.'

Pinkie's heart sank. He hadn't thought they would ask that. He removed his baseball cap and snapped off the mask.

The soldier looked at him suspiciously. 'Where's Charlie?'

'Sick,' Pinkie said. And he saw the soldier take an almost involuntary step back.

'Did you have any contact with him?'

Pinkie shook his head. 'Don't know the man. They took me off another run.'

The soldier seemed relieved. 'Put the mask back on.' He turned and shouted to the engineers at the barrier, 'Let him through.' And the soldiers peeled back the rolls of barbed wire to make a path through to the bridge.

Pinkie pulled his mask into place and slipped into first gear. The truck grunted and lurched forward towards the bridge. On the far side of the water, glass skyscrapers rose sheer into the mist. Company logos betrayed ownership. *The McGraw-Hill Companies. The Bank of America.* Pinkie ran anxious eyes along the skyline, looking for the snipers he knew had their rifles trained upon him. But he saw no one. He drove slowly up the ramp, past an empty blue security booth and stopped in front of the bridge. It was raised from the south side at an angle of around forty-five degrees. It was designed to let large vessels pass beneath it, but it created a very effective barrier. Someone, somewhere, threw a lever, and the bridge began a slow descent until it became, once again, a roadway passing south across the water into Canary Wharf, and the Isle of Dogs beyond.

Pinkie eased the white Merc slowly across to the other side, and in his side mirror saw the bridge begin to rise again. He glanced at the clipboard on his dash. The route and drop-off points were clearly marked. He would have to follow it meticulously to avoid arousing suspicion. He knew there were other checkpoints at Trafalgar Way and at Westferry Road, below the Bank Street roundabout. His exit on the return leg was through the checkpoint on West India Avenue, heading for Westferry Roundabout. But until then, he was in no man's land. An island of self-imposed quarantine in the heart of East London.

Pinkie had often wondered why it was called the Isle of Dogs, when in fact it was really a peninsula, a deep loop in the river. Only now did he realise that the loop had effectively been cut off from the north bank by the network of wharfs and waterways built to serve what had once been the busiest docks in the world. Apparently it was where Henry VIII used to keep his dogs, hence the name. At least, that's what Charlie had told him, just before Pinkie gently slid six inches of cold stainless steel between his ribs. He was a nice boy, Charlie. Shame he'd had to die.

Pinkie headed south, through Canada Square towards Jubilee Place, along canyons of tarmac between towering structures. There was no sign of life, not a single, solitary soul in the streets. Canary Wharf was like a ghost town. Opposite the tube station, the statue of a partially headless creature, half-man, half-horse, flanked by six stark leafless trees, gazed out east towards the hazy but distinctive shape of the Dome on the far bank of the river. An armless torso lay canted at an angle beneath the horse's belly, a head set into a niche in its flank. Pinkie allowed himself a tiny smile. And they called this art?

He swung right at Bank Street, and ahead of him saw the span of the blue-painted metal bridge carrying the Docklands Light Railway over the water between Canary Wharf and Heron Quays. There was no evidence here of the vandalism that blighted the city centre. Nothing was boarded up. Shops and restaurants were shut, but exposed to the world. The Slug and Lettuce. Jubilee Place Mall. Anyone who did not belong here, anyone who might be a carrier of the virus, would be shot on sight. So nobody ventured out, even the residents, because questions were only asked afterwards – by which time it would be too late.

Pinkie caught a movement out of the corner of his eye. A white golf buggy, driven by a man in blue uniform, a rifle sticking up at his side. It was just a flash of white and blue, and then it was gone, turning quickly into a darkened loading bay. Many of the original security men here had joined the vigilantes and commandeered the buggies. The big mystery was where they had got the guns. But wealthy and powerful people lived here. And where money and lives were at stake, anything was possible.

First stop was an underground car park on the south side of the square. Pinkie turned down the ramp and into a gloomy, deserted parking area that covered the entire footprint of the building. A low roof supported on metal beams. There were a handful of vehicles here, but no sign of life. Of course, he knew there must be someone watching. He pulled up and left his engine idling, and jumped down to throw open the doors at the back of the truck. The next half hour was spent loading boxes on to the pneumatic ramp, then lowering it to the ground and unloading them on to the concrete. Pinkie was fit, but it was hard work, and by the end of it he was sweating profusely. There was nothing on the boxes to indicate what was inside, but he was pretty certain it was tinned food. As many as twenty vehicles a day made the circuit, trucking in supplies for the nearly twenty-five thousand people who lived on the island.

As he shifted the final box, a bare arm fell out from behind a stack right at the back. Charlie's hand was locked in a position which gave the impression he had been clutching a cricket ball that someone had just removed. There were specks of blood on his forearm. Pinkie kicked it quickly out of sight and glanced around to see if anyone watching might have seen it. But still, he saw no one. He moved some boxes to ensure that Charlie made no more unwelcome appearances, and jumped down to swing the heavy doors shut again, locking the corpse away from prying eyes.

It was hot and uncomfortable inside his mask. Sweat was running into his eyes. He heaved himself back up into his cab. This was going to be a long couple of hours.

III.

Amy lay on her back gazing up at the ceiling. Her right leg was raised and propped on MacNeil's shoulder. He knelt in front of her and his big hands worked down the muscles of her calf, strong flat thumbs kneading giving flesh. He worked around her knee, and then down her thigh, in long sweeping strokes. She wished she could feel it. It was the strangest thing, knowing she was being touched, and yet having no sensation. She doubted if she would ever get used to it.

Occasionally she thought she had the faintest impression of pins and needles in her feet, and hope would flood back. Maybe one day life would return to these useless appendages. Maybe one day she really would walk again. The doctors said no. But on optimistic days she would tell herself that doctors could be wrong. And then on pessimistic days she feared that the pins and needles were only a figment of her imagination. Just wishful thinking.

But for MacNeil there was no question. Of course she would walk again. And she must keep the muscles supple and strong. It would be an awful thing to let them wither. And so he spent hours working her legs, exercising the muscles in groups, bending her legs at knee and ankle. Back and forth, back and forth. He had endless patience, it seemed. They never spoke during these sessions. He worked in silence, and she enjoyed a tranquillity she had never known before. Sometimes she closed her eyes and just drifted, her mind empty of all thoughts. At other times she would let it range over things that troubled her, problems at work, the estrangement of her brother. And often she would find answers, or partial solutions, or comfort in thoughts which had not occurred to her before.

Today she broke their unspoken code of silence. 'I've brought her home,' she said.

'Who?' MacNeil frowned and paused in mid-stroke.

'Lyn.'

'Who the hell's Lyn?'

'The little girl with the cleft palate.'

MacNeil leaned forward to look at her. 'What are you talking about, Amy?'

'That's what I'm calling her. Lyn. She's got to have a name, and I've always liked Lyn. I had a cousin called Lyn in Hong Kong, and I used to always wish my parents had called me that.'

'I like Amy,' MacNeil said. He started working her leg again. 'What do you mean you've brought her home?'

'I'm going to do her head. A reconstruction. It would help to know what she looks like, wouldn't it? She'll be very distinctive with that disfigured upper lip. Easily recognisable, I'd think.'

'You mean you've got the skull with you here?'

Amy nodded.

'Won't it stink?'

'A bit. But I'll work at the French windows upstairs. You know, where there's a little balcony overlooking the garden. As long as it's dry, I'll keep the windows open and it should be okay.' She drew herself up on to her elbows. 'Take me up and I'll show you.'

MacNeil liked the space at the top of the house. There was room to breathe here, and the sense of elevation helped. It couldn't have been more different from his claustrophobic little bedsit in Islington. He helped Amy set up a table at the French windows and gather together the materials she kept in a large cupboard against the back wall. He had never seen her working on a skull before, and had been quite taken aback by the row of heads that stood along the shelf in the middle of the cupboard. A bald man, a young woman, a boy, two older women, an unfinished man with a serious head injury.

She gathered her books and charts and dowels and cakes of plasticine around her, and MacNeil watched, fascinated, as she set up the skull on a pedestal, manoeuvring her wheelchair into the best position for working on it. The smell wasn't too bad with the windows open.

'You're going to build a face over the skull itself?'

'No, I'm going to make a plaster cast of the cranium, then cast the mandible in a cold-cure resin. We don't want to damage what might be evidence.'

He watched, fascinated, as she began her preparations. 'How do you know what the face looked like just from the skull? I mean, they all look the same, don't they?'

Amy grinned. 'Just like the Chinese?'

MacNeil felt his face colouring. 'You know what I mean.'

She nodded and smiled and said, 'I'm going to bore small holes at thirty-four reference points around the skull, and then glue little wooden dowels into them, just two-point-five millimetres in diameter. The dowels are marked at average soft tissue depths, according to a scale determined by a man called Helmer, who calculated them from ultrasound measurements made on living people. So they're pretty accurate. Then I'll sculpt the face, using what they call the American method. It's a scientific rather than an artistic process. You join the average tissue depths with strips of plasticine about five millimetres wide, effectively building up the layers of muscle beneath the skin. The teeth and the jaw will determine the shape of the mouth, and in particular the cleft lip. The shape of the nasal bridge is decided by the dimensions of the nasal bones. There are charts and measurements to shape the line of the eyelids, and of course race will play a part in that.'

'Where did you learn all this stuff?'

Amy shrugged. 'I was always interested in it. But after the accident, it was one of the few things I didn't need legs to do. Of course, I've had a lot of help from my mentor at BAHID.'

MacNeil knew that Amy was a member of the British Association for Human Identification. It was an informal academic association of experts from various fields of forensic expertise, from pathologists and policemen to lawyers and dentists. But he didn't know anything about mentors. 'You have a mentor?'

'Yeah. It's not unusual for some of the older practitioners, usually retired, to take some of the younger ones under their wing. My mentor's a retired anthropologist. Sam. We communicate by email and instant messaging.'

He watched her work for a while, marvelling at the dexterity of her fine, long fingers. She had the most beautiful pale, ivory skin, and lips that curled in what always looked like a smile, a reflection of a disposition which had been sorely tried by trauma and tragedy. He wanted just to pick her up and hold her, to possess her, to absorb her into himself. He had never felt like this about any other human being before. He was surprised, even shocked, by the feelings she aroused in him. Feelings he never knew he had.

'Scotland the Brave' jangled in his pocket. He took out his mobile and glanced at the screen. MARTHA, it said, and he was about to cut it off.

'Is it her?'

He glanced up to find Amy looking at him gravely. He nodded.

'You should answer it, then.'

And something about the look in her eyes made him

feel guilt at having spent the morning avoiding doing just that. He hit the green button. 'What do you want, Martha?'

'Where in God's name have you been, Jack? I've been trying to get you for hours.'

Something in her voice set alarm bells ringing. 'What's wrong?'

'It's Sean.' He heard her voice crack.

'What about him?'

'He's sick, Jack.'

IV.

Pinkie swung south-west along Manchester Road, past the Christ Church and St. John with St. Luke. Through gaps in the houses, and beyond the trees in Island Gardens, he could see the twin domes of the Old Royal Naval College at the University of Greenwich·on the far side of the river. The air was cold, rising up from dull grey water, and veiled in a thin mist. Beyond the Docklands Light Railway station he turned left into Ferry Street, swinging right then past the Poplar Rowing Club and along a street of red-brick new-build apartments overlooking the Thames.

The Ferry House pub on the corner was closed, but the

gates into St. Davids Square stood open. Charlie had told him that he always took a fag break here, and if anyone was watching, they'd never objected. Pinkie drove on into the square, past the Elephant Royale Thai restaurant. Six-storey apartment blocks rose all around, with white-painted balconies and French windows. What light there was played blue in a pool and fountain at the centre of the square. The river side of it was open to the view across mud flats to Greenwich. There, the three masts of the *Cutty Sark* rose above everything else.

Pinkie spent fifteen minutes unloading boxes, watching carefully for any sign of life at any of the windows which overlooked the square. There must have been dozens of pairs of eyes on him, but he saw nothing. He wondered how these boxes were divided up. Did they come out in ones or twos? Was there a rota? How did they settle disputes? He could not imagine what their lives were like, but even though he could not see them he could feel their fear. It was in the air, in their silence, and in the absolute absence of any sign of human life.

He finished unloading and closed up the truck, then strolled casually towards the riverside walkway, pulling a pack of cigarettes from his pocket. But he had no intention of smoking them. To his left, a door led into the lobby of

Consort House, numbers eight to forty-two. He sat for a moment on the wall next to the canopy and took out one of the cigarettes. He let his eyes wander along the line of the roofs opposite. It was now or never. He knew he would be seen going in, but who was going to stop him? Unless they had a gun. And who was going to open their door, or check on the old lady? They were all too afraid. He crushed his unlit cigarette and threw it away as he stood up. He pulled the door open and walked inside, waiting for the bullet in his back. It never came. In the lobby he drew a deep breath and took the elevator to the top floor. Stepping into the hall he ran his eye quickly past the numbers on the doors. Number 42A was next to the far wall. He moved quickly along to the window at the end of the corridor and glanced out across the water. A group of seagulls chased each other low across the river, swooping and diving and shrieking, before soaring skywards and beyond his field of vision. He knew she wouldn't answer the door, and it would make too much noise to kick it in. But he had other skills. He drew a slim plastic pack of thin metal rods from his pocket and examined the lock for a moment before drawing one out.

The hall beyond the door was carpeted, and absorbed the sound of his footsteps. He closed the door gently behind him and moved carefully down the hall towards the daylight spilling from the room at the far end. He paused at its open door, pressing himself back against the wall and tipping his head to look inside. It was a large, open room with windows looking out over the Thames, and patio doors opening on to a narrow balcony. The walls were covered with paintings and framed family photographs. Old-fashioned, chunky, patterned furniture made the room seem smaller than it was, but homely somehow. Pinkie liked the feel of it. He could live in a place like this. It reminded him of his grandparents' house. Except that they could never have afforded to live here.

He heard a chattering sound coming from beyond the angle of the door, and he took a cautious step in to determine what it was. An elderly lady with silver hair cut in a bob, a fringe dipping over her eyes, sat at a desk, fingers dancing with well-practised ease over a computer keyboard. Wire-rimmed spectacles were pushed back on her forehead, and the table beside her was covered in papers. She had a stunning view out across the river. But her eyes were fixed on her monitor. What a waste, Pinkie thought. People spent far too much time at computers.

He stepped into the room. 'Hello,' he said.

The old lady turned, alarmed, piercing blue eyes staring at him in startled disbelief. 'What – who are you?'

Pinkie smiled. She made him think of his grandmother. 'Your salvation, granny.' He slipped the gun from beneath his overall, its barrel extended by its silencer, and fired a single shot. It made a neat hole in her forehead, but the exit wound was messy, and blood and brain was spattered all over the window. She fell forward, face-first, and her blood soaked into the carpet. Pinkie winced. He didn't like to leave a mess. Cleanliness, tidiness. These were virtues that his mother had dinned into him. Honesty, kindness, loyalty. Diligence. If a job's worth doing, it's worth doing well. Never start something you can't finish.

He crossed the room to look at the family pictures on the wall. There she was. The matriarch. Head of the family. Children and grandchildren around her. Happy and smiling. And Pinkie felt a fleeting sadness that it was he who had taken all that away. It was a pity, really.

A sound like a baby crying startled him. He turned, pistol raised, to see a black cat with white bib and socks sniffing at the dead head of its mistress. It knew something was wrong, but had no idea what. Pinkie slipped his gun away. 'Aw, puss,' he said. 'Who's going to feed you now?'

The cat responded to his tone, and walked towards him, tail erect, slightly curled at the tip. Pinkie stooped and picked it up, and it let him cradle it in his arms, stomach exposed for him to rub gently. This was an old cat, well used to human handling. It was almost choking on its purr.

Pinkie carried the cat through to the kitchen and put it down on a worktop while he searched the cupboards for cat food. It was below the sink. He opened two tins and emptied them on to a couple of plates. That would keep the poor old thing going for a bit. It arched its back as it ate and he ran his fingers gently along its spine. 'Poor pussy,' he said. 'Poor old puss.'

CHAPTER SIX

I.

It was all depressingly familiar – the place they had bought together with the money he had saved, and Martha's inheritance. Even so, there was a crippling mortgage which he was still paying. It was a modest, two-bedroomed ground floor flat, the lower half of a modern terraced house in the leafy south London suburb of Forest Hill. At least there was a garden at the back for Sean, and MacNeil had been able to drive to Lambeth in twenty minutes outside of rush hour.

They had arrived here, mother, father, newborn baby, with such high hopes. But eight years on, this street was now just a painful reminder of how all their dreams had come to naught. A place haunted by failure.

It had never been a marriage made in heaven. He had only been twenty-seven when he first arrived in London, fresh-faced and naive from a job in rural Inverness-shire. The Met was a challenge, the Big Smoke an adventure. He met Martha in his first month. At a police party. She had been going out with a DC at the time, but it was a relationship nearing its end. She and MacNeil had been instantly attracted to each other. Sex was the driving force behind their relationship. They did it every chance they got, anywhere they could. They rented a little studio apartment in Lewisham, and spent most of his days off in bed eating ice cream, having sex and getting drunk. It was a crazy roller coaster existence, free from any responsibility, devoid of any thought of the future.

And then one day she told him she was pregnant, and their life changed.

Neither of them knew how it was possible. They had taken precautions. But there it was. Martha was torn. She desperately wanted children. But not just yet. She raised the subject of abortion, but MacNeil wouldn't hear of it. He had no religious convictions himself, but his parents had been lifelong members of the Free Church of Scotland, and while he didn't believe in their God, their morality had been seared into his soul. In the end, she was glad he had talked her out of it. Especially the day that Sean was born, and she held him in her arms and couldn't stop the tears from streaming down her face. And through them had seen that her big, tough Scottish husband was crying, too.

MacNeil pulled up his car at the foot of the path and locked it. What had once been a single arched doorway was divided now into two – one maroon door, one white. MacNeil climbed the steps, his heart frozen by fear. Two words is all it had taken to blow the remnants of his life out of the water. *Sean's sick.*

Martha opened the door before he got to it. He was shocked by her appearance. Her face was a bloodless white, deep shadows smudged beneath tired eyes. She seemed so much older than when he had last seen her, strained and tense. Was it really only a week ago? There had been no hint, then, that there was anything wrong with Sean. The schools were shut, and they'd had little or no contact with anyone. How in God's name had he got infected? It was all he could think to ask her. And there was more than a hint of accusation in it.

'I don't know.' She shook her head, and he heard the desperation in her voice. They went inside. 'Maybe it was you. We haven't been anywhere. Maybe you brought it in with you.'

MacNeil tipped his jaw and held his peace, containing the anger that rose in him like bile. 'Where is he?'

'The Dome. I called the doctor last night. By four this morning he was coughing up fluid. I can't believe how fast it's been. The ambulance came at first light.' She glared at him accusingly. 'Why didn't you answer the phone?'

'You don't give me many reasons to want to talk to you these days.' He looked around the living room. It was chaotic. Sean's Arsenal football strip was hanging up to dry on the clothes horse. His games console was lying next to the TV. MacNeil relented. 'I was working.'

'Of course you were.' Martha was unable to keep the bitterness out of her voice. 'Aren't you always?'

He looked at her and felt that familiar guilt. He knew she had cause. After the baby she hadn't been interested in sex any more. And somehow they didn't have much to say to each other. What little time off he had he spent with Sean, and she seemed to resent that. She grew more and more remote. He spent more and more time at work. The atmosphere in the house was awful. He just wanted to be out of it, to be anywhere else but here. Marry in haste, repent at leisure, they said. 'I'm sorry.' MacNeil shrugged. 'It must have been terrible for you, on your own.' He moved towards her, intending to take her in his arms, a belated offer of comfort.

She held out a hand. 'Don't,' she said. 'If Sean's got it, I might too.'

He immediately delved into his jacket pocket and pulled out the small bottle of tablets he had been issued at the start of the emergency. The one they wanted back in the morning. He held it out. 'Here, take these.'

'What is it?'

'It's a course of FluKill. They get handed out to all the cops.'

'What if you need them?'

'I don't care. Please, I want you to have them. Take them now.'

'You're only supposed to take them if you get it.'

'Well, if you've got it, the sooner you take it the better. Here.' He thrust them at her.

She took the bottle and looked at the label, and then at MacNeil. 'A pity you weren't around when Sean needed them.'

That stung. Not least because it was so unfair. 'You're the one who wanted me to leave.'

She put the bottle in her pocket. 'Maybe I'll take them later.' She paused. 'Will you take me to the Dome? I don't have clearance to drive around the city. And there aren't any taxis.'

He nodded. 'What did they say?'

'About what?'

'His chances.'

She looked at him. 'They didn't say anything. They don't have to. Everyone knows what the survival rate is.' Her eyes filled and she pulled in her lower lip, biting down on it until it bled.

MacNeil couldn't meet her gaze. He stared at the carpet, and remembered how he and the boy would rough and tumble on it. When Sean had been about three, they had watched an old Clint Eastwood movie together on the TV. *The Good, the Bad and the Ugly.* You never imagine what lines will stick in a kid's head. Eli Wallach had called Eastwood a 'double-crossing bastard'. And as MacNeil and Sean had mock-fought the next day, the boy had suddenly shouted at him, 'You cross double bustard!' And MacNeil and Martha had spent the next half hour in hysterics.

'We'd better go, then.'

It seemed almost bright in the street, although the light was still misty, and colder even than it had been first thing. But the house had been so gloomy and depressing, it felt almost cheerful outside.

MacNeil saw curtains twitching as he held the passenger door open for Martha. The neighbours would all have seen the ambulance come to take Sean away. The MacNeils would be pariahs now, latter-day lepers. No one would come near them.

II.

They drove under the southern approach to the Blackwall Tunnel and turned off the roundabout on to Millennium Way. Ahead of them they could see the tent-like dome suspended from its superstructure of outward-leaning steel columns dominating the wasteland that was North Greenwich. The dual carriageway took them up through a derelict industrial landscape to a parking area next to the tube and bus station. There had been no tube trains or buses running for weeks, but the car park was full to overflowing. Masked soldiers at the entrance waved them on, and MacNeil drove past lines of ambulances to the blue hoardings erected around the Dome – this billion-pound millennium folly for which, beyond its short life as a concert venue, they had finally found a use. They were filling it with the sick and the dying. Its vast floor area had been honeycombed by partitions, and thousands of beds wheeled in to ease the pressure on city hospitals. A fleet of ambulances and medical supply vehicles lined up along the piers of the bus station.

MacNeil pulled his car up on to the central reservation before the roundabout at the end of the road, and they hurried up a ramp and through an access gate in the hoardings. The red asphalt which circled the Dome was littered with vehicles and masked medical staff coming and going. It was chaos. There were no notices to guide visitors, because visitors were not expected. Martha and MacNeil had no idea what door to go in, or who to ask for. There was no security, and no one gave them a second look as they walked into the vast, cavernous space enclosed by white plasticised canvas.

The din that filled the air was extraordinary. The roar of the space heaters overhead. The thousands of voices raised above the sounds of the sick. The sneezing and coughing and groaning and retching. A bed was wheeled past by pale-looking orderlies in white pyjamas. The young man on it was dead, barely covered by his blood-and-vomit-stained sheet, open eyes staring into the void. MacNeil wanted to be sick. His son was here somewhere. In this hell. If he was going to die, then he'd rather take him home to die there. He grabbed a nurse by the arm and she wheeled around. 'What is it?' He could see the dog weariness in the shadows of her face, eyes clouded like cataracts. She was suffering from death fatigue, and a lack of patience with the living.

'My son's here somewhere. He was brought in this morning.'

A fleeting moment of humanity cut through her tiredness. 'Go outside and follow the road round to Gate C. That's where the new arrivals are brought in.' And she was gone again, off into the honeycomb.

MacNeil took Martha's hand, and they escaped for a few brief moments into the fresh air, and relief from the sounds of the dying. They ran around the perimeter of the Dome pushing and bumping their way through groups of workers who called after them in anger. But there was something compelling now about the need to find their son. Double doors stood wide open at Gate C and they ran in to find a temporary reception desk, where a record of the patients being brought in was being made on a computer. An older nurse seated on the other side of the desk looked at them warily from behind her mask. 'Can I help you?'

'Our son was brought in this morning,' MacNeil said. 'Sean MacNeil. He's eight years old.'

'We have no facilities for visitors here. I'm sorry.' But she didn't sound it. 'We have an emergency number. The switchboard is manned twenty-four-seven.'

There was a clipboard on the desk beside her, with a

floor plan and names written in pencil. It didn't occur to MacNeil immediately that the reason they pencilled in the names was because it would be easy to rub out and replace them. If he'd thought about it, he'd have realised it made sense, given the turnover. Instead, he instinctively reached over and grabbed it.

'Hey!' The nurse tried to snatch it back, but MacNeil held it out of her reach. 'I'll call the police,' she said, a hint of hysteria creeping into her voice.

'I am the police,' MacNeil said. He ran his eye quickly down the floor plan. There were more names than he could absorb. The floor had been divided into sections, and there were half a dozen pages beneath the top one on the clipboard. 'I can't see him,' he said to Martha, a hint of panic now in his voice. He flipped through the pages.

The nurse sighed deeply and ran her fingers lightly over her computer keyboard, then she reached over and took the clipboard back from MacNeil. She found Sean on page three. 'Section 7B,' she said. 'Follow the arrows painted on the floor. Seven is yellow.'

Sean was in a subdivision of section seven with three other children. He and two of the others were on drips. There were patches of high colour on his cheeks, but otherwise he was deathly pale. His bed sheets were soaking and twisted around his tortured body. He was only semi-conscious and seemed delirious, racked by occasional bouts of uncontrollable coughing. They could hear the liquid rattling in his lungs and throat. A masked medic in white overcoat and gloves stopped them from getting any closer. 'What the hell are you people doing here?'

'That's our son,' Martha said, her voice barely a whisper, so that she had to clear her throat and say it again, more loudly.

The medic glanced wearily at Sean and shrugged. 'I'm sorry.' Everyone was sorry.

'What are you doing for him?' MacNeil asked.

The medic unhooked the clipboard from the foot of Sean's bed and scanned the chart. He sighed. 'We've put him on steroids. He's following the usual pattern. He's developed ARDS.'

'What does that mean?' Martha clutched the arm of her estranged husband.

But MacNeil knew what it meant. Early in the emergency, all police officers had been briefed on symptoms and the course that the flu almost invariably took. It would start, like any other flu, with body aches, fever, sore throat, a cough. And then degenerate quickly into a progressive and irreversible respiratory decline that was called Adult, or

Acute Respiratory Distress Syndrome – ARDS. It started like pneumonia, but wouldn't respond to antibiotics or antivirals. He knew that steroids were a last resort, but even they were unlikely to stop the progressive inflammation, leading to protein leakage, fibrosis and finally death.

'It means it's all down to how strong your kid is,' the medic said. 'How effective his immune system is at fighting it.'

MacNeil looked at the tormented little boy in the bed. He seemed so small and vulnerable. Grown men were dying from this flu. Big, strong, tough men cut down like straw in the wind. What hope did a child have? He closed his eyes, overwhelmed by a sense of helplessness. He was the boy's father, for God's sake! He was supposed to protect him, to keep him safe, to see him grow into adulthood. MacNeil opened his eyes again as he heard his son convulsed by a relentless, retching cough, and he felt tears filling them. 'How long?'

The medic shrugged. He was just as powerless to do anything about it as the boy's father. 'If he makes it through the next hour,' he said, 'then maybe he has a chance.'

III.

Outside, MacNeil pulled his mask aside and drew the cold January air deep into his lungs. He put his arm around Martha's shoulder and felt her whole body shaking from the sobs she was trying to contain. They walked in a trance through the comings and goings, oblivious to the world around them. Back out through the gate and down on to Millennium Way. There were more hoardings on the far side of the road, and they passed through an opening, a hand-painted sign pointing them towards the Motel Millennium where accommodation and food was available at two hundred metres. But all they found was dereliction. Crumbling brick houses boarded up. A vacant lot strewn with debris, weeds and grass poking up through cracks in the tarmac. A rusted lamp post leaned at an impossible angle. Great mounds of excavated earth were piled up along the perimeter of the old Ordnance Wharf. This, then, was the great millennium dream. Bleak, derelict, bankrupt. A sad reflection of their own lives. A marriage in tatters, a child hovering in that impossible place between life and death.

The skyscrapers of Canary Wharf pushed up through

the mist on the other side of the mirrored loop in the river. Harbingers, or so their architects had hoped, of a new age of prosperity and regeneration. But, in fact, as soulless as the people who had built them, deserted now, stalked by fear.

A sound like crackling came from across the water, echoing over its slow, sullen ebb. Martha lifted her head, like an animal sniffing the air. Instinct, rather than interest, provoked her question. She had no real interest in the answer. It was just something to say. 'What's that?'

'Probably gunfire.'

She frowned. 'Who's shooting?'

MacNeil's response was mechanical. Like Martha, he felt the need to speak, to find words to fill an empty void in which they would otherwise drown in unwanted thoughts. 'The Isle of Dogs has been sealed off. There's no flu on the island, and a bunch of people with guns and some big financial backing are making sure that no one brings it on.'

'Can they do that?' Martha was incredulous. For just a moment she forgot why they were here.

'Apparently. You can leave if you want, but you can't go back. There's a stand-off with the army, and the government seems to have backed down from confrontation. Occasionally there's an exchange of fire. But I think it's just posturing. If anyone got shot for real, then I guess they would send in the troops.'

There was another bout of crackling, and then silence. The slow chug of a tugboat pulling rafts of yellow containers downriver was the only sound to break it.

They walked slowly without speaking for several minutes. Then MacNeil said, 'This is my last day.'

He felt her face turn up towards him, but he didn't want to meet her eye. 'What do you mean?'

'I gave in my notice. I finish at seven tomorrow morning.'

'I don't understand.' He heard the confusion in her voice.

'What's not to understand? I quit my job.'

'Why?'

'Because you had custody of Sean. Because I knew if I didn't make the time to see him now I never would.'

She didn't speak for a long time. And then she said, 'It's a pity you didn't think of doing it sooner.'

'Don't start.' He let his arm slide from her shoulder, and felt the same old anger again. It was always like this when they argued. 'I don't want to do this now. Sean's the only thing that matters.'

She slipped her arm through his and squeezed it. 'You're right. I'm sorry. Maybe if we'd both thought more about Sean and less about ourselves, things would have been different.'

Different for Sean, certainly, he thought. But he doubted if either he or Martha would have been any happier. If it hadn't been for Sean's unexpected arrival, their relationship would have burned itself out and they would both have moved on. How many couples, he wondered, were trapped in loveless marriages because of a child conceived in carelessness? And how unfair was that on the kid? All Sean had ever asked of them was their love. And while they had given it, it had never been unconditional. And now he lay dying, and all they had left were their regrets and their guilt. Each as culpable as the other.

'What are you going to do?' Martha asked. 'For a living.'

MacNeil shook his head. It was something he'd been avoiding. 'I've no idea.'

'Maybe,' she said suddenly, 'maybe if Sean – if he pulls through – maybe we should think about giving it another go. For his sake.'

MacNeil gazed bleakly through the chill winter haze, and had a sensation of falling weightlessly into space. 'Maybe we should,' he said, without conviction.

IV.

Amy ran her cursor over the drop-down menu on her computer screen and selected SEND INSTANT MESSAGE. She had already chosen Sam from her list of messaging buddies. She typed quickly.

– Sam, I'm thinking of asking for them to try to get a DNA sample from the tissue Tom recovered from the bone marrow. What do you think?

She hit the return key and sent the message. It went off with a *wwwooo-oop* sound. She waited, watching the window on her screen for Sam's reply. She had chosen a headshot of herself as her avatar which would appear on Sam's screen with her message. Sam, for some reason, had picked a colourful picture of a parrot. Amy had always meant to ask the significance of it, but then forgotten in the course of conversation – if text messages could be called conversation. They were more instant than emailing, but not as tying as a phone call. You could just leave the window open and return to it to pick up a conversation when you wanted. She had already had numerous conversations with Sam that day, providing the retired anthropologist with a briefing on the bones.

Another *wwwooo-oop* alerted her to Sam's reply.

– *Why?* was the response.

– *Why the DNA, or why am I asking you?*

– *The DNA.*

Their exchanges were often characterised by an almost childish flippancy, the only real way they had of expressing the mutual affection of two people who had only ever met in the ether. But Sam seemed grumpy today. Amy's fingers rattled over the keyboard.

– *There's an outside chance she might be on the DNA database.*

– *If she's from a developing country like you think, that's unlikely.*

– *True, but we'd kick ourselves if she was. Never overlook the obvious, you always tell me.*

– *The yield from the marrow will probably be pretty low.*

– *We could take pulp from one of her teeth.*

– *I thought you had the skull there.*

– *Oops, so I do. Bone, then. I could ask Tom to cut a wedge from the femur. In fact, he's probably already done that to get to the marrow.*

There was a long pause. Amy watched the cursor blinking blankly at her from the screen. Then,

– *Worth a try, I suppose.* Another pause. – *What other tests has Tom ordered up?*

– *I don't know. Toxicology, probably.*

– *That won't yield much. Qualitative rather than quantitative results. If there are drugs present, it'll only be a trace. No way to tell how much.*

Amy nodded at the screen, as if Sam might be able to see her. She knew that Sam was right. And it was frustrating. Somehow, you felt you ought to be able to tell more about a person from their bones.

– *Okay, thanks, Sam. Talk later.*

Amy looked across the room at her cast of Lyn's skull. Even without the flesh to give it emphasis, the cleft in the maxilla was a substantial disfigurement, displacing the teeth it was supposed to hold in a straight, even line. She grabbed the lever on the right arm of her wheelchair and propelled it smoothly across the floor to the table by the window. She had drilled the holes and glued the dowels in place. And now that the glue had set she could start to build the layers of 'muscle' that would give definition and personality to the face. She started preparing the strips of plasticine, but her sense of frustration had not gone away.

It was the emotion she felt most frequently, and it often led to depression. It came from her inability to do her job, the thing she had been trained for, the work she had grown to love. While her brain was still sharp and clear, and her fingers had lost none of their skills, her limited mobility meant she could no longer fully function as the forensic odontologist she had been. There were things she simply could not do from a wheelchair. She got lecturing work, of course, but that was not something she had ever enjoyed. She hated the sympathy she saw in people's eyes. It diminished, somehow, the value of what she had to say.

She had written some papers, and published some research. She provided a consultancy and advice service for the FSS, and her opinion had been sought more than once by investigating officers from forces outside of the Met. She had even started specialising in pattern bruising, on both the living and the dead. Tool marks, they called them – marks left by a ring in a murder case, belt buckle bruises in a rape, stabbing and incisive injuries inflicted during a fight. The principles of analysis were identical to bite mark analysis, which had always been one of her specialities, and it was possible to do it from a wheelchair. Still, her limitations were frustrating.

But she had always tried not to give in to self pity. That would have been just too easy. And so she shrugged off her frustration and lay the first strip in place across the cheekbone of the skull. Which is when the thought first came to her, and she wondered why it hadn't occurred to her before.

She reached for the phone and pulled Tom's home number from its memory, then listened as it rang at the other end.

'What!' Tom didn't sound happy.

'Tom?'

'Jesus, Amy, I'd just dropped off. It's been a long shift, and I'm on again at seven tonight.'

'Sorry, I wasn't thinking. Can you talk?'

Tom put his hand over the phone and there was a muffled exchange between him and another male voice. Then the hand was removed. 'This isn't a good time.'

'I'll call later.'

But he relented. 'Was it important?'

'It can wait.'

She heard him sigh deeply. 'Aw, shit, Amy, I'm awake now. You might as well tell me.' His voice went ambient and he said, 'I'm still listening. I'm just going to make a cup of tea. How's it going with the skull?'

'It's going well.'

'Given her a face yet?'

'Hey, come on, I'm not that fast. It'll be a few hours.' She paused. 'Tom, what tests did you order up on the bone marrow?'

He cursed as he dropped some piece of crockery. 'Shit!' Another muffled exchange, then, 'You know, in the end I didn't think it would be worth it, Amy. I mean, anything we get from toxicology is going to be really inconclusive.'

'That's what Sam thought.'

'You've been discussing it with Sam?'

'Yeah. Is that alright?'

'I guess.'

'We thought maybe we could get a DNA sample from the marrow.'

'It's possible. I'm not sure how useful it would be though, unless we had something to compare it with.'

'And I had another thought,' Amy said. 'We could run a virology test. PCR. See if she'd had the flu.'

'Half the bloody city's got the flu!' Tom didn't sound particularly impressed by her thought.

'Yeah, but that might be what killed her.'

'So why would anyone try to cover that up?'

Amy shrugged to herself. 'I don't know,' she said. 'It just seemed like something we should know. I mean, the information we're going to get from a skeleton is limited enough. We might as well find out everything we can.'

She heard him sigh again. Then a pause. 'Tell you what. Why don't you call Zoe and ask her to do it? It'll give the little bitch something to do, rather than stand smoking on the steps all day.'

V.

The wind had stiffened, picking up cold, damp air from the estuary and carrying it upriver into the heart of the city.

MacNeil and Martha made their way back around the perimeter of the Dome. It had been a long hour, and then MacNeil had made them wait another fifteen minutes. There was no point in going back too soon. But in truth, it was just a way of putting off the news they didn't want to hear. Ignorance was hope.

A group of soldiers, rifles pressed across their chests, trotted past them at the double, young boys with frightened eyes behind army-issue gas masks designed for a biological war in Iraq which had never materialised following the failure to find weapons of mass destruction. A little further around the curve of the Dome, several gates beyond theirs, they could see the unmarked black vans lined up to take the dead to the official disposal centres. The council-run crematoriums throughout the city had been overwhelmed by numbers, and the government had set up emergency facilities to dispose of the growing backlog of bodies. There were literally thousands awaiting disposal daily, and nowhere to keep them. It was considered a health risk for bodies not to be burned within twenty-four hours. Family funerals were impossible. Even commemorative religious services were banned because of the risks of spreading infection at public gatherings. The government had promised memorial services at a later date. And so the process of grieving remained unfulfilled, and the distress amongst relatives was almost unbearable.

The double doors at Gate C still stood open. There was a different nurse behind the desk, but she was engaged in earnest conversation with a group of orderlies, and did not look in their direction as they walked past. MacNeil led Martha through the maze, following the yellow arrows until they reached section 7B. The beds were still occupied. Four children. But Sean wasn't one of them.

Martha clutched MacNeil's arm. 'Where is he?'

MacNeil saw a medic beyond the next partition. He was re-attaching a drip to a young girl's arm. It was not the young man they had spoken to earlier. MacNeil grabbed him. 'The boy who was in the right-hand bed in 7B, where is he?'

The medic pulled his arm free, irritated by MacNeil's aggression. He glanced back along the passage between the partitions. 'The dark-haired kid?'

'Yes.'

'He died.'

CHAPTER SEVEN

MacNeil stood in his son's bedroom, looking from the window into the back garden at the swing he had assembled from a kit and concreted into the grass. He could still hear Sean shrieking in delight as MacNeil pushed him higher and higher, terrified and exhilarated at the same time. *Don't stop, Daddy, don't stop!*

A train rumbled past the foot of the garden, beyond the high wooden fence, and the vibration of it shook the house. It was something they had stopped even noticing.

MacNeil let the net curtain drop and turned back into the room. Posters of Arsenal players adorned the walls, a red and white scarf draped over the bedside chair, pennants hanging from a wire strung across the ceiling. In the next room, he could hear Martha sobbing, and he kicked Sean's football at the far wall in a sudden explosion of frustration. The ball rebounded into the chest of drawers, knocking over a framed family photograph. The glass shattered. MacNeil stooped to pick it up, and shook the photo free of its broken frame. They'd had it enlarged from a snap taken on a family holiday on the Costa Brava. The three of them crouching together in the sand, a crowded beach behind them, sunlight coruscating across an impossibly blue sea. They'd asked some young woman to take it with their camera, and it had turned out to be the best picture of them they'd ever had. A moment of happiness caught forever. And lost now for eternity.

He sat on the edge of Sean's bed, holding the photograph in his hand, and thought of his own parents for the first time in a very long time. Somehow the loss of his child made his feud with his parents seem futile and foolish. We all had only one life, and it was too short to waste on something as destructive as anger.

He had told himself time and again that it was not his fault, but he knew he had done nothing to bring about a rapprochement. He had never been close to his parents, and called them only occasionally from London. And when he had, there had always been a tone. Veiled barbs. How nice it was to hear from him – when what they meant was why hadn't he called before? His mother was the master of the acid reproach delivered with a silvered smile.

When Martha had told him she was pregnant he had delayed in telling them. He knew they would not approve. They didn't even know that he was living with someone. Sex before marriage, in their world, was a sin. And the longer he put it off, the harder it became. Until the point where he decided not to tell them until after the wedding. He and Martha had married in a London registry office with a couple of friends as witnesses.

And when he finally told them, his parents had been mortally offended. Not just because his vows had not been taken before God, but because they had not been invited. To their own son's wedding. And when they learned about the coming baby, and put two and two together, that had been the last straw.

He had taken Martha and the baby north only once. A trip he had dreaded, and not without cause. The atmosphere had been awful. While his parents had fussed and fawned over their grandson, they had been cool with him, and just short of rude to Martha. The day before they left, MacNeil had had it out with them, while Martha was walking the baby in the pram. A dour, painful, prickly confrontation in which the things left unsaid had almost been worse than those spoken. He had not been back since.

Now, as he sat on the bed his son would never sleep in again, he thought of them for the first time without anger. Remembered things he had forgotten. Things from his childhood. Laughter, kindness, safety. He had always felt safe with them, secure in a love that was real, if severe and perhaps lacking in warmth. It was very Scottish, very Presbyterian. You could feel affection, but you mustn't show it.

He took his mobile phone from his jacket pocket and turned it back on. It beeped and told him he had several messages. He didn't feel inclined to hear them. Instead, he scrolled through the numbers in its memory until he found his parents' telephone number. He should have known it, but he didn't. It was another element in their estrangement – they had moved house after he left, and it had never felt like home to him. The house where he had grown up was home, and he harboured just the smallest resentment at their selling of it.

He listened numbly while the phone rang in a house nearly six hundred miles away. In another time, another world. He wasn't sure quite why he felt the need to call them, but he did. Perhaps he simply wanted to curl up into

childhood again, insulated from reality, free from responsibility. His father answered the phone. Very correct, very
precise, rhyming off the number in full.

'Dad, it's Jack.'

There was a long silence at the other end. 'Hello, Jack.
To what do we owe the honour?'

'Sean's dead, Dad.'

This time the silence was interminable. Then eventually
he heard his father draw a long, slow breath. 'I'll get your
mother,' he said, in a very small voice.

It was more than a minute before his mother came to the
phone, and he heard the tremor in her voice as she spoke.
'Aw, son . . .' she said, and the tears rolled down MacNeil's
face.

Martha was in the hall when he came out of the bedroom.
He knew from the way she looked at him she could tell
he'd been crying.

'Who were you talking to?'

'Mum and Dad.'

He saw her tense. 'And what did they have to say?'

'Not much.'

'They didn't suggest it was God's way of punishing us,
then?'

He looked away. 'No.' They stood for a long time without saying anything. Then he said, 'I have to go.'

'Work, I suppose.' There was more than a hint of accusation in her tone.

'A little girl was murdered.'

'Your son's dead, Jack.'

'I can't change that. I can't even find someone to blame for it.'

She stood with her arms folded across her chest, barely in control. And then tears filled eyes already red from spilling them. 'Stay,' she said.

'I can't.'

'Won't.'

He shook his head. 'I can't, Martha. I'm not sure there'd be any point.' He brushed past her towards the front door. Then he stopped and turned. 'Would there?'

All the tension seeped out of her and she went quite limp. 'Maybe not.'

'Take the FluKill,' he said. 'I'll only have to give them back tomorrow.'

She took the bottle from her pocket and looked at it for a moment. And then she turned and strode to the bathroom at the end of the hall. She flung the door open and unscrewed the lid of the bottle, emptying its contents down the toilet. She looked back at MacNeil defiantly. 'To hell with the fucking FluKill,' she said. 'I hope I catch it. I hope I die.' And she pulled the handle, flushing away any hope of salvation.

CHAPTER EIGHT

I.

The auricles, or external ears, were the last feature to be added to Amy's facial approximation of the child she called Lyn.

The mouth had taken her the longest time. Normally, the junction between the canine and the first pre-molar on either side would determine the positions of the corners of the mouth. Each lip would be equal in height to the corresponding enamel of the upper and lower anterior incisors. But in this case the cleft palate had so distorted the upper jawbone that Amy had been forced to exercise a degree of imagination, in addition to her experience, to flesh out the disfigurement of the upper lip.

She had spent more than an hour working on it, so absorbed that it wasn't until she moved away to look at it objectively that she felt the full shock of its ugliness. It was brutal. And if she had empathised with the child before, now her heart went out to her unreservedly.

Gently she worked the soft tissue of the ears into place. There was no clue on the skull that made it possible to determine the size of the ears. The nose was the general guide, both to the length and position of the ears, but it could only ever be a rough estimation. The length and style of the hair was impossible, even to guess. Amy knew that Lyn would have had hair of similar colour and consistency to her own, but whether it was short or long, pigtailed or ponytailed, they would probably never know.

Amy had always worn her hair long. It was beautiful, fine, shiny black hair, and she had always been proud of it. Until one foolish moment of drunken bravado at a party at med school, when she had taken it into her head to cut it short and spiky. Herself. It was a disaster. She had wakened the next day, hungover but sober, to look at herself aghast in the mirror. She wept for nearly an hour before going out to buy a long, black wig. But it had never sat right, and in the end she had resigned herself to the months of waiting for her own to grow back.

She still had that wig somewhere at the back of the wardrobe in her bedroom on the floor below, and when finally she had finished the ears, she took the stair lift down to search for it. She was clutching it in her lap when she wheeled out of the bedroom to find MacNeil standing at the top of the stairs.

At first she was startled to see him, and then immediately knew the worst.

'Oh, Jack, no . . .'

'Don't come any closer,' he said. 'I might be carrying. I just . . . well, I couldn't bear to tell you over the phone.'

'Jack, I don't know what to say.' He looked so utterly helpless. Like a small boy. A big man reduced by tragedy.

'There's nothing to say.'

And he was right. There were no words adequate to express her feelings. She wanted to show him how she felt, to hold him, the only thing she could do to offer comfort. But it was clear, even from his body language, that he didn't want her anywhere near him.

'Have you told Laing?'

He shook his head. 'He's been leaving messages on my voicemail for the last three hours.' He looked at his watch. 'I really need to go.'

'You're not thinking of going back to work?' She was shocked.

'What else is there for me to do, Amy? I need a focus. Something to stop me thinking, a reason to go on.' He glanced up the stairs. 'Have you finished her yet?'

'The first rough. I was going to try an old wig of mine on her.' She held it up. 'Do you want to see?'

He stood at the far side of the attic room and watched as Amy leaned forward, placing the wig on the head she had fashioned on the table by the window. She took a full minute, adjusting and arranging before finally she was satisfied, and the electric motor of her wheelchair whined and propelled her to one side, revealing the child.

For a moment, MacNeil was shocked by the graphic disfigurement of the upper lip, and then his eyes saw beyond it to the face of a child. A face full of innocence and youth. Rounder than Amy's, a flatter brow, perhaps a distinctive racial subtype. And somehow Amy had given her life, captured her spirit from somewhere amongst all those bones. Bones MacNeil had picked through in a leather holdall in a London park at first light. Sean had still been alive then, and MacNeil had had a reason to put one foot in front of the other. He knew now that he wanted to find this little girl's killer more than anything else on earth.

*

As he was leaving, his phone went. He glanced at the display and saw that it was Phil, the Scenes of Crime officer who had shown him the Underground ticket recovered from the site in Archbishop's Park. He took the call.

'Jack, I called the office, but they said you hadn't been around for a few hours.'

'What is it, Phil?'

'We got a date off that magnetic strip. No idea how significant it might be. It was October fifteenth. Just a couple of weeks before the emergency.'

MacNeil couldn't think how the date might be relevant. He glanced up to see Amy watching him from the top of the stairs. 'Is that it?'

'Well, no. We managed to lift a partial thumbprint off the front side of it. Enough to make a match, if we can find one. We're running it through the AFIS now.' It seemed a lot to ask that a partial thumbprint recovered from a three-month-old discarded Underground ticket found on a building site would lead them anywhere. But if its owner was on the computer, the national Automated Fingerprint Identification System would match them up pretty fast.

MacNeil hung up and opened the door. 'Jack.' Amy's voice made him turn in the doorway. Her face was creased with anxiety. 'Take your FluKill now. Don't wait to see if you're going to have symptoms.'

He nodded. 'Sure.' He turned away.

'Jack.' Her voice was imperative, and he turned again. 'Promise me.'

He drew a deep breath. He hated to lie to her. 'Promise.'

Outside, he looked up into a grey and purple bruised sky, and it spat tiny drops of rain in his face. He remembered standing helplessly in the hallway as Martha emptied the pills down the toilet. They said that twenty-five per cent of the population would catch the flu. Between seventy and eighty per cent of them would die. He had been directly exposed to it, and the odds weren't good.

II.

Amy steered her wheelchair across the vast expanse of floor in her attic living room, the whine of its motor piercing a silence laden with depression and regret. If anything, the cloud had thickened, and the afternoon seemed darker. But she couldn't face the glare of the electric lights.

The daylight from the window cast deep shadows across Lyn's face, animating it in a way that somehow full light on it did not. And from those shadows, the little girl stared back at her. From a distance the hair looked real. Only the putty-coloured plasticine betrayed the fact that this was a head sculpted from inanimate materials. Amy felt impotent to do any more. She had given the child back her face, but not her identity, and beyond that she was helpless. Trapped in her wheelchair while others sought her killer.

She wondered if things would ever be the same between her and MacNeil again. Grief could change people, scar them irrevocably. Especially the loss of a child. And then there was the very real possibility that either, or both of them, might be struck down by the flu. It was easy for her to forget, locked away here in her ivory warehouse where once the air had been filled by cinnamon and clove, that out there in the real world, the able-bodied world, people were dying in their thousands. In their tens of thousands.

Her entry buzzer cut through the silence and startled her. For a moment she thought that perhaps it was MacNeil returning, that maybe there was something he had forgotten. And then she remembered that he had a key and would not need to buzz. She wheeled her chair across to the entry phone and lifted the receiver. 'Yes?'

'It's Tom.' He knew the entry code to the outer gates.

'Come on up.'

She pressed the buzzer and waited a few moments for him to open the door. And then she heard him on the stair. When finally he emerged from the staircase into the attic he looked pale and tired.

'What's wrong?' she asked, concerned.

'Oh, just the usual.'

'Harry?'

'It's because I'm on nights at the moment. He just can't seem to stay home alone. I used to worry about AIDS, now I wonder what else he might be bringing home with him.'

'Where does he go?'

'Oh, God knows. He won't tell me. We had a blazing row after you phoned, and there was no way I could get back to sleep.'

'Oh, I'm sorry,' Amy said, suddenly full of guilt. 'That was my fault. I shouldn't have called you at home.'

Tom waved a hand dismissively. 'It's been brewing for days. It was bound to blow up sometime.' He crossed to the kitchen. 'Okay if I make myself some tea?'

'Go ahead.'

'You want a cup?'

She shook her head. 'No, thanks.' She watched him for a while, preparing his tea in a strange, brooding silence. Then, mug in hand, he crossed to the window to take a look at the head. He stood, his own head canted at an angle, staring at it for some time.

Then, finally, 'God, she's ugly,' he said.

And Amy felt unaccountably defensive. 'No, she's not. There's something beautiful about her. Almost serene. If someone had cared to spend the money they could have fixed that lip, or at least improved it. You have to see past that.'

Tom looked at her curiously. 'It's just plasticine,' he said. 'She's not real.'

Amy detected an odd antagonism in his tone. 'She was once.'

Tom sipped thoughtfully at his tea, never taking his eyes off her, until she felt quite discomfited by his stare. Then he said, 'So what was he doing here?'

'Who?'

'Oh, come on. You know who I mean. MacNeil. I saw him leave.'

Amy felt her face flush. 'He came to see the head.'

'Oh? And did he think she was beautiful, too?'

'Don't be ridiculous.'

'Oh, so I'm ridiculous, am I? Since when did police officers start coming round your house to see your facial reconstructions?'

She said nothing.

'I wondered this morning, when you seemed to know all about him and his wife being separated.' He paused. 'What's going on, Amy?'

She didn't want to lie to him. 'It's none of your business, Tom.'

'Amy, he's the *ape man*! A big stupid gay-hating *ape*. I can't believe you're having a relationship with him.'

'Why not?'

'Well, for a start, because you never told me. I thought I was supposed to be your best friend.'

'You are.'

'Not any more, apparently.'

'Now you really are being ridiculous.'

'Am I?' Tom puffed himself up with indignation. 'How do you think we could ever co-exist, Amy. You, me and the *ape man*?'

'He's not like you think he is.' Amy knew that this was all slipping away from her.

Mirthless laughter exploded from Tom's lips. 'Oh, of course he's not!'

'He's not! He's not homophobic. He doesn't hate you; he just doesn't understand you, that's all. He might even be a little afraid of you.'

'Oh, yes, shaking in his boots.'

Amy was angry with him now. 'You're so obsessed with your sexuality, Tom, you let it define everything you are. You're gay, and proud of it, and want the world to know – which is great. But you thrust it in people's faces, and you don't realise how intimidating or embarrassing that can be. Especially to a Presbyterian country boy from the Scottish Highlands.'

Tom glared at her, filled with fury. 'You lied to me,' he said, barely keeping it under control.

'I did not! I didn't tell you, that's all.'

'Which is lying by omission. And friends don't do that. Friends tell one another everything.'

'And you'd have approved, I suppose?'

'No, of course I wouldn't.'

'So in other words, I can't have a relationship without your approval.'

'He's the *ape man*, for God's sake. What the hell do you see in him? And even more to the point, what the hell does he see in you?' It was out before he could stop it.

Amy turned deadly pale, and her whole world concentrated itself into a silent centre so filled with hurt it took her several moments before she could speak. 'In a cripple, you mean? What does he see in a cripple?' Her voice was very small, very quiet.

The colour rose high on Tom's face. 'No,' he said quickly. 'No, that's not what I meant at all.'

'I think you'd better go.'

'Amy . . .'

'Go. Please, Tom, just go before either of us says anything else.'

He seemed to realise that there was no way back. At least not now. Bridges had been burned. He lay his cup on the table. 'I'm sorry, Amy,' he said. 'I'm sorry I came.'

III.

The night they met, or at least the night it all began, nobody had been more surprised at the way it turned out than Amy. They'd encountered each other several times at the lab, and she knew there was some kind of animosity between him and Tom, but she had no idea then what it was. She had only recently started doing freelance work for the FSS, and MacNeil was just another policeman. A big, taciturn Scot who treated her like she didn't exist. Until the office night out.

It was Tom who had persuaded her to go. Someone was leaving, and they had booked a room in a wine bar in Soho for the farewell do. Amy was persuaded to leave her car at home so that she could drink, and since most London taxis these days carried ramps for wheelchair access, she ran out of arguments for not going.

She was shy and self-conscious. She had only been working at Lambeth Road for a matter of weeks, and didn't know many people, and so she had clung to Tom during the early part of the evening. But, as usual, Tom drank too much, and it wasn't long before he found himself a man and disappeared off into the night, leaving Amy to fend for herself. She ended up sitting in a corner on her own, nursing an empty wine glass, and no one thought to offer to refill it for her. Until a big shadow fell across the table, and she looked up to see MacNeil looking down at her. 'You want another one of those?'

Really, all Amy wanted to do was go, but here was Tom's *ape man* offering to buy her a drink. And very nicely, too. So how could she refuse?

He returned with a glass of Pinot Grigio for her and a whisky for himself and sat down beside her. 'You don't look like you're having a great time.'

'Neither do you.'

'I'm not.'

'So why are you here?'

He shrugged. 'One has certain social obligations.'

She laughed. 'That's the first time I've ever heard a policeman talk about social obligations.'

He smiled ruefully. 'Aye, well, they like us to use big words in the force these days. You know what a defensible space situation is?'

She looked at him blankly. 'I've no idea.'

'It's a garden.'

She laughed again. 'You're kidding.'

He straightened up and composed a serious expression. 'M'lud,' he said solemnly to some imaginary magistrate, 'I was proceeding in a westerly direction on the south footpath when the accused person and other unknown assailants emerged from the defensible space situation at the apex of the highway.' Then he relaxed and grinned. 'You know, they send us to foreign language classes to learn to speak like that.'

'You seem pretty fluent.'

'I was always good with languages. I speak pretty good profane.'

'I like your accent.'

'Do you? Most people down here make fun of it. And in

131

Scotland they'd call me a teuchter. That's a daft boy from the Highlands, for your information.'

'I'm glad you told me. And are you?'

'Am I what?'

'A daft boy from the Highlands.'

'Oh, aye. None dafter.'

She looked at him as if for the first time. There was something unexpectedly open about him. No hint of side, or angle, and he didn't seem to mind making fun of himself. He was a big man, with big hands which, she was sure, could do some damage if he chose to use them as weapons, and yet there was an appealingly gentle quality in his manner. It was in looking at his hands that she noticed the ring.

'How long have you been married?'

'Eight years,' he said without hesitation.

'Any kids?'

He smiled, and she saw the affection in it. 'Aye, a wee laddie. Eight years old. Great kid.'

'What's his name?'

'Sean. Named after his father.' When she frowned, he explained. 'Sean is Irish for John, but I preferred to be called Jack. My father's called Sean, you see. And his father, and his father's father. Way too many Seans in the family, Irish roots going way back. But I couldn't quite bring myself to break the tradition, and it was Martha who said, what about Sean? Sounded good to me.'

'Martha. That's your wife?'

'Aye.'

The party was breaking up. Someone from toxicology came over and said a bunch of them were going on for a curry if they wanted to join them. But Amy said she had better be getting home. And MacNeil said he had, too. The place emptied quite rapidly, and MacNeil said, 'I'll get you a taxi, if you like.'

'Thanks.' She let him help her out into the street with her wheelchair. The streets were crowded with drinkers who had spilled out of pubs and bars into the warm summer air. MacNeil steered her down to the corner where a bunch of yobs speaking some Slavic language were drinking cans of Fosters. One of them looked at Amy and made some comment, eliciting laughter from the others. MacNeil grabbed his shirt by the collar and nearly lifted him off his feet. His can went clattering across the pavement. 'You got something to say, sonny, say it to me. And say it in a fucking language I understand.' His pals were startled and instantly on the defensive, but wary, and kept their distance.

'Don't, Jack, don't. Please,' Amy said, and reluctantly

MacNeil let go of the youth, pushing him back into the arms of his friends.

'Sorry,' he said to her, embarrassed, and he wheeled her on down to Shaftesbury Avenue.

'Why did you do that?'

'I hate unfairness.' He kept his eyes dead ahead.

'What was it you imagined he'd said?'

'Something unpleasant. Something about you.'

'You get used to it,' she said. 'I've been called a "chink" all my life, "slanty eyes" sometimes. And worse. Now it's "slanty-eyed cripple".' As soon as she said it she thought how bitter it sounded. And she didn't want to be bitter. She had seen what bitterness could do to people.

On Shaftesbury Avenue he hailed a taxi. The driver apologised. He didn't have a ramp.

'We can wait for the next one,' Amy said.

'Don't need to,' MacNeil told her. And he lifted her out of the wheelchair as if she weighed nothing at all, a child in his big, strong arms, and he put her into the taxi before lifting in the wheelchair. 'I'll go with you,' he said. 'Then there won't be a problem at the other end.'

On the drive across town she said, 'You really don't have to do this, you know.'

'Nothing else to do.'

'You've a wife and child waiting for you at home.' There was a long silence. He was looking out of the window at the passing lights and didn't respond. 'Haven't you?'

He turned to face her, and in the fleeting light of a passing streetlamp she saw a look in his eyes like a wounded animal. He couldn't hold her gaze. 'No,' he said eventually. 'No, I haven't.'

It seemed like a very long time before she summoned the courage to ask. 'Why not?'

'We've separated,' he said simply. He was looking at his hands in his lap, and turning his wedding ring around and around. This time she knew he wasn't going to elucidate, and she knew better than to ask.

The Tower of London was discreetly lit as they drove past and across Tower Bridge to the South Bank. The taxi dropped them at the corner of Gainsford Street and Shad Thames.

'I'll see you to the door,' MacNeil said when he'd got her out and back into her wheelchair.

'There's no need, really. I'm a big girl. I come home in the dark all the time.'

'Aye, but not when I'm around to worry about it. It's alright, I'm not looking to get asked up for coffee. I never drink the stuff.' He paid the driver, and Amy punched in her entry code at the gate. He pushed it open and they crossed the courtyard to the ramp which led up to her front door.

She frowned. 'That's odd.'

'What is?'

'The light's out above the door. I always leave it on when I go out.'

'Just to advertise to burglars that the place is empty?'

She gave him a look. 'I need to see to get in.' She unlocked the door and opened it into the stairwell. The whole apartment was in darkness. There was a light switch within easy reach of the wheelchair, but it produced no light.

'Where's the fuse box?' MacNeil asked.

'On the top floor.'

MacNeil looked at the redundant stair lift at the foot of the stairs. 'How the hell do you get up and down when the power's out?'

'It's never been out before.'

He closed the door and picked her up out of the wheelchair again. She put her arms around his neck, and remembered how safe she had felt as a child, carried up the stairs to bed by her father who would sing to her every night as they went. *Carry me, carry me 'cross the world.*

'You'd better show me,' MacNeil said, and he carried her in the dark up two flights of stairs to the sprawling attic room at the top. Here street lights shone through the windows, casting a pale yellow glow across the room. He lowered her gently into the top floor wheelchair and opened the door of the fuse box. He flicked a switch and all the lights came on. He shook his head. 'Must have been a power surge or something. Tripped the fuse. You want to have some kind of battery back-up on those stair lifts if you don't want to get stuck.'

'I could always call you to carry me up and down.'

'I'd be here like a shot.'

Something in the way he said it made her heart skip a beat then pulse a little faster, and he seemed suddenly self-conscious. Her mouth went dry, and she couldn't believe that he might be interested in her. Not in that way.

Later, he told her the reason he'd hesitated was because he had no idea how to kiss someone in a wheelchair. It explained his clumsiness as he took a step towards her, and then stopped, before dropping awkwardly to his knees and taking her face gently in both of his big hands and kissing her.

It was a moment that would live with her always. A moment when she felt as if God had given her back her life.

CHAPTER NINE

I.

MacNeil parked outside the police station which stood in what Scots would have called the *gushet* between Kennington Road and Mead Row. It was a word MacNeil had used several times when he first arrived in London, but which nobody seemed to understand. He looked once in a dictionary and couldn't find it. The closest he got was the word 'gusset', which described a triangular piece of cloth sewn into a garment to reinforce it. And so he'd figured that must be it. And it described the positioning of Kennington Road Police Station precisely – built in the triangle created by two streets intersecting at acute angles.

He had been back to Islington to shower and change,

and felt less contaminated now. Less *mingin'*, some of his colleagues might have said. It was another Scots word, but one which this time had been unaccountably hijacked by the English to become trendy London slang.

DCI Laing, however, was sticking with good old-fashioned Glasgow profanity. 'Where the fuck have you been?' he bawled at MacNeil across the detectives' room. 'In here.' And he pointed an aggressive finger into his office. No one else paid much attention. They were used to Laing by now.

MacNeil stood in front of the DCI's desk. 'I had some personal business to attend to, Detective Chief Inspector.'

'There's no such thing as personal on this job, sonny. I'd have thought you'd know that by now.'

'Well, to be perfectly honest with you, Mr Laing, I don't give a shit what you think. And if you've got a problem with that, feel free to fire me.' He had meant to tell the DCI about Sean, but somehow this didn't seem like the moment.

Laing glared at him. 'If you don't want me to fuck with your pension, MacNeil, I'd suggest you keep a civil tongue in your head.' He didn't appear to see any irony in that, and MacNeil bit back a retort. 'I've had some prick from the Deputy Prime Minister's office chasing me for a written explanation of why one of our officers held up work on the

Archbishop's Park site this morning. And I couldn't even send them your report, because I don't have it.'

'It'll be on your desk in the morning.'

'I want it on my desk before I leave tonight.'

MacNeil stood and surveyed the paperwork accumulating in drifts on his desk. Reports and files and summonses, a hundred different Post-its stuck to the sides of his computer and all along his desk lamp, scribbled notes from dozens of investigations making a tower on the spike in his out-tray. Normally at this time the office would have been buzzing. Today there were no more than half a dozen officers and clerks sitting at desks. There were telephones ringing constantly, because there weren't enough people to answer them.

DS Rufus Dawson slapped a Post-it on the screen in front of MacNeil. He was a big red-haired Irishman with a strange hybrid accent which owed as much to his upbringing in New Zealand as his Irish heritage. An inveterate joker, always with a ready one-liner and an infectious laugh, he had been uncharacteristically subdued in recent weeks. There wasn't much he could find to laugh about these days. 'Phil called from Lambeth Road with a name and address. A match for the print they found on the Underground ticket. He said he was going to fax more info.' He was about to go again, but something in MacNeil's demeanour stopped him. He gave him a long look. 'You alright, mate?'

'Yeah, fine, Ruf, thanks.'

He peeled the Post-it off the computer and looked at Rufus's scrawl. Ronald Kazinski, was the name on the piece of paper. There was an address in South Lambeth. He got up and went to see if Phil's fax had come in. It was sitting in the in-tray.

Kazinski was thirty-one. He had dark, thinning hair in the smudged mugshot that accompanied his details. High cheekbones and wide-set eyes. He had been an undertaker's assistant at a south-side crematorium for the last two and a half years. Shortly after the start of the emergency he had been pressed into government service at the official body disposal centre set up south of the river in the derelict Battersea Power Station. His fingerprints were in the AFIS computer because he had a police record for reset. Now instead of handling stolen goods, he was disposing of dead bodies. MacNeil wondered if he had also been responsible for disposing of the bones of the little Chinese girl in Archbishop's Park. It was an odd coincidence that his print should have been found on an old Underground ticket picked up near where the bones had been dumped.

And coincidences, odd or otherwise, were not something in which MacNeil was inclined to believe.

He pulled on his coat and called over to Dawson, 'If Laing's looking for me, you can tell him I've gone to talk to Kazinski.'

II.

In the Middle Ages, the site of Battersea Power Station was known as Battersea Fields, an area frequented by vagabonds and undesirables. In the 1800s it was used for pigeon shooting and county fairs. The Duke of Wellington and Lord Winchelsea were alleged to have fought a duel here, from which both walked away unscathed. The power station, with its four iconic chimneys, was built in the 1930s and belched thick, black smoke into the air above the city for half a century before being shut down in the 1980s. They took off the roof to remove the giant turbines, and for nearly thirty years the building had been exposed to the elements. Ambitious plans by a private consortium to convert the site into a leisure, retail and hotel complex, while retaining the power station's distinctive outer shell, had been temporarily shelved by the government. A makeshift roof had been raised over the main hall, and the four chimneys were once again belching smoke into the skies over London. But it was not coal ferried up the river on barges that they were burning. It was human bodies. Victims of the pandemic. The smoke, however, was just as black, and hung over the south side of the river in a ghostly pall.

MacNeil drove past hoardings which hid the site from prying eyes. Hoardings raised by developers in more optimistic times. They created a bizarre screen of painted green fields and trees beneath a clear blue sky. Above them the red-brick towers of the power station pushed up into the real sky, dark and angry, and pierced on each corner by the tall white chimneys that bled off the fumes from the furnaces below. To the south-west, tall cranes stood idle over unfinished apartment blocks. To the north-east, the new Covent Garden Market – which described itself as *The Larder of London* – was deserted. And all along Chelsea Park Road, giant posters shouted slogans at empty streets – *The Industrial Revolution is Over; The Information Age Has Ended;* and *I Think, Therefore I Can. Welcome to the Ideas Generation.* MacNeil glanced up at the smoke hanging overhead and thought, welcome to hell.

He turned into Kirtling Street and drove up to the gatehouse, drawing up outside blue-painted metal gates.

Opposite the gate was an army jeep with a machine gun mounted in the back. Two soldiers sat smoking through cotton masks. A security man in green uniform appeared on the other side of the gate. He too wore a white cotton mask, and kept his distance. MacNeil got out of his car and stood looking at him through the bars of the gate. 'You got papers?' the man called.

MacNeil held up his warrant card. 'Police,' he said. 'I want to talk to one of your employees. A Ronald Kazinski.'

'Hold on,' the security man said. He went back into the gatehouse, and MacNeil saw, beyond the gate, a low building of odd angular-shaped white plastic and glass. It housed a model of the developer's plans for the complex. But they had never imagined this. On the grass next to it were two larger-than-life bronze statues. A man, and a woman holding a baby, both with their hands raised in salute. To what, was anyone's guess. To life, maybe, MacNeil thought. In which case there was something more than ironic about it. But they did seem to complement the sloganising posters he had seen earlier. There was something almost Stalinesque about them.

An electronic lock released the gate and it started swinging slowly open. The security man called from the door of the gatehouse, 'Drive straight up to the administration block and ask for Mr Hartson. He's in charge.'

MacNeil drove past the saluting statues and through another gate to a brick-built office block that rose halfway up the outer wall of the power station. Across a wasteland of crumbling asphalt, diggers and cranes stood motionless, like so many dinosaurs frozen in time. A line of unmarked black vans queued at the gates of a huge opening into the main hall, waiting to deliver their macabre cargo, before heading back to any of a dozen hospitals to reload and return. Latter-day ferrymen plying their trade back and forth across the River Styx.

He parked outside the office block and pushed open double doors into the entrance hall. A woman at a desk looked up from behind her mask. He waved his warrant card at her. 'DI MacNeil for Mr Hartson. He's expecting me.'

Hartson's office was at the top of the building. A huge glass partition along one side of it looked down into the main hall of the former power station. Hartson was a man of about sixty, tall, lean and bald, and he had about him the obsequious air of an undertaker. MacNeil was drawn to the glass. The scene below was one he could barely have imagined. Thousands of naked bodies laid out three deep on wooden pallets stretching as far as you could see, cast in their piles like so many mannequins in a doll factory, arms and legs intertwined, strangely luminous, barely human. Fumigating mists obscured the detail, like the fog that would lie along the Thames on an autumn morning. Ghoulish figures in blue bio-suits, faceless behind tinted plastic visors, moved amongst the wisps and tendrils of it in slow motion, like astronauts on the moon, removing bodies from the trucks to pile on yet more pallets. One of the furnaces seemed designated for clothes and bedding. Bodies were slid into the other three, still on their pallets, by giant forklifts. In those few moments when the furnace doors remained open, the fires within cast a vaporous orange light through the fumigating mists, before giant cast-iron doors slammed shut again, their vibration felt throughout the building like seismic tremors.

MacNeil let his eyes drift over the piles of discarded humanity below him, and wondered if Sean was down there somewhere, the seed of his loins awaiting cremation with all the others. It was not a thought he could bear to dwell on, and he turned back into the office.

'Sobering vision, isn't it,' said Hartson. 'There, but for the grace of God, go you and I.' He wandered past MacNeil to the window, and MacNeil saw his mask catch a momentary flicker of orange as one of the furnace doors opened to receive more dead. 'I used to be devout,' he said. 'A good Catholic.' He turned back to MacNeil. 'Now I wonder.' But then he dismissed his cosmic reflections in an instant. 'What do you want with Ronnie?'

'Just a word. You know him personally?'

'I know every man here. Death has a way of bringing the living together. We're all very close.'

'Then you know he has a criminal record?'

'Oh, yes. His file was made available to me when we were recruiting for the facility. But it's in his past, I think. His experience in dealing with death took precedence. He's an affable young man. Hardworking, conscientious.'

'You won't mind if I borrow him for half an hour?'

'I wouldn't mind in the slightest, Detective Inspector. But he's not due on until midnight.' Hartson's smile bore the gravitas of a man used to being the bearer of bad news. 'We work around the clock here. Twenty-four-seven, as our American friends would say.'

MacNeil glanced back down into the halls of Hades below, and for just a moment thought he saw Sean's small body amongst all the others, tiny and twisted, sandwiched between a large, fat woman and an old man. And then the image was gone, vanished forever in a swirl of white smoke.

III.

Kazinski lived with his mother in a 1960s council estate on the southern edge of Lambeth. High- and low-rise apartment blocks built to pluck people from the slums of 19th-century industrial London, and deliver them to a better life in a brave new world. The architects who designed them might have been emissaries of the devil, because they had instead removed the impoverished working classes from real communities, and brought them to a place which now resembled something worse than the hell from which they were supposed to have escaped.

At least half of the flats were boarded up, windows broken, others burned out. Crumbling concrete cladding bore the black streaks of insurance fires that for many had been the only way out. Tarmac concourses were strewn with broken glass and empty beer cans, a landscape punctuated by burned-out vehicles, like the carcasses of so many dead animals. The detritus of abandoned households – old mattresses, discarded clothing, broken furniture – was washed up against the ramps and walkways, like seaweed on a beach after a storm. Streetlamps had been smashed, many of them torn down. It would be a no-go area after nightfall, dark and dangerous. This was the brave new world.

MacNeil parked on the street and stood looking through the open gates of the estate. It was hard to believe that anyone still lived here. And yet, he could see, along the covered walkways on each floor, freshly painted doors, and windows with clean, white net curtains. Like the occasional good tooth in a mouth full of decay. Across the road, a multi-storey block had been abandoned. Every window boarded up, rolls of barbed wire dragged around its perimeter.

Glass crunched underfoot as he walked across a children's play area, where doubtless architect's drawings would have depicted a happy gathering of multicultural kids kicking a ball about. Even had that ever been a reality, it was long gone.

MacNeil had a strange sense of foreboding as he entered Kazinski's block. There had not been a solitary sign of life. The world felt like a vessel whose captain had given the order to abandon ship, but nobody had told MacNeil.

The stairwell smelled of urine and stale beer, and something else he couldn't quite identify. The walls were almost obscured by graffiti. He heard his own footsteps echoing all the way up to the sixth floor. On the second, he turned into the open walkway that ran along the outside of the block, leading to the individual flats. Every second doorway was boarded up. Others had been daubed with red paint, crude crosses warning that this home had been visited by the flu, a strange, frightening throwback to the days of the Plague. What misery, MacNeil wondered, lurked behind these doors?

Kazinski's flat was number twenty-three. The door had been newly painted. Pillar-box red. To cover up the mark of the flu? Or to guard against it? MacNeil had no way of knowing. There was a polished brass knocker at head height, and he banged it three times. After a moment, he saw the lace curtain twitch in the window to his left.

'What do you want?' A woman's voice came muffled from behind the glass.

'Police, Mrs Kazinski. I want to talk to your son.'

'Let me see your card.' This was a woman used to dealing with cops.

MacNeil took out his warrant card and pressed it against the window. The curtain was dragged to one side, and by the daylight it let in, MacNeil saw the pale, pasty face of a woman in her fifties, features sharp and pinched, the genetic inheritance of generations of poverty. The curtain fell back into place.

'He's not here.'

'Don't tell me stories, Mrs Kazinski.' He knew she would not open the door to him, and it would take too long to get a warrant and officers to break it down.

'He left for work this morning.'

'He doesn't start work till midnight.'

'No, he started at midday. He told me.'

'Then he lied to you, Mrs Kazinski. I've just come from Battersea.'

'No. He's a good boy, my Ronnie.'

'Was he at home last night, Mrs Kazinski, or was he at work?'

She hesitated, clearly not knowing which was the right answer to give.

'What time did he get in from work this morning, Mrs Kazinski?'

'I don't know, it was late. I mean early. Five, maybe six. I was asleep. He was on the five o'clock shift last night. They work twelve hours.'

'It was his day off yesterday. They told me at the power station.'

'No!' He heard the confusion in her denial. The hurt in her voice. Why had her son been lying to her? MacNeil believed now that she was telling the truth. That Kazinski

151

really wasn't there, and that she didn't know where he'd gone if it wasn't to work. 'What's he done?'

'I don't know that he's done anything, Mrs Kazinski. I just want to talk to him, that's all.'

'You people never just want to talk.' She was transferring her anger and hurt at her son's lies and directing them at MacNeil. It was something he was familiar with. It was always the fault of the police when the people you loved got into trouble.

'You can tell him I was looking for him.' MacNeil folded his warrant card into an inside pocket. 'And you might like to ask him what it was he was doing last night when he told you he was at work.' He thrust his hands in his pockets and headed back along the stairwell, Mrs Kazinski's imprecations following him along the walkway. But still, she wasn't going to open her door under any circumstance. Even to abuse him to his back.

A few paces from the stairs, he heard a scuffle of feet, a voice whispering in the darkness beyond, and he stopped in his tracks. 'Who's there?'

A skinny youth stepped out into the walkway. His hair was gelled into spikes, and the triangle of a red and blue bandana covered his nose and mouth. His forehead above it was peppered with acne. He wore a hooded sweatshirt that looked two sizes too big for him, and a pair of khaki cargo trousers with the crotch almost at the knees. From a hand crudely tattooed with letters on each knuckle, a scarred baseball bat dangled to the ground. Three other youths, one of them black, stepped out behind him. They all wore bandanas and carried baseball bats or crowbars.

A noise behind him made him turn, and he saw another two young men emerge from a doorway which had been daubed with red paint. He felt the hostility in the eyes that fixed upon him and knew he was in trouble. He glanced over the side of the walkway. Even if he survived the jump he would break both legs.

'Wot you want wiff Ronnie?' the acne youth said.

'We've got business,' MacNeil replied, hoping that Ronnie might be on terms with these boys, and that they would leave him alone if they thought he was a friend of the ex-con.

'Yeah, right,' Acne said. 'You're the fuckin' fuzz, aintcha? Fuckin' rozza.' MacNeil said nothing. Acne nodded towards MacNeil's coat pockets. 'Got 'em onya, 'ave ya?'

'Got what?'

'The fuckin' drugs, coppa. Know what I mean?'

'I don't have drugs.'

'Course you do. They give 'em tcha. All the cops got 'em, din they? Fuckin' FluKill.'

'Maybe.'

'Give us 'em, then.' He held out his hand.

'I'll give you my FluKill if you give me some information. That's a fair exchange, isn't it?' MacNeil tried very hard to keep the tremor out of his voice.

Acne frowned. 'Wot kinda fuckin' info you looking for, rozza?'

'I want to know where Ronnie goes when he's not at work.

Acne looked at him as if he was insane. 'You wot?'

'I want to know where he hangs out.'

'Sssa Black Ice Club, innit?' the black youth said.

'Shut the fuck up,' Acne told him.

For a moment, MacNeil forgot his plight. 'In Soho? All the clubs up there were shut down weeks ago.'

'At's wot you fink, mate.' A cold smile narrowed Acne's eyes. 'Not that it fuckin' matters wot you fink, does it?' He held his hand out again. 'Cough up.' And he roared at his own joke. 'Funny, eh?'

'Sorry,' MacNeil said. 'I'm afraid I lied.'

'You wot?' Acne looked perplexed.

'I haven't got any FluKill.' And he swung his left fist full into the boy's face. He knew he had to take the initiative, catch them off guard, if he was to stand a chance. He felt bone and teeth break beneath his knuckles, and immediately stooped to scoop up the baseball bat as it fell from Acne's hand. He grasped it with both hands and swung around. The bat, at full extension, caught one of the youths behind him square on the side of the head, and he went down like a sack of coal. The door to MacNeil's right had been boarded up with plywood. He kicked it as hard as he could, and the sheet of wood splintered into darkness in a cloud of dust. MacNeil plunged through it into the unknown, the voices of his assailants raised in pain and fury at his back.

He was in a length of hallway from which the floorboards had long ago been ripped up. He ran from rafter to rafter and turned into another doorway. From here he could defend his position. They could only come at him one at a time. And the first of them came, screaming down the hall like a demented spirit. A crowbar embedded itself in the plaster beside MacNeil's head. He hadn't even seen it coming. He swung his bat and caught the black youth in the mouth, and the kid fell backwards, blood bubbling through split lips. MacNeil braced himself against the door jamb and waited for the next attack. But it didn't come. The black kid, still whimpering, staggered back out through the gloom to the walkway. He heard the murmur of voices, and then someone cursing loudly. And then silence.

All MacNeil could hear now was the rasp of his own breathing in the dark. As his eyes grew accustomed to it, he looked around the room behind him. The floorboards were gone here, too. There was a torn mattress pushed up into one corner, and the rusted remains of an old bedstead. A window giving on to the walkway was boarded up. MacNeil fumbled for his phone. He could call for help, but it would take time, and he didn't know how long he could hold these kids off. But there was no time even for a call. A whooshing sound came down the hallway, along with a dazzle of flickering white light. A flaming bundle of rags soaked in petrol. MacNeil could smell the fumes, and thick black smoke immediately forced him back into the room. It was insane. They didn't care if they burned down the whole block.

He reacted instinctively, in panic as much as anything, and threw himself at the window. The whole board tore itself free of the nails which held it, and he went out through the window frame with it, pulling his knees up to his chest, catching his shoulder and his head as he went. He landed on top of one of his attackers, the board a barrier between them, and he heard the air being forced from the youth's lungs in a deep, painful retch. MacNeil didn't wait to see who it was. He scrambled to his feet and ran for the stairwell, legs nearly buckling beneath him. In his panic he had lost the baseball bat. But it didn't matter. He was on the stairs now. He was on his way down, three, five at a time. Behind him, he could hear them whooping and shrieking, out for blood and revenge. If they got him he was a dead man.

He could see daylight falling in through the open doorway at the foot of the stairs. Half a flight, and then once he was out he could sprint for the car.

He drew a lungful of sweet, fresh air as he swung through the doorway out on to the concourse, and a baseball bat caught him full across the chest, forcing it all back out. His momentum carried him on for several steps before he fell amongst the broken glass and felt it cut into the flesh of his palms and cheek. He rolled over and saw a tall, gangly black youth in drainpipe jeans grinning down at him, his bandana pulled down to his neck. Three others emerged from the stairwell behind him and pulled up short. Acne had discarded his mask, his face thick with blood drying around his nose and mouth. He held a metal bar in his hand now, eyes filled with hatred and fury.

MacNeil lay on the tarmac, pulled up on to one elbow, still trying to catch his breath. He knew there was no way he could reach the car before them. These kids were like wild, wounded animals. They were armed, and they meant to kill him.

Acne confirmed his intent. 'You'ra fuckin' dead man, rozza!' He lifted the iron bar clutched in his hand and took a step towards him. Then his chest burst open in a spray of pink. The youth barely had time to register surprise, before toppling forward on to his face without a sound. His weapon clattered noisily away across the flagstones.

MacNeil looked at him in amazement. He had no idea what had happened. The others stood frozen in disbelief.

'Wot the fuck . . . ?' The black kid who had smacked MacNeil in the chest with his baseball bat moved towards his fallen friend, and the right side of his head just vanished. He spun around, toppling on to his back, his one remaining eye staring sightlessly up at the cloud overhead.

'Jesus fuckin' Christ, he's fuckin' shot!' MacNeil heard one of the others shout. 'Someone's got a fuckin' gun!' And then he heard them sprinting off in different directions, like animals scattering at the report of a hunter's rifle. They were gone in moments, and MacNeil was left lying on his own with two dead kids at his feet. He swung around and got quickly on to his knees, remaining crouched there, eyes flickering along the skyline of the surrounding apartment blocks, trying to spot the marksman, wondering if he would be next. But he saw no one, and there was no third shot. He got to his feet on shaky legs and looked at the two youths lying in slowly gathering pools of their own blood. He winced, as pain seared across his chest, and drew a sharp breath. He put a hand to his chest, and gently pressed. He didn't think there were any broken ribs, but he knew he was going to be black and blue.

As he walked to his car, he scanned the semi-derelict buildings that rose up all around him. Someone, somewhere, from one of these abandoned apartments, had saved his life. He had no idea why, and it was only later that it struck him as odd that he had not heard either shot.

He slumped behind the wheel of his car and took out his phone.

CHAPTER TEN

Pinkie watched through wooden slats as MacNeil sat behind the wheel of his car. He could see his mouth moving as he spoke into his phone, and he could imagine what the cop was saying. Maybe, Pinkie thought, he could even read his lips.

He rested the barrel of his rifle again on the window ledge, and nestled his chin against its wooden butt so that he could look through the sight. He focused the cross-hairs on MacNeil's mouth, but his face was partially obscured by reflection. Pinkie's finger caressed the trigger. How easy it would be just to squeeze, ever so gently, and watch that face dissolve in front of his eyes, like those stupid boys across the street.

But Mr Smith had told him that if anything happened to

the investigating officer it would only draw unwanted attention. And, anyway, it hadn't been right, the way they had ganged up against him. Six against one. It wasn't fair. And Pinkie always backed the underdog. He liked to see a man triumph against the odds. He had watched events unfolding on the walkway, unable to get off a shot. MacNeil had done well to escape down the stairs, and once the yobbos were out in the open, well, they'd been easy meat. He had particularly enjoyed their consternation. And then their fear. And MacNeil? His expression had been a joy to behold. It was fun to give a man back his life. Almost as much fun as it was to take it. But what had made it all the sweeter was MacNeil's confusion. His utter lack of comprehension. He had no idea how, or why, he was still alive. And never would.

Pinkie withdrew his rifle and began the slow, meticulous process of disassembling it, lovingly wiping down each piece with an oiled cloth, to slot it back into its allotted place in its felt-lined case. They said that sometimes a silencer would reduce accuracy over distance. But Pinkie had never found that. He never took a shot if he thought there was a risk of missing. And he had never missed.

If a job's worth doing, it's worth doing well.

He appreciated those simple things his mother had taught him. She'd had wisdom beyond her years. Her only mistake had been in the company she kept. The succession of men who came to the house had not always treated her well. He could remember hearing her cry out the night it happened. A lack of judgement on her part. But Pinkie had always liked to imagine it was only because she'd been so trusting. She had always seen only the best in people. Especially her boy, her precious son.

He looked around the front room of this tenth-floor apartment, fading daylight falling in shadowed strips across the littered floor. Evidence of down-and-outs, or junkies, in the discarded cans and cigarette ends, the bundle of filthy clothes abandoned in the far corner, the mattress on the floor. Perhaps these shadow people would return when it was dark. Pinkie did not relish the thought of being here when they did. Who knew what contamination they might bring with them. And Pinkie was nothing if not fastidious. He disliked human contact of any kind. Just being in this place left him feeling unclean. He would shower and change as soon as circumstances allowed.

Meantime he was trapped here, for as long as MacNeil remained at the scene. He snapped shut the polished case that held the pieces of his profession and settled down to wait.

It was nearly twenty minutes before the uniforms

arrived, and an ambulance, and an unmarked van which deposited two men and a woman in strangely luminescent white protective suits. Pinkie watched as MacNeil spoke to them, and the group assembled around the bodies of the two youths beneath the block opposite, before turning to follow MacNeil's pointing finger. For a moment, Pinkie felt exposed, as if they could see him, and he drew back from the boards at the window. A reflex action. But of course they saw nothing.

The street lights had come on, and dusk was falling fast. Lights appeared in the few remaining inhabited flats on the estate, frightened residents peering out in the gathering gloom before drawing curtains and turning on TV sets to blot out the real world.

When Pinkie looked again, MacNeil had begun walking back to his car. Time, he thought, to move. He gathered his things and hurried down the deserted staircase. By the time he emerged into the area at the back of the block, once designated a parking area for residents, MacNeil's car was turning the corner at the end of the street. A smear of brake lights in the cold twilight.

Pinkie put his case in the boot and started up Mr Smith's BMW. It purred smoothly, leather seats softly creased. He eased it over traffic bumps into the lane that led out to the street behind the estate. He turned left, and left again, and breathed a sigh of satisfaction as he saw the lights of MacNeil's car ahead of him. With luck the cop would lead him straight to Kazinski, and the useless lives of those two boys would have found some meaning in death.

CHAPTER ELEVEN

It was dark in Kennington Road, lights all along the police station falling out across the deserted street below, reflecting in the darkened windows of the shops and restaurants opposite.

Laing waved MacNeil into a seat and shut the door. There were more people now out in the detectives' office. It was almost seven, a changeover in shifts. A brief congregation of officers and staff who met only rarely when their rotas diverged. And in just a few minutes, all across the city, the curfew would begin. A signal for most people to lock down their homes for the night and wait for morning. A signal for others to emerge under cover of darkness to embark on a rampage of looting and vandalism. It was not a time anyone wanted to be out on the streets.

MacNeil had spent the last two hours writing up his reports on the bones found in Archbishop's Park, and the two youths shot dead on the housing estate in South Lambeth. Laing had just finished going through them, half-moon reading glasses still perched on the end of his nose. He was shaking his head. 'Weird,' he said. 'Fucking weird.'

'What is, sir?'

'These kids that got shot. Not some casual shooting, some lunatic with a gun. It was a real pro job. A professional weapon in professional hands.' He regarded MacNeil speculatively. 'Do you think there was a connection?'

'With Kazinski?' Laing nodded, and MacNeil shook his head. 'I can't see how. No one knew I was going there, or why.' He'd had time in the intervening hours to think about it, and was quite spooked. Someone had saved his life. Someone had shot those kids to stop them beating hell out of him with iron bars and baseball bats. Without that someone, it was MacNeil who would be lying on Tom Bennet's autopsy table right now instead of those boys. He could imagine how much satisfaction that would have given Bennet.

'So you've just got some kind of guardian angel looking out for you, then?' Laing said.

MacNeil could only shrug. How easily that gunman could

have shot him, too. From some empty apartment in the abandoned block opposite, from where he must have been watching, even before MacNeil arrived. But watching for what? What on earth had he been doing there?

In normal circumstances, the flats would have been sealed off, and officers drafted in to search them unit by unit, until they found the gunman's vantage point. And then forensics would have combed it for any tiny piece of evidence that might have been left at the scene. But they simply didn't have the manpower, and the approach of darkness and the curfew would only have complicated things. Perhaps Laing would order some kind of search in the morning. But in any event, it would no longer be any of MacNeil's business. In twelve hours he would not be a police officer any more. He would be a former cop, former father, former husband. Everything behind him, only uncertainty ahead.

Laing held out his hand. 'I'll take those pills off you now, Jack.'

It took MacNeil a moment to drag himself back to the present and realise what Laing was asking for. He shook his head. 'I'm sorry, sir. I don't have them.'

Laing glared at him. 'You've taken them?'

'No, sir, I've lost them.'

Laing glared at him, disbelief burning in his eyes. 'You'd better fucking find them, then. These bloody things are like gold dust. They're not on my desk first thing tomorrow, you're in big shit, son.'

MacNeil just nodded. What were they going to do? Shoot him? 'I'll need curfew clearance to go up to Soho, Mr Laing. If you could enter it up in the computer.'

'What for?'

'To check out the Black Ice Club.'

Laing regarded him as if he had two heads. 'You mean you think those kids were telling the truth?'

'I don't think they meant to. But, you know, the black kid just sort of blurted it out.'

'Well, if it's open for business, it's doing it illegally.'

'I doubt if it's advertising the fact, sir.'

'You'd better put in a courtesy call to the local bobbies. Let them know you're in the area.'

'Fine.' MacNeil got to his feet and turned towards the door.

'MacNeil.' He turned as Laing stood up and extended a hand towards him, before pulling it away again, as if from an electric shock. 'Sorry, forgot. No shaking hands. No spreading germs.' He grinned awkwardly. 'Just wanted to say, you know, good luck. You're a fucking idiot, MacNeil, but I don't wish you any harm.'

MacNeil managed a pale smile. 'Thank you, sir. I'll always remember your final words of kindness.'

Laing grinned. 'Fuck off.'

MacNeil was nearly halfway across the detectives' office before he realised that things were not as they should be. A bunch of coloured balloons danced above his desk on the end of a string. Most of his colleagues were gathered in a semi-circle beyond it. Someone had filled a trayful of plastic cups with orange juice, and on a cue they all leaned forward to lift one, and began a refrain of 'He's a Jolly Good Fellow'.

MacNeil stood, frozen with embarrassment, as they sang their ragged but hearty way through to the last line. *And so say all of us.* Someone shouted, *Hip, hip!* And there were three loud cheers before cups were tipped and orange juice downed. Rufus thrust a cup in his hand. 'Sorry we couldn't do anything stronger, me old son.'

'You don't know how jealous we all are,' someone shouted.

'Lucky bastard,' someone else said, to much noisy agreement.

MacNeil turned to see Laing standing grinning stupidly in the open door of his office.

DS George Murray leaned back behind his desk to pull out a box wrapped in brightly coloured paper, and peppered with the cartoon faces of smiling kids. 'We had a bit of a whip-round,' he said. 'But we had no idea what to get for the man who has everything.' A lot of loud laughter. 'So we got something for your kid instead. A box set of the Lord of the Rings trilogy on DVD.'

'And if you haven't got a DVD player, you're just going to have to buy him one, you mean Scots git,' Rufus said.

MacNeil stared at the box they had gone to so much trouble to buy and wrap. How could they have known? How could they possibly have known? And yet it seemed so cruel. Like kicking a man when he was down. For just a few moments this afternoon, when so much else had crowded his thoughts that he hadn't been able to think, he had found it possible to forget. And then felt guilty about it when he remembered. But this was the wickedest reminder of all.

And all he could see were their grinning faces, gathered around, watching for his reaction, waiting for his face to crease with the smile they knew so well. And all he could hear was Sean shouting excitedly, *Don't stop, Daddy, don't stop!*

A wave of nausea rose up through him like the chill of a winter draught. The detectives' room burned out on his retinas. The cup of orange juice fell from his hand. He felt his eyes burning, and he turned and hurried from the room. Grown men didn't cry. Certainly not in front of their peers.

He ran down the stairs, a voice shouting down the stairwell after him, full of concern and consternation. 'Jack, are you alright . . . ?'

He ran past the reception desk and burst through the front door on to the steps, passing between the pillars and grabbing the handrail. He retched several times, but nothing came up. Tears burned his cheeks and blurred the street lights. He slumped down on to the top step and tipped his head forward into his open palms.

He heard the door swing open behind him, and Laing's angry voice. 'What the hell are you playing at, MacNeil? These guys went to a lot of trouble for you tonight. Just being here for some of them was a big thing . . .' His voice tailed away as he saw his DI bent over on the top step. 'For Christ's sake, what's wrong with you, man?' The anger had leeched itself from his voice. Now he just sounded shocked.

MacNeil straightened himself up and quickly wiped the tears away from his face. He didn't want Laing's pity. He couldn't face that. But he knew he couldn't avoid telling him. He stayed sitting on the top step, gazing down the street towards the Three Stags pub where he'd too often spent too much time avoiding going home. Beyond it, the park and the Imperial War Museum seemed drowned in a pool of darkness. The Days Hotel across the road was empty, its staff laid off weeks ago.

'Sean died,' he said. 'This afternoon.'

He didn't look round for a reaction, and none came. Nothing but silence. A very long silence, and then slowly Laing eased himself down on to the top step beside him, and both men gazed south along the darkness of Kennington Road.

'We couldn't have kids,' Laing said finally. 'Elizabeth was always dead keen. She wanted children. That was her *raison d'être*. A bright, intelligent woman with a great career, and all she wanted was to get pregnant and stay home with the kids.'

MacNeil felt his boss turning to look at him briefly, then gazing away again. 'I wasn't that interested. It never bothered me, you know, until they said it wasn't possible. And then I wanted nothing more in this world. Funny that, isn't it? How you only start wanting something when you canny have it.' He scratched his head. 'And you look around you, and you realise that most of the scum we put behind bars . . . most of them got kids. Seems like there's nothing easier in this life. And so everyone just takes it for granted.' He paused. 'It's been one of the great regrets of my life, not having kids. I can't imagine what it must be like to have one, and then lose him.'

He put a hand briefly on MacNeil's shoulder, then stood up, and MacNeil was grateful that it wasn't pity he felt. It was sympathy, even empathy, not something of which he would ever have thought Laing capable.

'Go home, son,' Laing said. 'You're all finished here, now.'

MacNeil shook his head. There was nowhere he could go that he would have called home. He needed a focus. He needed something to get him through this night. 'Someone murdered that little girl,' he said. 'I'll not be finished here until I find him.'

CHAPTER TWELVE

I.

The West End was eerily quiet, washed out beneath colourless streetlamps, and under the constant, watchful eye of the CCTV cameras. MacNeil had been in one of the control rooms once, watching the bank of screens flicker from camera to camera. All that they had seen moving, apart from soldiers, were rats. Thousands of them. Cautiously venturing out from the dark of the sewers, inheritors of a city abandoned to them by the humans. They must have wondered what had happened. But it hadn't taken them long to stop wondering. They had grown bold quickly, and now joined the looters in their nightly endeavours to pick the city clean.

MacNeil drove up Haymarket. He could never quite get used to seeing the streets so empty, so devoid of life. Before the emergency, even in the small hours of the morning there would be taxis and private cars, and groups of revellers spilling out from clubs and pubs with late licences. But since the curfew, nothing stirred, and if it did, it would probably be shot.

The fountain and statue of Eros at Piccadilly Circus were still fenced off. The huge neon ads for Sanyo and TDK that once clad the corner buildings above Gap seemed like black holes in their absence. All colour and animation was bled from what had once been one of the liveliest corners of town. The green news-stand on the corner was battened down and all locked up. Nobody these days was buying the sightseeing bus tour tickets it used to sell. A megastore on the corner brooded darkly behind charred plywood. If the looters couldn't prise the boards free, they set them on fire. And they would almost invariably be gone by the time the army arrived.

Somewhere in the distance he heard the siren of a fire engine, and saw the faint orange glow of far-off flames reflecting in the low cloud that still hung over London. He went right, instead of left, around the roundabout to turn into Shaftesbury Avenue. It was the only plus side of the curfew. There were no traffic lights, and he could ignore one-way streets and roundabouts. The Mayor of London had tried hard to reduce traffic in the city. If only he had thought of this. It was far more effective than congestion-charging.

Immediately ahead of him, two trucks and an armed personnel carrier blocked the road. More than a dozen soldiers stood about in groups of two and three, removing their masks to smoke in isolation, before replacing them to rejoin their colleagues. But as soon as MacNeil's car turned off Piccadilly, they were on instant alert, SA80s swung in MacNeil's direction, twitchy fingers on sensitive triggers. One of them stepped forward, hand raised. MacNeil braked and pulled up short. The rifles trained on him made him tense, but he was confident that as soon as they checked his registration number on the computer, things would get more relaxed. He was wrong.

The lead soldier glanced over his shoulder as someone called something from one of the trucks, and he was immediately joined by five others who fanned out around the front of MacNeil's car. They were clearly jumpy.

'Get out of the car with your hands up,' the lead soldier shouted. 'Do it! Now!'

MacNeil was not going to argue. He opened the door

and got slowly out into the road, keeping his hands well above his head. It was disconcerting that he could not see the soldiers' faces behind their masks and goggles. It made them seem less human. It was hard to imagine entering into any kind of negotiation. 'I'm a cop,' he said. 'I've got clearance to be out.'

'Not on our computer, you don't.'

MacNeil cursed under his breath. Either Laing had forgotten to enter it up, or there was some glitch. They moved in close around him, the barrels of their rifles inches now from his face. 'I've got ID. I can show you.' He started reaching slowly for his inside pocket, and one of the soldiers swung his rifle around and clubbed him on the side of the head. A bright light flashed in his eyes and he fell to his knees. 'Jesus,' he said, his voice just a whisper. 'I'm a fucking cop.'

Hands pulled him roughly to his feet and slammed him up against the side of his car. Someone pushed his face down on to the roof and forced his hands up behind his neck, then kicked his legs apart. 'Move and you're a dead man.' The voice hissed very close to his ear. His head was pounding, and he felt hands frisking him and going through his pockets. His warrant card was slapped down on the roof of the car next to his face. He saw the light from the streetlamps reflecting on the badge with its crown and royal insignia.

'Where did you steal this?'

'I didn't steal it. Take a look at the photograph, for God's sake!'

The warrant card disappeared from his field of vision and there was a moment of hiatus. Then, 'Doesn't look anything like him,' he heard one of the soldiers say. And he cursed the day he'd decided to get his hair cropped short.

'Put him in the truck.'

They started dragging him across the roadway.

'Jesus, just phone my boss, will you? It's DCI Laing at Kennington Road Police Station. He was supposed to enter my authorisation into the computer.'

Several pairs of hands dragged him roughly over the lip of the drop-down gate at the back of the truck and left him sprawling on the studded metal floor. Someone slapped his face and banged him up against the canvas side flap. His warrant card skittered away across the floor.

'Don't fucking move!'

He was vaguely aware of a young soldier at the back of the truck with a laptop computer and a short-wave radio. The light from the screen reflected on the boy's face as his fingers spidered over the keyboard. But MacNeil had no time to reflect on his situation before a deafening explosion rocked the truck on its wheels. The shockwave pushed the canvas cover inwards as if from a physical blow, before sucking it out again. Breaking glass showered the streets around them like rainfall and a huge flash of searing white light turned the night sky briefly into day.

Voices outside of the truck were raised in panic. He heard someone shout that it was the bank in Chinatown. 'They've blown up the fucking bank!'

From where he sat, MacNeil could see the troops, who moments earlier had manhandled him into the truck, deploying north along the avenue towards Chinatown. No one was worrying much about him any more. The young coms officer at the back of the truck was shouting into his short-wave, calling for reinforcements. MacNeil made an instant decision, something he would almost certainly not have done given time to reflect. He reached forward and snatched the soldier's rifle, which was lying on the bench beside him. The soldier turned from his radio and grabbed at it. But too late. He found himself on the wrong end of his own gun, with MacNeil grim, determined and frightened, at the other.

'I'm legit, kid. I'm a cop. Check me out on the computer.' He bent down cautiously to retrieve his warrant card.

The kid sat frozen with fear and humiliation and shook his head.

MacNeil pulled the magazine from the rifle and tossed it out into the street, and then the rifle after it. 'I'm going,' he said. 'Don't come after me.' Even as he turned, the young soldier made his move. He didn't relish trying to explain to the others how he'd lost his gun and his prisoner. But he was no match in size or strength for the big Scotsman. MacNeil grabbed his jacket and ripped off his mask. 'Don't even think about it, sonny. Or I'll breathe on you.'

The threat was more effective than any physical intimidation. The young man recoiled from the policeman's breath, and MacNeil pushed him back into the truck before jumping down into the road and running to his car. Nobody had thought to remove the keys from the ignition, and it fired first time. MacNeil reversed at speed into Piccadilly Circus, and with tyres spinning, turned into Regent Street, and then Air Street, accelerating across Brewer Street into Lower John Street and up into the deserted Golden Square. It would be a risk, he knew, leaving his car here, but he would be able to move around more freely on foot.

None of the street lights along the far side of the square were working, forming a deep pool of darkness into which he drove and parked his vehicle. He got out and stood by the car, hearing the tick, tick of cooling metal, and listening intently for any hint of activity nearby. The explosion at the Chinatown bank had started a blaze which lit up the night sky beyond the nearest buildings. He could hear sirens and the crackle of gunfire and raised voices echoing around empty streets, and decided that it was safe to move.

He stuck to the network of narrow streets and lanes which fanned out like a spider's web across Soho to the north of Shaftesbury Avenue. Bridle Lane, Great Pulteney Street, Peter Street. The devastation here was extraordinary. Stolen vehicles discarded and set alight. Almost every building – shops and offices – violated by looters. The pedlars of sex and pornography who sold their wares in the streets and alleys of Soho had been cleaned out. *Slinky's, For the Liberated and Enslaved – Corsets – Rubber – Leather.* The lap dance joints and tattooists and cinemas had been stripped bare. Broken glass and discarded merchandise lay in drifts along streets where doors hung off twisted hinges and windows were black holes. Pubs where he had drunk, and restaurants where he had eaten, were barely recognisable. Soho Spice, The Blue Posts.

Dean Street was shrouded in darkness. The explosion at the bank down on the avenue seemed to have affected power supplies. There were no street lights. But the reflection of an eerie, flickering light licked faintly up the walls of its deserted clubs and restaurants from the fire in Chinatown. Broken glass on the pavements sparkled like frost, and a cold wind carried on it the smell of smoke and burning rubber. The cream-painted walls of a piano bar on the corner with Meard Street were streaked black from the blaze which had gutted it.

MacNeil flitted quickly through the dark to the east side of Dean Street and headed north. Fifty yards brought him to the steel-shuttered facade of the Black Ice Club. There had been clear attempts to force an entry, but metal grilles had so far kept the looters at bay. MacNeil was not sure what he had expected to find. If the club was still in operation, it was hardly likely to be advertising itself. He stood perfectly still, listening. And he felt, more than heard, the faintest thump, thump, thump. The monotonous, endlessly repetitive dance music that so characterised the tastes of today's kids. Not, he supposed, that it had been all that different in his day. It was all a matter of what you grew up with, and grew out of.

He could not have said for certain that the music was coming from inside the Black Ice Club. But he would have risked money on it, if he'd had to. There had to be another way in. At the end of the block, opposite the Wen Tai Sun Chinese News Agency, a narrow lane led beneath overhead offices, into a cobbled courtyard filled to overflowing with wheely bins which hadn't been emptied in months. Rats scurried in panic around his feet as MacNeil moved warily through the dark of the alley into the courtyard beyond. There were black-painted railings, and steel-barred windows, and fire escapes that zigzagged up the sides of brick-built office blocks. A pencil-thin line of light showed all around a thick steel door. As he approached it, MacNeil sensed the music getting louder. And now he heard it, rather than felt it.

It seemed extraordinary to MacNeil that people would want to be out partying given the dangers of infection, and the lawless, lethal streets that they would be required to negotiate safely after curfew. Never mind the fact that it was illegal. But then, he thought, a restless generation of kids with energy and money to burn simply weren't going to stay at home and watch telly with mum and dad. He supposed they probably got a kick out of it, living life on the edge. Better than drugs. But he was willing to bet that the patrons of the Black Ice Club, on the other side of that steel door, would be rich kids from Chelsea and South Ken. Kids from privileged homes, with daddy's money in their pockets. Not the sort of place a crematorium worker from a South Lambeth slum was likely to frequent.

He hammered on the steel door and stood back, waiting. Nothing happened. He hammered again, and this time a small metal hatch slid open. Light and music spilled out into the darkness of the courtyard, and a face peered suspiciously into MacNeil's. 'What do you want?'

'A drink.'

'Don't know you.'

'I'm a friend of Ronnie's. Ronnie Kazinski. He told me a thirsty man could get a drink here any time. And I've got a hell of a drouth.'

'How did you get through the curfew?'

'How does anyone?'

'Most people arrive before it starts and leave when it finishes.'

MacNeil shrugged. 'I guess I must have been lucky.'

The bouncer looked at him for several long moments before sliding the hatch shut. For a while, MacNeil thought he wasn't going to open up. And then he heard the scrape of metal bolts being withdrawn, and the door swung in. The bouncer was a big man, but not as big as MacNeil. His head was shaved, and he wore a leather waistcoat over his naked chest. A beer belly hung low over baggy jeans. A grubby-looking white surgical mask covered the lower half of his face, and he regarded MacNeil warily before flicking his head to indicate that he should come in.

'Cheers, mate,' MacNeil said. 'Where's the bar?'

'Downstairs.'

II.

As he went down the stairwell, the music rose to greet him like a physical assault. A brain-numbing level of decibels. Coloured lights were soaked up by black walls, and when he reached the dance floor, maybe two hundred people moved in one undulating wave of sweating humanity, lost in some primordial trance, swaying to sounds that owed more to distant tribal roots than to a sophisticated modern society. They all wore white surgical masks, like a uniform. And in the ultraviolet overhead strips, the masks glowed weirdly in the dark, like a strange, luminescent sea of floating gulls.

There was a small stage on the far side of the dance floor, and two scantily clad females wearing pointed white hoods with slits cut for eye holes swung their hips and gyrated in slow hypnotic circles. A bar stretched along the length of the wall to the right. Two young barmen wearing army-style gas masks were busy serving customers lined up three deep. People lowered their masks to drink, then pulled them back into place. Used glasses were set in circular racks that slid into huge dishwashers to disinfect them for further use. Steam rose in great clouds from behind the bar into air already thick with heat and sweat. A perfect incubator for infectious disease.

MacNeil shoved his way through the drinkers to the bar. Anyone who objected was likely to get an elbow in the face. Vocal protest was drowned by the music. A dyed blond barman with black roots regarded MacNeil warily. MacNeil was older than the usual clientele, much more conservative, and he still had his coat on, in spite of the heat. Besides which, his face was bruised and lacerated on one cheek with tiny cuts from the glass on the forecourt of the South Lambeth flats. 'Whisky,' he shouted. 'Single malt. Glenlivet if you have it. And a little water.' It seemed like a long time since he'd had a drink, and now the anticipation of it was almost overwhelming. But just the one. He knew that more than one would weaken resolve and lead him into a downward spiral of sorrow drowning.

A glass with half an inch of amber, and a small jug of water, were banged on the bar in front of him. He handed over a fiver and got no change. He diluted his whisky fifty-fifty and took a sip. He turned to the barman. 'That's not Glenlivet!'

'You said if I had it. I don't have it.' No apology.

MacNeil took another sip. It was just some anonymous blend. He was disappointed by the taste of it, but enjoyed its warmth burning all the way down into his stomach. Then he tipped the glass and it was gone in an instant. He thought about all the times he'd had just one more, anything to put off the moment when he would have to go home. Back to Martha. He thought about all the times Sean had been asleep by the time he got back. All those missed moments. All those wasted hours. And he turned and shouted at the barman for another.

When it came he caught the barman's wrist and leaned over the bar. 'Is Ronnie in tonight? Ronnie Kazinski?'

But the barman raised a hand to shoosh him as the music stopped, suddenly, on a single drum beat, and reverberated around the club for several seconds. The sea of masks stopped heaving, and there was some sporadic applause as the dancers and drinkers all turned expectantly in the direction of the stage. From a door somewhere at the back, a young man who looked to be in his thirties emerged carrying an artistically tied white cloth bundle suspended on a pole over his shoulder. It looked for all the world like the cartoon bundle in which a stork would deliver a baby. And for a brief moment, a fleeting memory of Laing winged its way through MacNeil's thoughts.

The hooded dancers had melted away, and somehow left behind them a small folding table centre stage. There were some cheers and whoops as the man placed his bundle on the table. He was dressed all in black. Even his mask was black, and he was almost subsumed by the black wall behind him. The white upper-half of his face glowed in the fluorescent strip lights, and seemed to dance around, disembodied, above the glowing bundle on the table. His hair was thin and wispy, and scraped back across a balding scalp. He spoke into a microphone, leaning on the pole, and his dead voice boomed out above the heads turned, as one, towards him.

'Art,' he said, 'real art, is about life on the edge. It's about pushing the boundaries as far as they will go, and further. What is a life lived within boundaries set by others? We must make our own boundaries, and draw them in ever widening circles, encouraging others to go with us. We are not our parents, or our parents' parents. We are we. And we are here and now. The future is ours, and only what we make it. Only by treading that razor-sharp path between life and death, between good taste and bad, between acceptable and unacceptable, will we find true meaning in our lives.'

He looked around the upturned faces watching him in breathless silence. They knew that he was going to do something awful. It's what most of them had come for. This was underground art. It was what had made the club cult before the emergency. MacNeil looked on, fascinated, unexpectedly caught by the hypnotic quality of the performance, completely unprepared for what was to come.

The man in black leaned over the table and theatrically pulled one end of the knot that held the bundle, and it fell open, revealing a strange, bloody-looking mulch that seemed devoid of form or shape. There was a gasp from the crowd. The man's eyes shone like coal, black beacons in circles of white. He whipped his mask aside and seized the mulch in both hands, raising it, dripping, high above his head.

His voice, too, rose in pitch. 'This is life,' he said. 'And death.' Only the hum of the sound system breached the silence in the club. 'It is just two hours since the heart in this child beat in its mother's womb. Just two hours since it was ripped from its umbilical, denied any future, bereft of a past. Abortion. The rejection of life. The curse of our age.'

MacNeil watched in disbelief, frozen by horror. He heard a solitary voice whisper, 'Oh, my God!'

'Only in life can we find death, and only in death can we find life.' The man in black suddenly dropped his hands level with his face. He paused for just one moment before gouging with his mouth at the bloody mass he held in them. Gorging himself on it.

Someone in the crowd vomited. There were just a couple of voices raised in disgust or dissent. The only other sounds were the guzzling and snorting of the man on stage as he fed on the contents of his hands. Then just as quickly as he had begun, he finished, dropping the remains of his meal into the bundle on the table. His face was smeared red around his mouth.

'Thank you, thank you,' he called, and he retrieved his props and vanished in a flourish back through the door from which he had come.

The lights immediately plunged low, and the music started where it had left off, assaulting the body and the senses. The sea of masks rose and fell in a frantic, stormy swell.

MacNeil was shocked and shaking, and wanted to throw up. He turned back to the bar and the waiting whisky and found the barman grinning at him from behind his mask.

'Quite something, eh?' he shouted. He was enjoying the revulsion written clearly on MacNeil's face. 'Who was it you were looking for?'

MacNeil threw back his whisky and banged the glass breathlessly on the counter. 'Ronnie Kazinski.'

The barman frowned for a moment, then enlightenment dawned. 'Oh, yeah. You mean the crem guy?'

It took MacNeil a second or two to realise that *crem* meant *crematorium*. 'That's him.'

'Why don't you ask Foetus Man?' he shouted, flicking his head towards the stage. 'They're big pals, those two.'

III.

The corridor behind the stage led to toilets at the far end. MacNeil could smell stale urine the moment the door from the club closed behind him. But it muted the assault of the music, and for that he was grateful. A harsh yellow strip light reflected off dull linoleum, and MacNeil brushed past framed black and white photographs of some of the celebrated performance art which had made the club its name. The dressing room was the last door on the left. A sign said *Private*. MacNeil pushed the door open, and Foetus

Man turned from the wall mirror above his dressing table, still cleaning the mess from his hands and face with hot, wet towels.

'Can't you fucking read?'

MacNeil crossed the room in two strides, grabbed him by his lapels and slammed him hard against the wall, knocking all the breath from his lungs. 'Yeah, I can read. And right now I'm going to read you your fucking rights, you sick bastard.' He held him pinned to the wall with one hand and showed him his warrant card with the other. 'I'll figure out the charges later. Body snatching, foetus theft, murder, maybe. Someone as sick as you should be locked up for a very long time.'

'Hey,' Foetus Man protested. And he started to laugh. 'Come on, man. You didn't think any of that was real, did you? I mean, give us a break. I'd have chucked up all over the joint.' He nodded towards the bloody bundle still sitting on the dressing table. 'It's just jam and bread roll. Can't stand the canteen food, so I bring my own packed lunch.'

He pulled himself free of MacNeil's slackening grip.

'It's just performance, man. People like to be shocked. They like to think it's real. But deep down they know it's just a bit of fun.'

'You call that fun?'

'It's pushing the boundaries. I'm engaging the audience, provoking an emotional response. It makes them question stuff, stretches their limits.'

He sat down again and continued wiping his face, and MacNeil watched his reflection in the mirror keeping a wary eye on him.

'I mean, where would I get a foetus from, man? I got the idea watching this documentary about a Chinese guy who did it for real. I mean, really did it. Now, that *was* sick. Me? I just enjoy a sandwich.' He finished cleaning himself and stood up. 'Was there something else you wanted?'

MacNeil looked at him, filled with anger and contempt and a large residue of the revulsion his performance had induced. He tried to focus on what had brought him here in the first place. 'I'm looking for Ronnie Kazinski,' he said.

Foetus Man shrugged. 'Ronnie who?'

The dressing room door opened, and MacNeil looked past Foetus Man into the mirror and saw the reflection of a young man in jeans and a leather jacket. He was not a tall man, and he had managed to emphasise the smallness of his head by gelling thin black hair down over his skull. For a moment MacNeil thought he knew him. There was something familiar in the high cheekbones and wide-set eyes. He had bad skin, pasty and white, that looked as if it hadn't seen daylight in months. An odd memory flashed through MacNeil's mind. A woman's face behind a net curtain, features made mean by generations of poverty. And he remembered where he had seen this man before. A smudged image on a faxed printout. Ronald Kazinski.

Kazinski stopped in the doorway and saw MacNeil's reflection looking back at him. His eyes flickered to meet Foetus Man's and he knew immediately he was in trouble. He turned and ran, sprinting back up the corridor like a man possessed, sneakers squeaking on the linoleum. MacNeil went after him, slower, his big frame lumbering through harsh yellow light until he hit the door at the far end, bursting through it into the glowing sea of masks and the assault of the music. Kazinski had cut a swathe through it towards the stairs at the far side, and MacNeil followed in his wake, shouldering bodies out of his way as he went, until finally the sea parted voluntarily before him.

He took the stairs two at a time, and the heavy metal door was slamming shut as he reached the landing at the top. The bouncer with the bald head and the leather waistcoat stood in his way. He put a hand out to stop him. 'Where do you think you're going, pal?'

It took the merest flick of his neck, MacNeil leaning forward as if to kiss him. He felt the bridge of the man's nose splinter beneath his forehead and the bouncer staggered back, a look of astonishment in his eyes. The back of his head smacked into the wall and his mask turned red as blood soaked into white cotton. MacNeil heaved the door open and was out into the night. He heard the clatter of overturned bins, a smell of stinking refuse whipped up on the edge of an icy wind. Light spilled across the courtyard from the open door, and he saw the shadow of the fleeing Kazinski as he dived up the alleyway towards the street. Rats scurried and screamed underfoot as MacNeil ran after him.

When MacNeil emerged from the alley, Kazinski was sprinting up the centre of Dean Street, being rapidly swallowed by the dark. He was like a hare to MacNeil's bulldog. MacNeil saw him turn into St. Anne's Court, a narrow pedestrian street between tall brick buildings, and knew he was going to lose him. But as he reached the corner, he saw that there was something going on beyond the far end of the lane. The flicker and glow and crackle of flames. Voices raised in laughter and howling derision. Looters. Kazinski pulled up and glanced back towards MacNeil, caught between the devil and the deep blue. MacNeil could almost hear the wheels grinding as Kazinski tried to decide which was the lesser of two evils. But he found a third way instead. A narrow passage that ran south, at right angles to St. Anne's Court, opposite the shattered Georgian windows of what had once been a cake shop. It was no more than three feet wide, and he hurtled down it, covering twenty yards or more before realising that the opening into Flaxman Court at the far end of it was choked with upturned bins and debris tipped from the windows of looted offices. MacNeil heard him curse in the darkness, and slowed to a walk to try to catch his breath. There was no way out for Kazinski. He'd turned into a dead end and wasn't going anywhere.

As MacNeil approached, Kazinski backed off until he couldn't go any further. 'Your mother thinks you're at work,' MacNeil said.

'What do you want?'

'Why did you run?'

'I can smell a cop at fifty paces.'

'Yeah, it's the smell of urine from creeps like you pissing their pants.'

'I got rights.'

'Yes, you have. You've got the right to bleed quietly. You've got the right to a decent funeral. Not that you'll get one. Not these days. But then, you'd know all about that.'

Kazinski tried to break past him, ducking and squeezing

to scrape between MacNeil's right side and the wall. But MacNeil was nearly as wide as the alley itself. He just leaned to his right and pressed Kazinski against the wall. Then he grabbed the back of his collar, almost lifting him off his feet, and threw him bodily against the barrier at the end of the lane. Kazinski fell in a crumpled heap, and refuse and rubble cascaded over him.

'Tell me about the bones,' MacNeil said.

'What bones?'

MacNeil sighed. 'I've got a thumbprint on an Underground ticket found where you dumped them. You're going down for murder, Ronnie.'

'I never killed her!' There was panic in Kazinski's voice. 'Honest, mate. I was just to get rid of the bones.'

'You didn't do a very good job.'

'I was supposed to sneak them into Battersea, dump them in the furnace. At first they wanted me to get the whole body in. But there was no way I could have got her in there past security. So I said, gimme the bones. I can get them in. They didn't want no traces, see? They had to be destroyed.'

'Why?'

'I dunno. I didn't have nothing to do with it, honest.'

'So why didn't you burn them?'

'Because that hole was going to get filled in with concrete

this morning. It meant I didn't have to take no risks, and they wouldn't have been any the wiser.'

'Who's they?'

'Dunno.'

'Bullshit!'

'Honest, mate. They just paid me to get rid of the bones.'

MacNeil leaned in towards him. 'Ronnie, you're going down for these guys unless you tell me who they are.'

'Jesus, mate. I don't know their names. This guy approached me after work one day, made me an offer I couldn't refuse.'

MacNeil shook his head. 'You're going to have to do better than that, Ronnie. Where did you pick up the bones?' He heard Kazinski sighing deeply in the dark.

'I don't know the address. It was a big house. You know, some rich geezer's place.'

'Where?'

'It was somewhere near Wandsworth Common. Root Street, Ruth Street, something like that. It was dark. I dunno. They picked me up and dropped me off in a car.'

'During curfew?'

'Sure. It didn't seem like a problem. Nobody stopped us.'

MacNeil stood and looked down at him for several moments. He needed much more than this, and he was sure that Kazinski had more to tell. 'Come on, get up,' he said.

Kazinski didn't move. 'What're you gonna do?'

'I'm taking you in, Ronnie, on suspicion of murder.' He didn't see the pole coming out of the dark until it was too late. He heard the hollow clang of it against his skull, and his knees folded under him. Kazinski dropped the length of scaffolding tube his fingers had found amongst the rubble, and it rattled away across the tarmac as he leapt over the prone figure of the policeman and sprinted back the way he had come.

MacNeil was doubled over, gasping, lights flashing in his eyes. How could he have been so careless? He cursed, and spat on the ground and tasted blood in his mouth. It took him a full minute to recover enough to stagger to his feet, leaning one hand against the brick wall to support himself until he was able to stand without falling. His head was still ringing like a bell. There was no point in taking things too fast. Kazinski was long gone.

It was several minutes before he emerged shakily into St. Anne's Court and saw a dark shape sprawled on the ground a few yards to the east. He wondered for a moment what it was. There hadn't been anything there five minutes ago. He stepped towards it and saw that it was a man lying face down, black liquid pooling on the ground beneath him. Sticky blood, coagulating in the chill wind. MacNeil knelt down and felt that he was still warm. He pulled the body over and Kazinski gazed up at him with staring eyes. His white shirt was soaked with blood, but MacNeil could still see where the three bullets had passed through it. All in the vicinity of his heart. He was quite dead.

CHAPTER THIRTEEN

I.

MacNeil slumped to the ground and sat with his back against the wall. There was still a fire burning somewhere beyond the west end of St. Anne's Court, but the looters had moved on, because all he could hear now was the crackling of the blaze.

Someone had shot Kazinski three times in the chest. Someone who had been waiting out here in the lane. MacNeil had heard no shots. Even with the ringing in his head he could not have missed them. He remembered Laing's verdict on the sniper who had shot the kids in South Lambeth. *It was a real pro job. A professional weapon in professional hands*, he had said. This, too, had all the hallmarks of a professional. A clean, efficient execution. A weapon with a silencer. Someone did not want Kazinski talking to MacNeil, or anyone else. And it occurred to him that perhaps it was the same professional. Perhaps the marksman who had saved his life that afternoon had been waiting there for Kazinski. And now he had got him.

MacNeil tilted his head gently back against the brick and breathed deeply. He felt something like hysteria slip slowly over him, like a shroud. Everything seemed somehow out of control. His life, the city, his job, this investigation. It was as if he were being swept along on a tide of events he was powerless to affect. He was tired. He had barely slept the night before, and he had been on duty now for nearly fifteen hours. If he closed his eyes, he could sleep. Right here on the pavement, with a dead man at his feet.

But there was an anger in him, a tiny voice that screamed and raged inside, and he knew it would never let him sleep. In the distance he heard gunfire, and the far-off echo of voices raised in anger. Like the one in his head. He crawled forward on his knees and dragged on a pair of latex gloves to start going through Kazinski's pockets. There was a wallet with an ID card, some bank notes, and a pouch with some loose change. A bunch of keys in his trouser pocket.

Cigarettes and a lighter in his jacket. Nothing remotely helpful.

MacNeil looked at the wallet again. There was a zip pocket in the back of it. He fumbled with big fingers to open it up. There were some receipts in there from better times. A couple of restaurant bills, a till receipt from a bar. And a dog-eared business card. MacNeil tilted it to try to catch what light there was, and ran a finger over the red embossed lettering. *Jonathan Flight, Sculptor*, it read in curlicued script. It had the address of a gallery in South Kensington.

MacNeil knew the name. The arts columns of the broadsheets had been full of him last year, and some of his work had been controversial enough to make the tabloids, where MacNeil had read about him. He specialised in grotesque, often overtly sexual body sculpture. A headless man with his erect penis partially inserted in the anus of a female torso. A woman with one arm missing, holding her severed breast in her remaining hand. A facial sculpture whose smile stripped away flesh to reveal teeth and jaw. MacNeil could not imagine who might buy stuff like that, or who would want it in their homes. But his exhibitions attracted thousands, and his work sold for tens of thousands.

He wondered what someone like Kazinski was doing with

Flight's business card in his wallet, or what his connection had been with the Black Ice Club. The only thing that linked them was extreme art, and Kazinski did not seem to MacNeil like either a connoisseur or a collector. He slipped the card into an inside pocket, zipped up the wallet and returned it to Kazinski's jacket. He sat back against the wall again and pulled off the latex. His head was pounding less severely now, but he ran his hand down the side of his face and felt a swelling on his cheek and knew that he would be black and blue by morning.

He sat for several minutes before deciding to do something he would never have contemplated in another life. He was going to leave Kazinski there on the pavement. He was dead. There was nothing that could be done for him. And if MacNeil called it in, he would spend the rest of his shift tied up in red tape. In eight hours he would walk out of the door of Kennington Police Station for the last time. And if he hadn't found the little girl's killer by then, he was pretty sure no one else would. So there was no time for red tape. This investigation had become something of an obsession. And he was about to cross a line into uncharted territory. A world alien to him, outside of the law, where he would be all alone. With just his angry voice for company.

CHAPTER FOURTEEN

Pinkie cruised west on Piccadilly towards Hyde Park Corner. He kept his eyes on the red tail lights at the far end of the boulevard, the faintest of pinpricks shining back through the darkness ahead of him. He had extinguished his headlights, and could see perfectly well by the light of the streetlamps. If he was stopped by soldiers he would simply say he was trying to avoid attracting attention. Private vehicles were being attacked in the street by looters every night.

He had a niggling sense that all was not well, and suspected he might know where it was MacNeil was headed. Although how he could have made that connection was a mystery to him. Pinkie could not imagine that Kazinski would have told him.

Poor Kazinski. If only he had burned the bones as he had

been paid to do, none of this would be happening. Pinkie would be at home, back in his real world life, where his mother would be preparing supper. Kazinski would still be alive. As would those kids in South Lambeth. And the old lady on the Isle of Dogs. All because the stupid little bastard hadn't done what he promised he would do.

Pinkie shook his head. It was extraordinary. One simple failure, one unscripted act, and look at the chaos that ensued. Spiralling out of control. This is what happened when you didn't see a job through to the end. How in the name of God was it all going to finish?

The mobile phone on the seat beside him began to ring. He reached across and pressed the green answer button and clamped it to his ear. 'Hello?'

'Hello, Pinkie, how's it going?' Mr Smith had such a restful voice. Pinkie could listen to it all day. Even though he knew it was just a veneer, a smoothing over of the turmoil beneath.

'Kazinski's dead, Mr Smith.'

He heard the pleasure in Mr Smith's voice. 'Well done, Pinkie. That should be an end of it, then.'

'I hope so, Mr Smith.'

But Mr Smith clearly detected the reserve in Pinkie's response. 'Why do you only hope so, Pinkie?'

'Because the cop got to him first. They had quite a tête-à-tête.' That was French, Pinkie knew, and he wondered if Mr Smith would be impressed. 'I don't know what he told him. Could have been anything.'

Mr Smith was silent for a long time.

'Hello? Mr Smith? Are you still there?'

'Yes, I'm still here, Pinkie. What are you doing now?'

'I'm following the cop. Looks like he might be heading for South Ken.'

Another silence, then, 'Do you think he knows?'

'I've no idea, Mr Smith.' He paused. 'Something odd, though.'

'What's that, Pinkie?'

'He never called it in. Kazinski's murder. Just left him lying there on the pavement.'

'I think our Mr MacNeil might be a little out of control, Pinkie. Which could make him very dangerous.'

'How do you mean, out of control? Why would he be out of control?'

'It's his last day, Pinkie. He quits the force at the end of his shift. And it's been an emotional day for him. He lost his son.'

Pinkie frowned. 'Lost his son?'

'He died, Pinkie. The flu. Policemen's kids are just as likely to get it as anyone else.'

'Aw, shit.' Pinkie focused on the distant pinpricks of red light, and now they signalled only grief. 'That's a shame, Mr Smith,' he said. And meant it. 'What do you want me to do?'

'Keep following him, Pinkie. Do what you feel you have to. And keep me informed.'

Mr Smith hung up, and Pinkie felt unaccountably sad. He wondered how his own father might have felt if he had died of the flu when he was just a kid. If his father had known he existed. If he had known who his father was. His mother, he knew, would have been bereft.

Kids didn't deserve to die. They hadn't done enough bad things yet to deserve it. What harm had that poor little girl done anyone? None of it had been her fault, but she was the one that Mr Smith blamed. She'd got on his wrong side. And the wrong side of Mr Smith was not a good place to be.

CHAPTER FIFTEEN

Amy sat out on the metal balcony at the back of the apartment looking down on to the empty concourse below. It was cold, and she had a travelling rug wrapped around her shoulders to keep her warm. But the fresh air was good, and she had left the French windows open to let it blow through the top floor. The skull still smelled. And although she had wrapped it in several plastic bags and taken it down to the bottom landing, it had left an unpleasant odour lingering in the air.

She loved to sit out here on summer evenings, screened from the gaze of her neighbours by the wisteria she had trained to grow all around it. On long, lazy summer after-noons it was a sun trap, and in the evenings it was fanned by the cooling movement of the air. A delicious retreat from life, a place to forget.

Now the wisteria was naked and gnarled, providing no kind of a screen, and it was hard to believe that fresh growth would appear in the spring, cascades of lovely purple flowers falling all around the railings, drawing the first honeybees of the year in search of nectar. This was only her second winter since the accident, and that first year she had found November through March to be the hardest months. Cold days when you wanted to be out walking, striding out with the wind in your face, the cold sting of rain on your cheeks. Hurrying home for a bowl of hot soup, curtains drawn against the night, curled up on the settee with a good book and a glass of soft red wine.

And here she was, huddled bleakly in her wheelchair, cold and depressed and letting dark thoughts creep in to cloud her usual sunny disposition. Her heart bled for MacNeil, and wept for the memory of the young man who had died at the wheel of his car that fateful night just thirty months ago. The young man she was to have married. The young man whose baby she'd been carrying.

It had been just seven days since the test proved positive. They had already decided to marry, and so it was just one more reason for celebration. They couldn't have been happier. Perhaps that's why fate had dealt them such a cruel blow. They had dared to be so happy. Happier than anyone else they knew. Happiness had radiated from every pore. She had been so happy she glowed. She couldn't stop smiling. Had anyone ever been happier in the history of the human race?

David had drunk only mineral water that night. He was driving, he said, and he had responsibilities now that he was to be a father. Amy had kept him company. She was pregnant. No alcohol for mum until after the baby was born. And then they could celebrate. Champagne to wet the baby's head.

How ironic that it should have been a drunk driver whose car ploughed into the side of theirs at the junction. Straight through the traffic lights on red. Experts called to give evidence at the trial judged that he had been doing more than sixty. Even more ironic that he had walked away unscathed. In another three years he would be out of prison, with most of his life still ahead of him, able-bodied and fit. A job waiting for him in his father's business. A forgiving family.

Amy found it difficult to forgive, but she had tried hard not to let it make her bitter. She had lost so much else, that to lose that core of sunshine that lit her personality would have plunged her into a dark world, depressed and defeated, and unable to face the challenges ahead. Challenges that would need all her reserves of courage and resolve and optimism.

But tonight she wasn't sure how much deeper she could dig into those reserves. She grasped the controller on the arm of her wheelchair and manoeuvred herself back into the attic of the warehouse, closing the French windows behind her and drawing the curtains against the night. Time, she thought, for a glass of red wine to cheer herself up. She went to the kitchen and poured herself one. If only now she could curl up on the settee with a good book.

The electric motor whined as she crossed the floor to gaze for the umpteenth time at the little girl whose face she had recreated. She wasn't sure about the hair. Something told her – instinct, the thing that MacNeil so hated when it came to analysis of evidence – that Lyn would suit her hair short. Not a bob cut. Something more primal – ragged and spiky. After all, a child from a developing country would not have had access to a stylist. And yet she had been here in London. Living here, perhaps. But not long enough, certainly, for a change of diet to affect her teeth. And there had been no surgery attempted to fix her lip.

Was she adopted? If so, who were her adoptive parents? Hadn't they reported her missing? Questions, questions,

questions. They had been rattling around her head all evening. An attempt, she recognised, to stop her dwelling on other things. But there had been no answers. Only flights of fancy. Speculation. Assumption. She knew no more now than she had this morning.

The phone rang and she crossed the room to answer it.

'Amy, it's Zoe.'

'Hi, Zoe.' Amy glanced at the time. It was after eleven. 'You're not still at the lab?'

'Yep.'

'You should have been home before the curfew.'

'Yeah, well, I'm stuck here now, aren't I? And it's all your fault.'

Amy gasped her indignation. 'My fault! How?'

'You asked me to run a virology test on the bone marrow Dr Bennet recovered from the skeleton of the little girl.'

'You've done a PCR test already?'

'I did more than that.' She sounded pleased with herself. 'I recovered not only the virus, but the RNA coding.'

Amy experienced momentary confusion. 'What? You mean you're telling me she had the flu?'

'She sure did. And the virus I recovered is definitely infectious. I mean, the pure RNA alone is still infectious. But the RNA and protein together, well, that's sheer dynamite.'

'Jesus, Zoe,' Amy said, alarmed. 'You should be working in a Level Three lab with infectious material like that.'

'Yeah, probably.' There was a hint of a yawn at the other end of the phone.

'You don't have lab three facilities there.'

'Nope.'

'But you used lab three precautions, right?'

'Well, not exactly.'

'Zoe!' Amy was shocked. 'You stupid idiot!'

'Hey, keep your hair on, Amy. It's cool. Honest. I know what I'm doing. I could have done it in my kitchen.'

Amy was furious. 'Is Dr Bennet there?'

'He's got a couple of autopsies.'

'Well, get him to call me as soon as he's free.'

'Aw, come on, Amy, you'll get me into trouble.'

'You *should* be in trouble, Zoe. You could infect yourself. You could infect everybody in the building.'

'It's all locked down and safe as houses. Honest.' She paused, nursing her silent resentment at Amy's anger. 'So I suppose you won't want to know what else I found, then?'

'What do you mean?'

'Hah. Got your interest now, haven't I?'

'Zoe . . .' Amy's voice carried its own warning.

'It's not real.'

Amy heard the words, but she didn't understand them. 'What do you mean it's not real?'

'The flu virus. It's not the H5N1 mutant that's killing everyone. It's been genetically engineered.'

Amy was having difficulty taking on board the implications of what Zoe was saying. 'How do you know that?'

'Well, it's all just code, right? When you boil it right down to basics, any virus is just a series of letters – code words. And somebody left some words in the code that shouldn't be there. I mean, for example, you would find the words Stu I AGGCCT and Sma CCCGGG in synthetic polio. And you know these create a restriction site that is easily recognised by treating the DNA copy of the virus RNA with a battery of restriction enzymes that cut the DNA at that site.'

'Woah! Jesus, Zoe, hold on! Speak English.'

'I thought I was.'

'Okay, think molecular genetics for idiots.'

She heard Zoe sighing at the other end of the phone. 'People have been collecting library sequence banks for the flu virus for years. I've got them all on file. Took only a few minutes on my laptop to compare the RNA of the virus we got from the girl with the sequence banks on the hard drive. The introduced restriction sites stood out like a sore thumb. I'm telling you, that kid didn't just have any old garden-variety flu. She had a twenty-four carat, genetically engineered humdinger.'

Amy sat for a moment replaying what Zoe had just told her. None of it made any sense. 'Is that what killed her?' she asked. 'This man-made flu?'

Zoe blew air through her lips three miles away across town. 'I haven't got the first idea.'

CHAPTER SIXTEEN

I.

MacNeil turned past the deserted South Kensington tube station into Old Brompton Road. The Lamborghini London franchise had been cleaned out long ago. The showroom windows were smashed; the floor space beyond, which had once been graced by some of the most expensive cars in the world, was empty and exposed to the elements. The Royal Bank of Scotland next door was all boarded up, its vaults cleared out by the bank itself and transferred to more secure premises. There was no point in the looters trying to break in, and so they had taken out their frustrations in a multicoloured display of graffiti comprising even more colourful language.

The bench in the tiny triangle of parkland at the road junction was normally inhabited by two or more drunks congregating to share their misery, to drink from cans in paper bags and fill the air with their cigarette smoke and hollow laughter. To MacNeil's shame, he had almost always heard a Scots voice amongst them. But they were long gone. The soup kitchens were closed, and men raddled by years of drink were easy prey for H5N1.

There was less damage here than in the city centre, less evidence of looting. Old Brompton Road was largely residential with small shops at street level. Pizza Organic, Mail Boxes Etc., Waterstones. Poor pickings compared to the big stores downtown. And no self-respecting looter was going to be seen dead breaking into a bookshop. Still, most of the shops were boarded up, and there were few lights on in the windows of the flats and offices above.

MacNeil dropped down to second gear and cruised slowly along the street checking the numbers. He found Flight's gallery on the corner of Cranley Place, next door to the steel-shuttered Café Lazeez. The windows of the gallery had been boarded up, and then pasted over with layer upon layer of peeling bill posters advertising everything from mail-order art to underground concerts in unnamed locations. There was some sort of crest above the door on the corner, and in Cranley Place itself, an entrance to the apartments above the gallery.

MacNeil turned into Cranley Place and found a spot to park. Rows of pristine, white-painted terraced town houses stretched off into the night, black wrought-iron balconies supported on pillared doorways. There were a few hotels and guest houses here, empty of course, but mostly these were private homes, great rambling houses divided and subdivided into luxury apartments. Prime real estate, light years removed from the scruffy two-bedroomed lower terrace that MacNeil had been able to afford in Forest Hill. On the far side of the street, on the shuttered windows of Knightsbridge Pianos, beneath a large sign which read BILL POSTERS WILL BE PROSECUTED, some graffiti artist with a sense of humour had sprayed BILL POSTERS IS INNOCENT!

Steel grilles protected the glass in Flight's door beneath a red and green decorative lintel. There were two bell-pushes on the electronic entry system. One marked STUDIO, the other marked FLIGHT. MacNeil stood back and looked up. Lights were on in the first floor studio. The apartment above it was in darkness. He stepped forward and pressed the STUDIO bell. After a few moments, a rasping electronic hum accompanied a man's voice issuing from a speaker set into the wall. 'Yes?'

'Mr Flight?'

A moment's pause, and then a voice laden with suspicion. 'Who wants to know?'

'Detective Inspector Jack MacNeil, Mr Flight. I'm investigating a murder in Soho tonight.'

'I've been here all evening, Inspector,' Flight said quickly.

'Yes, I don't doubt that, sir. I know you didn't kill him, but you might have known him. Can I come up?'

'What's his name?'

'Kazinski, Mr Flight,' MacNeil said. 'Ronald Kazinski.' There was another long silence, which MacNeil broke. 'Can I come up, sir?' he repeated.

'Have you had the flu?'

'No, sir. But I'm protected,' MacNeil lied.

'Put a mask on, if you have one. If you haven't, I'll give you one. And please wear gloves. I don't want you touching anything in my studio.'

'Yes, sir.'

The buzzer went, and MacNeil pushed the door open. A carpeted stairway led up to a first floor landing and a door marked STUDIO. There was a window in it, and Flight appeared on the other side of it, his face almost obscured by a double mask. Even from his side of the door, MacNeil could see that Flight was tall. He had a strangely cadaverous head covered with a steel grey stubble. Blue eyes blinked suspiciously at him through the glass. 'Let me see your hands,' Flight said, and MacNeil held up his latex-gloved hands. 'And your ID.' Patiently, MacNeil took out his warrant card and opened it up to the glass. Flight scrutinised it carefully, before unlocking the door and stepping away from it. 'You can't be too careful these days,' he said. 'And please keep your distance.'

MacNeil walked into Flight's studio. What had once been a polished wooden floor was stained and scarred and littered with the debris of an untidy artistic temperament. It was a large, well-lit space that covered just about the entire area of the gallery below. A dozen works in various stages of completion sat on the floor or on work benches. A grotesquely deformed head, intertwined arms, a mangled torso with breasts and a penis. The walls were covered with sketches. There was a potter's wheel, and tall cabinets with half-open drawers full of art materials – paints, inks, dyes, sculpting tools, tracing paper. Centre stage was Flight's work table, and the piece he was currently sculpting. An arm raised on its fingertips, partially fleshed, partially stripped down to the tendons and bone, half a head growing out of the armpit, an exposed brain sectioned through its centre revealing all its folds and colours and interior textures.

MacNeil wondered how it remained standing, until he saw the support spike that passed through the upper arm. For all its unnatural distortion, there was an unpleasantly life-like quality about it. Which was true of all of Flight's works.

Something of MacNeil's distaste must have been apparent to Flight. His eyes smiled, supercilious and superior. 'Don't you like my work, Inspector?'

'I prefer a nice picture I can hang on my wall.'

'Like?'

MacNeil shrugged. 'Vettriano.'

'Ah,' Flight said. '*The Singing Butler.* I've often wondered who bought those things.' He turned towards his work in progress. 'The brain's a fascinating subject, don't you think? Of course, you have to know a little about it. The brachium pontis. The colliculus superior.' He pointed to lobes and leafs of his sculpted brain. 'An amazing piece of engineering. It's extraordinary to think that just anyone can have one. Of course, they come in all models, from a Rolls Royce to a Mini.'

'And what do you have, Mr Flight?'

'I like to think I'm probably in the BMW bracket. What about you, Inspector?'

'Oh, probably a Ford Granada,' MacNeil said. 'Solid, reliable, doesn't need much servicing, and just keeps going till it gets there. So what can you tell me about Ronald Kazinski, sir?'

'Nothing, I'm afraid.' Flight began circling his sculpture, casting a thoughtful eye over its curves and planes. MacNeil saw now that he was, indeed, a tall man. Six-six, perhaps, and painfully thin, with long, feminine fingers. He was wearing a three-quarter-length white apron, like a surgeon's gown. Only it was smeared with clay and paint rather than blood. 'I've never heard of him.'

'He'd heard of you.'

Flight flicked him a look. 'Had he? Did he tell you that?'

'No, Mr Flight. He was dead. Don't you want to know how he died?'

'It's no concern of mine.'

'He was shot three times in the chest.'

'How unpleasant for him.'

'And he had your business card in his wallet.'

'Did he? Well, you know, there's probably a few thousand people of whom you could say that.'

'Most of whom are probably interested in art.'

'And Mr Kazinski wasn't?'

'He was a crematorium worker, Mr Flight. He lived in a slum south of the river.'

'Then I take your point.'

MacNeil let his eyes wander around the studio, flicking from one obscenity to another. He said, 'It's possible, of course, that he picked up your card at the Black Ice Club. Do you know it?'

'I've heard of it, of course. Avante-garde performance art. Shock for the sake of shocking.'

'Familiar territory for you, I'd have thought.' Flight cast him a withering look. MacNeil said, 'You've never been, then?'

'Really, Inspector, credit me with a little taste.'

'I do,' MacNeil said. 'Very little.' He looked around the studio. 'Most of it bad.'

Flight's patience with him was starting to wear thin. 'If that's all, Inspector, I'd like to get on, if you don't mind.' He nodded towards the arm and head. 'The hours of darkness are my most creative.'

'I'm not surprised,' MacNeil said. There was more than just something of the night about the cadaverous sculptor. He gave MacNeil the creeps. 'Thank you for your cooperation, sir.'

II.

Pinkie watched MacNeil back his car out into Old Brompton Road and turn towards South Kensington tube station. He waited until the tail lights were gone, and then he got out of the car and walked slowly across the road to the green, grilled door of Flight's apartment. He hesitated there and looked around. There were lights shining in an atrium conservatory on the other side of Cranley Place, but he couldn't see anyone moving around. Most of the other windows in the street were black holes, protective curtains drawn tight to shut out a scary world. Pinkie hated wearing a mask, but there was one good thing about it. It hid your face, and nobody thought it was strange. Any witness questioned by the police would always be certain of at least one thing. *He was wearing a mask, officer.*

He pressed the STUDIO buzzer. And after a moment, Flight's angry voice growled through the speaker grille, 'What is it now?'

'It's Pinkie.' There was a long pause before the buzzer sounded and the electronic lock clicked open. Pinkie stepped inside and flicked up the snib on the lock so that it remained unlocked when the door closed behind him.

He hated being locked in. He remembered the cupboard under the stairs where his mother locked him away when she had her visitors. She didn't want them to know there was a child in the house. But she had made it comfortable for him, with a light, and a drawing book and some games. And a mattress for him to sleep on. It was his little den, secret and safe. He had never minded being shut in there, until the night he heard her screaming.

Flight peered at him through the glass in the studio door, and Pinkie grinned behind his mask and waggled his gloved hands in the air. Flight opened up. 'What do you want?' He was careful to keep distance between them.

'You had a visitor, Jonathan.'

'A very rude policeman.'

Pinkie shook a finger of admonition at him. 'Don't be so judgemental, Jonathan. Poor Mr MacNeil lost his son today.'

Flight was unaffected. 'Perhaps that explains why he was so rude.'

'What did he want?'

'He wanted to know if I knew Ronnie.'

'And what did you tell him?'

'That I'd never heard of him, of course.'

'And he believed you?'

'Why shouldn't he?'

'Why did he think you and Ronnie would be acquainted?'

'Apparently Ronnie had my business card in his pocket.'

'Ahhh.' That explained it. Pinkie wandered across the studio and poked the exposed half of the brain with un-ashamed curiosity. 'Is this real?'

'Don't touch it!' Flight snapped at him. Then, 'Did you kill Ronnie?'

Pinkie smiled. 'I could do with a drink, Jonathan.'

'I'm working.'

'I could do with a drink, Jonathan.' Pinkie repeated him-self as if making the request for the first time.

It had its effect on Flight. He seemed nervous. 'We'll have to go upstairs.'

The living room of Flight's apartment overlooked Old Brompton Road and was what the design magazines would have called *minimalist*. Bare floorboards, polished and var-nished. Naked cream walls. A glass table and six chrome and leather chairs in the window. There were two red leather recliners with footstools, a long, low, black-lacquered side-board, and a wafer-thin plasma TV screen on a chrome stand. The only art in the room comprised a couple of Flight's own sculptures raised on tall black plinths. Pinkie looked at them with distaste. 'I don't know how you can stand to have that stuff in your home.'

Flight didn't grace the comment with a response. 'Whisky?' He opened up the drinks cupboard in his sideboard.

'Cognac.'

'I've only got Armagnac.' Flight sounded annoyed. 'It's very expensive.'

'That'll have to do, then.'

Flight poured a conservative measure into a single brandy glass.

'Aren't you going to join me?'

'I never drink while I'm working.'

'Make an exception.' Pinkie walked to the window and looked down into the street below. He heard Flight sighing and taking out a second glass. The unaccustomed sound of a car engine rose from the street, headlights raked the shuttered shops opposite, and a vehicle pulled up outside the gallery. Pinkie pressed his face against the window to see who it was, and recoiled as if from a blow. MacNeil was stepping out on to the pavement. Pinkie turned quickly towards Flight, who looked up in surprise, his bottle of Armagnac hovering over the lip of the second glass.

'What is it?'

Pinkie smiled. This was the bit he enjoyed most. 'Time for you to feature in one of your own sculptures, Jonathan.'

III.

MacNeil glanced up and saw that there were lights on now in both the studio and the apartment. He walked around into Cranley Place and pressed both buzzers. There was no response. He waited nearly thirty seconds before trying again. Still no reply. MacNeil was losing patience. He'd got as far as the King's Road before the thought struck him. A thought so breathtaking in the scope of its horror that it was almost unthinkable. But he couldn't stop thinking about it. And so he had felt compelled to return, if only to clear it from his mind. And now Flight was playing games. He raised his hand to bang on the door and shouted, 'Come on, Flight, open up!' His voice echoed angrily around the empty street, and the door moved under the beat of his clenched fist. MacNeil froze, his arm still in mid-air. His surprise gave way to an immediate sense of misgiving. The door had locked behind him as he left. He was sure of that. He had pulled it shut. Tentatively he pushed on the door with his fingertips, and it swung in. He stepped into the hallway and saw that the lock had been put on the latch. He inclined his head and peered up the stairs. A light still burned on the first landing.

'Flight? Mr Flight?' MacNeil's voice got soaked up by the carpet and went unanswered. He climbed the stairs slowly to the first landing. The lights of the studio shone brightly through the glass panel in the door, and MacNeil peered inside. There was no sign of Flight. He pushed the door. It opened and he walked in. The arm and head looked just as it had fifteen minutes ago. Flight did not appear to have done any more work on it. MacNeil looked around the other works in the studio with new eyes. A door at the back led to what appeared to be another room. MacNeil crossed the studio and opened it. In fact, it led into a large walk-in, windowless storeroom. There was a long wooden work-bench, scored and stained, a huge vice, and all manner of tools hanging from nails in the wall. Knives, saws, several different weights of chopper, of the kind you might find in a butcher's shop. A tray on the worktop was lined with scalpels of various sizes. There was an autoclave plugged into the rear wall next to an oscillating saw and a row of plastic bottles containing bleach. It was cold in here, the air sharp with the acid scent of disinfectant. And something else that MacNeil couldn't quite identify.

Several opaque containers lined up along a shelf were labelled SPRAY PLASTIC.

MacNeil had a bad feeling about this place, like the

touch of icy fingers on his neck. He shivered, and felt as if he were in the presence of something deeply sinister. There was an odd jolt, and the air was filled with a loud electronic hum and the rattle of glass. He turned, and saw that behind the door stood a huge refrigerator which reached almost all the way up to the ceiling. It was divided in two halves, upper and lower. He opened the upper door, and a light flickered on to reveal shelves full of bottles with glass stoppers. They were filled with various coloured liquids. There was a strangely familiar, if unpleasant, smell in the fridge. MacNeil turned one of the bottles around. Its label read *Formalin*, and MacNeil knew why it smelled familiar. It was the ever present perfume of the autopsy room. Formaldehyde. Used in medical laboratories and mortuaries as a preservative. Three small sausage-shaped objects lay in a glass saucer in the meat tray. MacNeil lifted it out and nearly dropped it. 'Jesus Christ!' His revulsion forced the words involuntarily from his lips, and his voice sounded excessively loud in this confined space. The three sausage-like objects in the saucer were fingers. Human fingers. He slid it quickly back on to the shelf and shut the door. He was shaking. He took a moment to compose himself and control his breathing before opening the lower door to reveal four deep freezer drawers. He hardly needed to open them to know what was inside.

But still the shock when he slid the top drawer out forced him to step back. A man's head stared out at him, eyes wide open, flesh chalk-white and faintly frosted. MacNeil had to force himself to open the others. Legs, arms, hands, feet. An entire torso in the bottom drawer. A woman.

MacNeil slammed the door shut and stood breathing stertorously, trying to stop the bile rising from his stomach. This was sicker by far than Foetus Man's jam and bread sandwich. This was real. He staggered out into the studio and looked around at all the body pieces that Flight had 'sculpted'. He strode across the studio floor and wrenched the work in progress from its support spike, raising it above his head and smashing it down on the edge of the table. The half head separated itself from the arm and rolled across the floor, and the exposed section of the arm split open. There was a crack like the report of a rifle, and the arm hung in two halves in his hand, the bone broken clean through. And bone, he now knew, it was. Human bone. Flight was no sculptor. He was plagiarising nature. Taking human body parts and manipulating them to his own twisted design. Disinfected, preserved, plasticised, painted, whatever the hell it was he did to them.

And MacNeil knew also that Flight had lied about knowing Kazinski. Knew that they must have been collaborating ever since Kazinski got his job at the crematorium. Supplier of body parts to the celebrated sculptor. He dropped the arm as if it were burning hot, barely able to control his anger and disgust. Is this where that little girl had been butchered? The flesh stripped from her bones, her skeleton disjointed. He looked back into the storeroom with its stained workbench and array of cutting tools and felt sick to his stomach.

'Flight!' he roared, but was greeted only by silence.

He ran out on to the landing and up the second flight of stairs two at a time. He called Flight's name again, but there was still no response. Three doors opened off a short corridor. He threw them open in turn. The first was a bathroom, cool blue ceramic, a glass shower. The wash-hand basin was a free-standing bowl set on mahogany. MacNeil saw himself, wild-eyed, staring back from a huge mirror that took up one wall. His face was bruised and scored, and he barely recognised himself. The second door led to a bedroom. Black silk sheets, a cream carpet, a faint smell of feet and eau de cologne. The third door opened into a large, spartan sitting room. Flight was sitting in a red leather recliner, one foot up on a footstool, one arm hanging over the right side of the chair. He was still wearing his surgeon's apron. Only now, it was blood that covered it, seeping from the signature three bullet holes in his chest. Flight's silver-bristled head was tipped forward. MacNeil moved slowly towards him and felt for a pulse at his neck. There was none, and the flesh felt cold already. But MacNeil knew he could only have been dead a matter of minutes.

He spun around, suddenly sensing his own vulnerability. There was no one there. Not a sound disturbed the silence in the house.

MacNeil glanced at the black-lacquered sideboard. The door of the drinks cabinet stood open. There were two glasses on top of it, next to a bottle of Armagnac. One of the glasses held half an inch of dark, smoky amber. The other was empty.

MacNeil sat in the other recliner and dropped his head into his hands, running them through the fuzz of his short-cropped dark hair. There was no one in the house, he was sure of that. And yet in the time it had taken him to drive to the King's Road and back, someone had come here and murdered Flight. Two glasses on the sideboard, one filled and untouched, the other empty. As if Flight had been interrupted in the act of pouring. One for himself. One for his killer.

Was it MacNeil who interrupted them? Was Flight's killer still in the house when he came in? He supposed it was possible that while he was in the studio the killer had slipped down the stairs and made his escape. Silent, unseen. Like a ghost. A ghost that was haunting MacNeil wherever he went, killing everyone with whom he had contact: the kids on the housing estate in South Lambeth, Kazinski, and now Flight. He looked at the sculptor, head slumped on his chest, and thought that he was no loss to the world. He knew he would have to call this one in. But he didn't want to be involved. An anonymous tip-off from Flight's own phone would bring the local police, although maybe not until the curfew was over. What they found here would be largely self-explanatory.

MacNeil stood up and crossed to the sideboard. He went through all the drawers, careful not to disturb anything that might prove useful to the cops when they came. He found old flyers for exhibitions of Flight's work, sketches and scribbled notes, a well-thumbed pack of Tarot cards, pens and pencils, receipts, some loose change. There was little else in the room that could be described as personal. MacNeil wondered where Flight kept the accumulated detritus of his own life. Or perhaps, since it was other people's lives he collected, preserving them in pieces for posterity, he kept little or nothing of his own.

In the bedroom, next to his bed, MacNeil found the only piece of furniture in the apartment that didn't look like it had been chosen from a Scandinavian mail-order catalogue. It was an antique roll-top bureau, a family piece, perhaps, from another life. MacNeil rolled back the top and found a mess of paperwork and accounts. Bills, receipts, invoices, an accounting notebook full of Flight's tiny, neurotic scribbles. A brass holder was stuffed full of letters, still in their envelopes. A few pieces of private correspondence, but mostly paid and unpaid bills.

Finally MacNeil found gold. In a shallow drawer at the back of the bureau, nestling in green felt, was Flight's address book. It was full to overflowing with business cards and addresses scribbled on folded scraps of paper. But here was the definitive collection of all Flight's friends and acquaintances, from both his private and business lives, although MacNeil imagined that the dividing line between the two was probably pretty blurred.

Carefully, he started leafing through the alphabet. But there were so many names, and with no idea of what he was looking for, MacNeil quickly gave up and flicked through to K, where he found Kazinski's telephone number. But no address. It would have been superfluous, a place Flight would never have gone, even in his worst nightmares.

He was about to thumb through the remaining pages, when MacNeil spotted a small square of paper, folded twice, and wedged in the spine. So he left the book open at K, pressed the spine flat and delicately retrieved the small scrap of paper. He unfolded it. There was a name scrawled on it, perhaps a nickname of some kind. *Pinkie*. And beneath it a telephone number. MacNeil could tell from the code that it was a mobile. Beneath the number was an address, but a line drawn across the paper seemed to separate the two, and MacNeil got the impression that they didn't necessarily go together. Although it was possible that they were related in some way. And then he went very still. And in his head he heard Kazinski say, *I don't know the address. It was a big house. You know, some rich geezer's place. It was somewhere near Wandsworth Common. Root Street, Ruth Street, something like that.* MacNeil's eyes were fixed on the piece of paper in his hand. The address was in Routh Road, Wandsworth.

MacNeil sat on the edge of the bed and held the paper between slightly trembling fingers, looking at the name and number and address until they blurred. He was hungry, and tired, and very possibly in shock. It was hard to concentrate. And then he had a thought. He reached for the telephone on the bedside and dialled the number on the piece of paper.

*

Pinkie sat in his car fifty yards away watching the lights burning in the windows of Flight's apartment. He wondered what MacNeil was doing in there, what delights he had discovered, what secrets uncovered. He had been so preoccupied with Flight's little house of horrors on the first floor that it had been a simple enough matter for Pinkie to creep silently down to the front door and out into the night. He tried to imagine MacNeil's surprise when he went upstairs and found Flight waiting for him. Pinkie had been unable to resist the temptation to arrange the sculptor in welcoming pose on his expensive leather chair. If MacNeil had come straight up, well then, he'd simply have had to shoot him. Even at the risk of Mr Smith's ire. Irritatingly, Flight's head had refused to play ball and kept falling forward, and Pinkie had felt compelled finally, for reasons of self-preservation, to leave before he was satisfied.

His mobile phone purred on the seat beside him. He picked it up and looked at the display. *Jonathan Flight*, it said, and he dropped it again, as if it were contaminated. It couldn't be Flight. He'd just killed him. He felt goosebumps rise up all across his neck and shoulders, before forcing himself to think logically. It *couldn't* be Flight. But it was someone calling from Flight's phone. So it had to be MacNeil. Where in the name of God had he got the number? Flight must have kept it in an address book, or in the memory of his phone. But how would MacNeil know to call it? Pinkie was spooked.

Tentatively he picked up the phone and pressed the green button to take the call. He put it to his ear and listened and said nothing. 'Hello?' he heard MacNeil's voice. 'Hello?' But still Pinkie said nothing. And then he grinned. Now it was MacNeil's turn to be spooked.

MacNeil listened to the ambient silence. He could hear someone breathing, someone listening but saying nothing, almost as if they knew who was calling. He wanted to hang up, to cut off the presence that was so eloquent in its silence. But there was something compelling in it, and he sat for a full minute saying nothing. Just listening. He felt evil in the silence, and the longer he listened to it the more oppressive it became, until finally he couldn't stand it any more, and he banged the receiver back in its cradle. He was shaking now, his mouth dry. He had the unnerving feeling that he had just had an encounter with the ghost that was haunting him, this killer of men and boys, and perhaps of a little Chinese girl with a cleft palate. And he had, too, the sense that this ghost was somewhere very close.

'Scotland the Brave' burst into jolly refrain, and MacNeil's heart nearly hit the roof of his mouth. He fumbled in his pocket for his mobile and saw Amy's name on the display.

'Hey, Amy,' he said, trying to sound as natural as he could.

'What's wrong?'

'What do you mean?'

'You sound weird.'

'I'm just tired, Amy.' He looked at his watch. It was after midnight. 'You should be in bed.'

'I can't sleep. I wish I'd never brought the head home with me. It's like she's here in the house, that little girl. Haunting me. I can't get her face out of my mind.'

Someone else, MacNeil thought, being haunted tonight.

'How is it going?'

He knew he couldn't tell her the truth. Someday, maybe, but not tonight. 'I've got a couple of leads,' he said. 'I think she might have been murdered in a house near Wandsworth Common.'

'My God, that's more than a couple of leads. How did you get to that?'

'Too complicated to go into now. How about you? Anything fresh? Any feedback from the lab?'

'Actually, yes. Pretty strange, really, and I've no idea if it's important or not. But she had the flu.'

MacNeil was taken aback. 'Died of it?'

'Impossible to tell. But she'd either had it and recovered, or she was suffering from it when she died.'

MacNeil thought about it. He had no idea, either, if there was any significance in it.

Then Amy said, 'What's weird about it, though, is that it wasn't the H5N1 human variant that's killing everyone else.'

MacNeil frowned. 'I don't understand.'

'It was another variation on the H5N1 bird flu virus. A man-made one.'

CHAPTER SEVENTEEN

I.

Amy hung up and stared at the head gazing back at her in the dim lamplight of the attic sitting room. Her eye was drawn again to the cleft lip. It was as if the child had been caught on a fisherman's hook and then thrown back, permanently disfigured, into an ocean in which she would always find herself swimming against the tide.

It could just as easily have been Amy. Some tiny glitch in the genetic code determining the course of a life, separating the smart from the stupid, the beautiful from the ugly. Amy was both smart and beautiful. It wasn't a genetic glitch which had determined the course of her life, it was a drunk behind the wheel of a car, and five seconds of madness.

They had other things in common, though – Amy and Lyn. A racial inheritance, perhaps even a cultural one. A girl born into poverty in China had little chance. Amy knew it only too well. She had been born in England, not China. She had been born into relative affluence, not poverty. But thousands of years of cultural preference for a son, rather than a daughter, had been hard for her parents to shake off. She had been the first born, but it was her younger brother, when he arrived, who had taken pride of place.

Had she been born in impoverished rural China, she may well have ended up in an orphanage, like millions of her peers. Abandoned by her family on the doorstep of a police station somewhere, so that they might try again for a son. The Chinese government policy of one child per family meant there were no second chances – unless you lived in the city, had money and knew how to buy your way around the system.

For as long as anyone could remember, in Chinese society, when the son married he brought his wife to live with his parents. And when the parents grew old, it was the responsibility of the son and his wife to look after them. But if you had a daughter, she would leave to look after her husband's parents, and you would have to fend for yourself in your old age. So it was little wonder that boys were prized and girls despised.

Amy wondered if it had been Lyn's fate to end up in an orphanage somewhere, unloved, unwanted, even by childless Western couples desperate to adopt – her deformity always working against her. And yet, here she was – or had been – living in London, this bastion of Western affluence and privilege. But only to meet a fate worse than any orphanage, murdered and hacked up and dumped in a hole in the ground.

A *wwwooo-oop* sound turned Amy's head towards her computer. The window of her most recent conversation with Sam was still up on the screen. And now Sam had sent a new message. Amy manoeuvred her wheelchair over to the desk to see what Sam was saying.

– *Amy, are you still around?*

The cursor blinked with endless patience, awaiting Amy's response.

– *Hi, Sam. Yeah, I'm still up. It's late.*

– *I couldn't sleep for thinking about your little girl.*

– *Me neither. She keeps staring at me.*

– *It's a terrible thing when you can put a face to someone, but not a name, or a history. I wish I could see her, too.*

– *I could take a photo of the head and email it to you.*

– *Maybe in the morning.* The cursor blinked for a bit. Then – *How is Jack holding up?*

– *I don't know. He sounded pretty weird when I spoke to him last. I think he's throwing himself into this investigation just to stop himself thinking.*

– *What do you mean, weird?*

– *I don't know. Just a bit . . . spaced, I guess.*

– *How is the investigation going?*

– *He seems to be making progress. He thinks he knows where she was killed.*

The cursor blinked again for a long time.

– *How on earth does he know that?*

– *I've no idea.*

– *Where does he think it happened?*

– *He said something about a house out near Wandsworth Common.*

– *That's not too specific.*

– *He wasn't being very specific.*

Their conversation lapsed. More blinking. This time two minutes, maybe three, passed without any further exchange. Amy found her eyes wandering across the room to the child's head once more. The girl was watching her, almost reproachful in her silence. Why couldn't Amy do more? How difficult could it be to find her killer?

Then *wwwooo-oop.*

– *Amy, did you ask for a DNA sample in the end?*

– Yes, Sam. Might be a day or two, though.

– I wouldn't get your hopes up for finding a match.

– I'm not. And then Amy remembered about Zoe. *– I did ask for a PCR test, though, to see if she'd had the flu.*

Another long wait.

– Why did you do that?

– You always tell me every little detail helps when you're trying to put together the pieces of the puzzle.

The cursor blinked some more.

– So did you get a result?

– Yeah. We've got a post-grad molecular genetics student training at the lab. Zoe. She's a bit of a ladette. But really clever. She'll be good when she grows up. Stupid girl took so long over the test that she missed the curfew, so she's stuck at the lab all night. Tom'll be pleased. He can't stand her!

– What did she find?

– The little girl did have the flu.

There was a short, cursor-blinking hiatus before Sam replied.

– Which doesn't really help with anything, does it?

– I suppose not. But here's something strange – Zoe said it wasn't H5N1. At least, not the version that's caused the pandemic.

– How does she know that?

– She said she'd recovered the virus, and the RNA coding. It's all

a bit beyond me, Sam. Something to do with restriction sites and code words that shouldn't be there. Anyway, she said this virus was genetically engineered.

Their conversation lapsed for so long, Amy began to think that Sam had gone.

– *Hello, Sam, are you still there?*

– *I'm still here, Amy.*

– *So what do you think?* Amy watched the hypnotic blinking of the cursor.

– *I think that changes everything.*

II.

Pinkie watched the drab rows of mustard-harled council flats drift by. It was fun driving about in the deserted city. No traffic, no lights. So much easier to get around. And he hadn't been stopped once. It was sufficient for him to slow to walking pace as he approached the army checkpoints. Their cameras fed his number into the computer in seconds and they waved him on. VIP. No contact required. Everyone was happy.

At Clapham Common, MacNeil had taken a right turn, and Pinkie was sure he had no idea he was being followed.

It was impossible at night to see a vehicle three hundred yards behind you with no lights. As long as Pinkie could see the merest hint of MacNeil's tail lights he wouldn't lose him. At least, not while he stuck to the main thoroughfares. The danger would be if he went off-piste and made turns that Pinkie couldn't see. Then he would have to get closer, and that would become dangerous.

The phone lying on the passenger seat fibrillated in the hushed interior of the car. Pinkie glanced over at the display and then answered the call.

'Hello, Mr Smith.'

'Hello, Pinkie. Where are you now?'

'We're on Battersea Rise, Mr Smith. Heading towards Wandsworth Common. I think Mr MacNeil is heading for Routh Road.'

'I'm afraid he is, Pinkie.'

'We're in trouble, then.'

'In more trouble than you think. The stupid cripple asked for PCR on the bone marrow.'

'And is that bad?'

'It's very bad, Pinkie. They found the virus.'

Pinkie shook his head. That stupid little shit, Ronnie Kazinski. He'd got them all into so much trouble. Pinkie almost wished he hadn't killed him, so that he could be made to see the consequences of his actions. 'What do you want me to do, Mr Smith?'

'I think we need to leave Mr MacNeil for the moment, Pinkie. We are required to take other action now.'

III.

Routh Road was at the end of a collection of streets they called 'The Toast Rack'. Not unreasonably, since Baskerville Road, which backed on to Wandsworth Common, and the five streets which ran off it at right angles, made a shape not unlike a toast rack. Although it might just as easily have been called 'The Comb'. Wandsworth Prison was a stone's throw away, on the other side of Trinity Road.

David Lloyd George had lived here once, in Routh Road. At number three. These were substantial detached and semi-detached town houses built in red-brick on three floors, nestling darkly behind walls and railings, and screened from the street by trees and hedges in gardens which had taken more than a century to mature. The kerbs were lined with BMWs and Volvos and Mercedes.

MacNeil parked on Trinity Road and walked down to the address on the slip of paper. It stood in darkness behind a black wrought-iron railing. There were no lights in any of the houses, but this one bore an air of sad neglect. The small front garden was overgrown and uncared for. Empty bins lay spilled on their side. Curtains or blinds were drawn on most of the windows. It was in stark contrast to the mani- cured gardens and well-kept facades of the other properties in the street. In daylight it would have stood out like a sore thumb, a single bad tooth in a dazzling smile.

The house was detached on its left side, but brick bomb shelters built between it and its neighbour during the Second World War meant that there was no way round to the back, except through the house. MacNeil stood in a pool of yellow light beneath a lamp post and looked at it appraisingly. It did not look inhabited. The gate protested loudly in the dark as he opened it and walked the few paces to the steps which led up to the front door. He could see now that this was an original door, recently restored to its former glory. Stained glass panels all around it would splash the hall beyond in coloured light on sunny days. The house itself was not as neglected as the garden. There was no nameplate on the door. There was a bell push to the left of it, and MacNeil pressed it and held it for a long time. He heard an old-fashioned bell ring distantly from somewhere deep within the house. But it elicited no response. He rattled the flap of the brass letter box, and then crouched down to lift the lid and peer inside. Apart from the faint light that seeped through the stained glass from the street lights beyond the trees, it was almost pitch-dark and MacNeil could see very little. There was an unlived-in smell that breathed out through the letter box from the interior of the house, damp and fusty, like bad breath, confirming MacNeil's earlier impression that the place was empty.

He went back down the steps and walked along the front of the house. The neighbours appeared to have converted their half of the bomb shelter into a walk-through shed with a blue-painted door at the front end. MacNeil reached over the fence and tried the handle. It wasn't locked. But suddenly the garden was flooded with light, a bright, blinding halogen light. MacNeil's movement had triggered the neighbour's security lamp. He took an involuntary step back and tripped over a shrub, landing in the long grass, exposed to the full glare of the halogen. A window on the first floor of the neighbouring house flew up, and an elderly, balding man in a pale blue nightshirt leaned out with a shotgun raised to his shoulder. He pointed it directly at MacNeil. 'Get out of the garden!' he shouted. 'Go!'

MacNeil stood up, brushing the mud from his coat, and shaded his eyes against the light. 'Or you'll what, shoot me?'

'I'm warning you.'

'Do you have a licence for that thing?'

'I'll call the police.'

'Too late. They're already here.'

The man let the shotgun slip a little from his shoulder, and he peered down through the leafless branches of a mountain ash at the figure in the adjoining garden. 'You're a police officer?'

'Yes.'

'Let me see some identification.'

'You're hardly likely to be able to read it from there, sir.'

'Climb over the fence and approach the front door. There's a security camera there. Hold it up to the camera.'

MacNeil did as he was told, snagging his coat as he climbed over the fence. He heard it tear behind him. He approached the security camera which was set just out of reach above one of the twin columns supporting the archway above an open porch. He held his warrant card open towards the lens. The man with the gun had disappeared from the window, but now his voice came from a speaker set somewhere in the porch. 'Okay, Inspector. Why are you creeping around my house at one o'clock in the morning?'

'It's the house next door I'm interested in, Mr Le Saux.' The name was on a plate on the door.

'It's empty.'

'So I gather. Who was last in it?'

He heard Le Saux's frustration. 'It's a letting concern. There've been a succession of people over the years.'

'But most recently?'

'A foreign couple. Although I never saw much of her. They were only here about six months, and let the garden go to wrack and ruin. A short-term contract, he said. Setting up a new production line somewhere. But I've no idea what business he was in. He wasn't very talkative.'

It felt odd conducting an interview on a doorstep with a disembodied voice. 'When did they leave?'

'Well, that's the odd thing. There were comings and goings up until just a day or so ago. Although that might have been the agents. The house seems to be empty now, but I don't know where they would have gone. Not back home, certainly, because no one can leave London right now.'

'Where *was* home?'

'I'm not sure. They might have been French. But his English was so good it was hard to tell.'

'And the wife?'

'Never spoke to her. She never seemed to leave the house. They had a young adopted daughter who started at the local school in September.'

MacNeil frowned. 'How do you know she was adopted? Did they tell you that?'

'Didn't have to, Inspector. She was Chinese, and they weren't. And after the child caught the flu, there was no further contact. Although neither of the parents seemed to catch it.'

'Did she survive?'

'I've no idea.' There was a pause. 'She was a poor soul, though.'

'Why do you say that?'

'She had a terrible facial deformity, Inspector MacNeil. The ugliest harelip I've ever seen.'

CHAPTER EIGHTEEN

I.

Pinkie walked quickly between towering warehouses, narrow metal footbridges running at odd angles overhead, cobbles underfoot. Past Maggie Blake's Cause on his left, and a row of fancy-goods shops all boarded up on his right. The wealthy, in their warehouse conversions, slept safe and sound behind barred windows, no more than gilded cages in this pandemic-stricken city. Once plague-carrying rats had streamed off the boats that docked here. Now the narrow canyon that was Shad Thames was utterly deserted, and deathly quiet, emptied by a different kind of plague.

Pinkie followed it around past Java Wharf until he found the address he was looking for. Butlers and Colonial. He climbed easily up over the electronic gate, straddling the spikes along the top and jumping down into the courtyard beyond. Lights were set in the heads of low posts that led him around into the rear square, and he saw the ramp leading up to Amy's door. He smiled to himself. It had taken him no time at all to find it.

Amy was restless. It was nearly two in the morning, and she didn't feel the least bit sleepy. She was tired, yes. But she could not have slept. Sam's final words had left her strangely uneasy. *I think that changes everything.* What had Sam meant? Try as she might, Amy had been unable to get any further response from her mentor. The window of their conversation remained on her screen, the cursor blinking beyond the end of several failed attempts to re-establish communication. *Sam, are you still there? Hello? Sam? Talk to me!* Nothing. Clearly Sam was no longer at the computer. Gone to bed, maybe. But why such an abrupt and enigmatic conclusion to their conversation?

Amy had finished the bottle of red wine and felt a little drunk. She had spent nearly half an hour talking to Lyn, telling her all about her brother. Telling her how Lee had resented her success. Her academic prowess and the prizes she had won at school. Acceptance then to med school, graduating top of her year. Her hugely successful practice in forensic odontology, her engagement to David. After a childhood of parental indulgence in which every sacrifice had been made for Lee, and Amy had been forced to fend for herself, it came as a huge blow to his ego that his big sister should be such a success while he was not. He had never had good grades at school, dropping out before A-levels, and ended up working as a sous-chef chopping vegetables in a restaurant in Chinatown. Every little gift Amy's success had enabled her to buy her parents he had viewed with jealousy and resentment.

And so he had positively glowed in the aftermath of Amy's accident. Full of kind words and ersatz sympathy. But Amy had sensed his glee. Big sister chopped down to size, confined to a wheelchair. Now he would be the one to take care of the family, buy the gifts, take his rightful place at the head of the table next to his father.

But he had not counted on Amy's determination to rise above her disability, and when she won her million in damages, he had felt that he deserved a share. That they all did. After all, hadn't Amy's success really been down to the sacrifices of her family?

For once in her life Amy had stood up to him. She needed that money to get herself back on her feet, metaphorically if not literally. Did he have the least idea how much it cost a disabled person to try to lead a normal life?

It had created a rift in the family, and Amy had moved away from the Chinese community, to the splendid isolation of her old spice warehouse in Bermondsey. They had been to visit once, the whole family, resentment in everything they saw burning in envious eyes. And they never came again. And so Amy's splendid isolation had turned into a not-so-splendid loneliness – until Jack MacNeil came into her life.

Poor Jack. She thought of him, out there somewhere in the night, fixated on a murder he was unlikely to solve, trying hard not to think about the son whose affection he had neglected. Something he had realised too late to change, and now never could.

She arched her back to flex muscles and try to change her position in the chair. She had been in it too long. Pressure points had become painful. She needed to lie in her bed and give her body a rest. But she couldn't face the thought of it while MacNeil was still out there. She wanted to be here for him if he needed her, and around when he clocked off for the very last time at seven. Perhaps a shower, she thought, would relieve some of the pressure and ease the pain. At the very least it would help her stay awake and alert.

*

Pinkie heard the stair lift before he saw her. He had already searched her bedroom, confident that he would have plenty of warning if the stair lift started up. He had heard her voice drifting down from the attic, and at first thought she had company. But as he listened, unable to pick out the words, he came to realise there was only one voice. Perhaps she was speaking to someone on the telephone. He could not have known that she was talking to the little girl whose flesh he had seen stripped from its bones by Mr Smith.

Now, from his vantage point in the coat closet, face pressed against the crack in the door, he had a clear sight of her for the first time. And she almost took his breath away. She was beautiful. Small and delicate, and so vulnerable with her useless, wasted legs. She sat sideways on the stair lift with her eyes closed, hands folded in her lap. There was something in her serenity that drew Pinkie, that forced an ache into his heart. In a quite bizarre way she reminded him of his mother. Her serenity had been her enduring quality. An almost zen fatalism that allowed her to accept all the brickbats that life had tossed her way. And he remembered, too, that night, locked in the cupboard under the stairs, that he heard her scream for the first time. And with the memory came the familiar trembling. And the darkness and claustrophobia of this coat closet started choking him. He had to fight to control his breathing or else Amy would hear him. And he didn't want to kill her. Not just yet.

He watched her transfer herself to the wheelchair at the foot of the stairs, and listened to the whine of its electric motor as it propelled her towards the bathroom.

It was his mother's third or fourth scream that had finally induced the panic that gave him the strength to force the door. Just ten years old, and not a particularly big boy. They were in the kitchen. His mother on her back on the floor, the man on top, his hands around her neck, cursing and telling her to shut up. He punched her, two or three times, splitting her lip, and she had grimaced with pain, white teeth streaked with blood. Her clothes were ripped, her belly exposed, one breast torn free of its bra. Pinkie had no clear idea what was happening, except that this man was hurting his mother. There was no premeditation in what happened next. He reacted instinctively, jumping on the man's back, tugging wildly at his hair, screaming at him to let his mother go.

The man had been shocked, turning in astonishment to knock the boy from his back. It had come as a surprise to him that they were not alone. Pinkie had fallen, striking his head on the edge of the door, momentarily stunned, bright lights flashing in his eyes. He had heard his mother screaming, frantic now. And the man bellowing and choking off her screams. He saw her legs kicking wildly as she fought for breath, the soles of her naked feet slamming on the floor. And somehow he had got back to his feet, dragging himself up by the worktop. Which is when he'd seen the knife block. Every waking minute since, he'd regretted not acting sooner. That he had not picked himself off the floor thirty seconds earlier. His mother might still have been alive. As it was, by the time he plunged the bread knife deep between the man's shoulder blades, she was already gone, and his own life was changed irrevocably.

Pinkie slid down the wall in the dark of the closet and folded his arms around his knees, pulling them into his chest. He hated it when he remembered like this. It was something he tried to bury, to hide away, but it always came back to him in the dark. He tried to stop himself sobbing, but still he felt the tears hot on his cheeks. He wanted to close his eyes. He wanted to leave this dream behind and slip gently back into that parallel world where every night, when it came time for bed, his mother still kissed him gently on the forehead and whispered, *sleep tight, little man.*

When finally he had gathered himself enough to control his breathing and wipe his face dry, he heard the shower running in the bathroom. He slid back up the wall and took a deep breath. This would be the perfect time, while she was in the shower.

Slowly, he eased the door open and slipped out on to the landing. The bathroom door was ajar, and he could see steam rising in the cold electric light, like fog at dawn on a winter's morning. He crossed the hall and paused at the door, leaning slowly into the gap so that he could see inside.

She had some kind of contraption to support her in the shower, almost standing. And through the steam, and the water streaming down the glass, he could see that she was quite naked, skin blushing pink under the hot jets of water. He saw the pink-brown circles of her areolae, the black triangle between her legs, and he turned quickly away in embarrassment. He had seen his mother naked once in the shower. He had wandered into the bathroom by accident, and stood unseen for almost a minute, watching her. Until she had caught sight of him and screamed at him for peeping. For being a dirty-minded little boy. It was one of the few times she had ever raised her voice to him, and he had never been able to look at a naked woman since without guilt.

He turned and hurried back across the landing and up the stairs in quick, careful steps. Up into the roof. At the top of the steps he ran his eyes rapidly around the huge attic living room until they fell upon her computer. A screen saver faded from one photograph to another, scenes in cool blue and green of some tropical rainforest, misty and damp. He sat himself at her desk and moved the mouse. The screen saver vanished and revealed the window of dialogue between Amy and Sam. The blinking cursor, Amy's final appeals. *Sam, are you still there? Hello? Sam? Talk to me!* Pinkie smiled to himself and spotted the address book icon on the dock at the foot of the screen. He clicked on it, and Amy's address book opened up in front of him. He typed in BENNET. And there, instantly, it appeared. *Tom Bennet, Flat 13A, 1 Parfrey Street, Fulham.* Lucky for some. But not for Tom. Or Harry.

Pinkie closed down the address book and left the screen the way he had found it, triggering the screen saver so that Amy would never know he'd been.

And then he saw her, watching him from the far side of the room, and all the hairs on his neck stood on end. 'Jesus,' he whispered. It was just like her. Uncannily so. Her mouth, repulsive, just as it had been in life. How could they know what she had looked like just from her skull?

For a moment he forgot where he was, and crossed the room to take a closer look. He shook his head, full of new-found admiration for the Chinese dentist in the shower. It couldn't have been more like the child if she had been working from a photograph. There was only one thing that Amy had got wrong. And it irked him.

She had towelled herself dry in the shower and now wheeled herself through to the bedroom. She debated whether just to slip on her dressing gown, or whether to dress in fresh clothes. She decided on the latter, and lay on the bed to pull on jeans and a sweatshirt over clean underwear. Then she manoeuvred herself into a sitting position and leaned over to slip her feet into her sneakers. Dressing was such an effort, but the doctors had said it was good exercise, vital to keep her body functioning.

As the stair lift carried her smoothly up to the attic, she closed her eyes and for the first time felt sleepy. She knew that if she lay down on the settee she would be gone in minutes. As she emerged from the stairwell into the roof space, she had the first premonition of something wrong. It would be hard to say what it was that alerted her. The slightest foreign scent lingering in the air at the top of the house, perhaps. Or just a presence, or the sense of there having been a presence, like a ghost or a spirit. Impossible to know what hidden senses might be at work in the subconscious. Whatever it was, she immediately felt uneasy.

She transferred to her wheelchair and crossed to her desk. Was there a message from Sam? She moved the mouse to banish the screen saver and saw her dialogue window with Sam just as she had left it. *Sam, are you still there? Hello? Sam? Talk to me!*

She was halfway across the attic when she saw the head, and her scream was quite involuntary. Fear stabbed at her, tiny invisible spears, and she looked around the room in a panic. There was no one there. She sat perfectly still, listening. Not a sound. Then she forced herself to look again at the child's head. The hair of the wig had been cut short, in uneven spiky clumps, just as she had imagined it earlier. She forced herself to grab the controller and move towards it.

The table was littered with fist-sized wads of black hair. A pair of scissors lay discarded amongst the cuttings.

Lyn stared back at her, her face changed quite radically by the altered hair. For a moment she wondered if it was possible that she had done it herself, and somehow forgotten. But even as she entertained the thought she dismissed it. And she knew with an absolute certainty that while she had been in the shower, someone had come into the house and cut the hair on the child's head.

No matter how insane that seemed, the evidence was there before her eyes. And it scared her to death. There was a chance that whoever had done it was still there. She was shaking uncontrollably as she reached for the phone, and dropped it on the floor. She retrieved it with difficulty and with trembling fingers dialled MacNeil's mobile. She heard it ring. And ring. And ring. And then his voicemail kicked in. She was about to hang up in despair, when she decided that she should leave a message anyway.

Her own voice sounded strange to her as she spoke, trying to control her hysteria. 'Jack, there's someone here in the house. Please, come quickly. I'm scared.' And she hung up and clutched the phone to her chest, and thought she had never been so frightened in her life.

CHAPTER NINETEEN

I.

MacNeil waited as the switchboard patched his call through. Then he heard Dawson's voice. 'DS Dawson.'

'Rufus, it's Jack.'

'Hi, Jack. How's it going out there?'

'I think I've found where the kid was living. A house in Routh Road in Wandsworth. A rental property. According to the neighbour it was occupied for the last six months by a family, possibly French, called Smith.'

'A likely story.'

'They had a little Chinese kid with a cleft lip. I'm sure it's our girl. But the parents were European. We need to find out who owns the house. The neighbour thinks it's let by an agency. Find out who the agent is and get them out of bed. I want to know who's currently renting the house, or who had it last.'

'I'm right on it.'

'Good man.' MacNeil gave him the full address.

'Jack . . .' Dawson paused, something clearly on his mind. 'About tonight . . .'

'Rufus, I'm sorry.' MacNeil pre-empted him.

'No, *I'm* sorry, Jack. We all are. Bad enough what happened without . . .' His voice tailed off. 'Shit, we all feel really bad about it.'

'Don't. You didn't know. And I appreciate the thought. I really do. Tell the guys thanks.'

He hung up and sat in the dark cocoon of his car, staring down the length of Trinity Road towards the prison. He'd heard that the flu had gone through the prisons like wildfire. Nature's own form of capital punishment. Indiscriminate, all possibility of appeal denied. Nothing was moving out there. It was perfectly still. No sound. No cats, no barking dog. No traffic. He could almost have believed he was the last man alive. It felt like he was.

'Scotland the Brave' demolished the silence. He glanced at the screen on his mobile. A voicemail notification. There was a message for him. He hesitated for just a moment, then decided not to listen to it. Whatever it was could wait. He had more pressing business.

He walked back down Routh Road and stood gazing up at the house. It was where she had spent the last six months of her life. Very probably where she had died. She had walked these streets with a little satchel, to and from school every day. Eyes averted, perhaps, to avoid the stares of the people she would pass on the way. What kind of teasing and cruelty must she have suffered at school? Even the teachers would have found it difficult not to let their eyes be drawn. How sad that everything else about her – her personality, intelligence, character, temperament – would have been blighted by a single physical defect. How sad that so much is judged on appearance, rather than substance.

He went through the gate into Le Saux's garden. He had warned Le Saux that it might be better to turn off his security lights, just for tonight, if he wanted to avoid being repeatedly disturbed. The blue door into the old bomb shelter opened into darkness. MacNeil felt his way through it, eyes adjusting to the little light that fell in from the street behind him. There were gardening tools, and watering cans and plant pots. It smelled earthy damp in here, and the chill cut right through his heavy outer coat. At the far end a door opened into the back garden. It was even darker here. No light made it through from the street out front. A high brick wall separated the two gardens. MacNeil felt along the top to see if there was glass set into the cement. But all he felt was soft spongy moss. He braced himself and jumped, pulling himself up, the toes of his shoes scraping for footholds, until he got one leg over, straddling the wall for a brief moment before dropping down on the other side, and into the garden of number thirty-three. He crouched in a short length of paved alleyway that ran along the side of a huge modern conservatory built out from the back of the house. And he listened to see if he had disturbed any of the neighbours. Le Saux had taken his advice. The security lights had stayed off, and there was no hint of activity in any of the neighbouring houses.

What he was about to do was illegal. But to get a warrant now, in the middle of the night, given all the circumstances, would have been next to impossible. It was unlikely he could even get a magistrate out of bed. If he found something in the house, then someone else could always come back with the proper paperwork and search the place legitimately. But MacNeil wasn't prepared to wait. He was strangely driven. Not only by the fact that in just five hours he would no longer be a police officer. But by a compelling sense of urgency. A feeling that time was somehow of the essence. The murder of the two boys at the flats in Lambeth. The execution of Kazinski in Soho. The carefully arranged corpse of Jonathan Flight in South Kensington. Everywhere he went people were dying. People that someone was very anxious to keep quiet. The killer's sense of urgency had transmitted itself to MacNeil, and he was determined to press on now, regardless of the niceties or the consequences.

Somewhere beyond the veil of clouds that masked the night sky, a nearly full moon was trying to force its way through. But only the merest trace of moonshine permeated the black folds of rain-laden nimbostratus. An icy wind rustled through the long, dead grass that choked the garden, rattling the leaves of evergreen shrubs left to grow ragged and wild.

MacNeil pressed his face against the glass of the conservatory and tried to see inside. But the dark was impenetrable. He skirted around its edge and caught his shin on a heavy marble planter and cursed violently under his breath.

Which was when he heard the movement in the grass. Bigger than any gust of wind might have made, more substantial than any domestic animal or urban fox. He stood motionless, listening. There was someone there. He could feel the presence, was almost certain he could hear the person breathing, staying very still, perhaps waiting for MacNeil to make the next move. Although he could not see the figure in the grass, whoever it was could probably see him. He decided to get pro-active. 'Who's there?' he called, and thought how foolish it sounded. As if anyone was going to tell him!

But his words spurred a sudden movement off to his left in the shadow of the undergrowth. He heard the rapid whoosh-whoosh of dead grass against running legs as a figure darted towards the back fence. He could barely see the intruder, a light, shadowy figure, someone quite a bit smaller than himself. MacNeil went after him, throwing himself through the wilderness of the back garden, abandoning any attempt at stealth. Just short of the high wooden fence that ran along the back of the garden, he grabbed a handful of what felt like jaggy tweed, and both he and the intruder fell hard amongst a pile of discarded plastic plant pots next to a dilapidated potting shed. The plastic whined and cracked and snapped beneath their combined weight. Whoever he'd caught squirmed and wriggled below him, tiny squeals of panic issuing forth in the dark. And then a light suddenly exploded in his face, blinding him. A torch. He grabbed the hand that held it, and its beam skewed off into the night. Another hand scratched and clawed at his face until he grabbed it, too, and turned the torch on to the face of his attacker.

He was almost shocked to see the pale, frightened face of a middle-aged woman with short, silver-grey hair. But although there was fear in her dark eyes, there was determination there, too. She bucked one way then the other, desperately trying to free her wrists from MacNeil's iron grasp. Her torch spun away into the grass, its beam pointing back at them, illuminating their struggle and casting its shadow against the fence.

'I'll scream!' she said in a voice made so tiny by fear that it barely penetrated the dark.

MacNeil said breathlessly, 'If you scream, then so will I.'

Something in his voice stopped her struggling. She lay on the ground below him, gasping for breath, a strange, wiry creature in a tweed jacket and skirt with a white blouse and pearl necklace. 'Who the hell are you?' she gasped.

'Detective Inspector Jack MacNeil. Who the hell are you?'

He saw her panic recede. 'My name's Sara Castelli,' she said in a voice that was unmistakably North American in origin. 'I'm an investigator with the HPA.'

'And what's the HPA?'

'The Health Protection Agency. I can show you my ID if you like?'

MacNeil let go of her wrists, but remained straddling her waist so that she was still pinned firmly to the ground. He reached to retrieve her torch and shone it on her.

'Please don't shine that in my face,' she said sharply, and he averted the beam to follow her hand into an inside pocket from which she pulled out a laminated HPA identity card on a chain. It had her photograph on it. And her full name. Sara Elizabeth Castelli. It also had her date of birth, and MacNeil made a quick calculation. She was nearly sixty, and he suddenly felt guilty that he had manhandled her so roughly. He rolled to one side and got quickly to his feet, holding out a hand to help her to hers. But she ignored it and got up unaided, brushing pieces of broken plastic and mud and dead leaves from her jacket and skirt. 'Ruined,' she muttered. 'You clearly have no idea how to treat a lady, Mr MacNeil.'

'Clearly,' MacNeil said. 'What are you doing here, Miss Castelli?'

'Mrs,' she corrected him. 'Castelli is my married name. But you may call me doctor.'

'Doctor. You haven't answered my question.'

She assiduously avoided his eye as she continued brushing herself down. 'Well, I might consider doing so if you were to show me some ID of your own. You could be anyone pretending to be a policeman.'

MacNeil showed her his warrant card. 'Well?'

'I'm trying to trace the source of the pandemic, Mr MacNeil. That's what I do. I trace the source of infections and make recommendations on how to contain them.'

'You're an American?'

'Canadian. Although I've spent most of the last twenty years in the States. Even took citizenship when I married Mr Castelli. Wouldn't have bothered if I'd known then that he owed more allegiance to the Sicilian flag than to the Stars and Stripes. You've heard of the movie, *Married to the Mob*, Mr MacNeil? Well, that was me. Turned out the Castelli family runs most of New York. Which went down well with the Justice Department when I worked there as a health adviser.' She glared at him defiantly. 'Anything else you'd like to know?'

'I'd be interested to hear why you think the pandemic started in the back garden of a house in Wandsworth, Dr Castelli.'

'Well, of course I don't think that. But I think someone who lived in this house might have been a carrier, or one of the first to be infected.'

'The house is empty.'

'Yes, I know.'

'So how were you intending to get in?'

'That's academic, Mr MacNeil. Now that you're here, you can break in for me.' She paused and crooked an eyebrow. 'That's what you were going to do anyway, isn't it?'

'What makes you think that?'

'Well, why else would you be sneaking around the back garden in the dead of night?' It was his turn to avoid her eye, and she pressed home her advantage. 'And you haven't told me what *you're* doing here, Mr MacNeil.'

MacNeil looked at this garrulous, defiant little woman with her coarse grey hair and tweed suit, and decided to come clean. 'I'm investigating the murder of a ten-year-old child,' he said. 'A little girl. I think she lived here.'

Dr Castelli's face darkened. 'Choy?'

'I don't know her name.'

'Well, there was only one little girl who lived here, as far as I know. And her name was Choy Smith.'

II.

His glove protected his hand as the glass broke inwards, landing in jagged shards on the carpet beneath the window. He reached in, unsnibbed the sash and slid it up.

'You do that very well, Mr MacNeil,' Dr Castelli whispered. 'Is it something you learned in the police?'

MacNeil gave her a look and held out a hand to help her over the sill and into the room. They had climbed up a tangled trellis on to the pitched roof above the kitchen, and slithered across it to this first floor window.

They stood now in what was clearly a study of some sort. MacNeil shone the doctor's torch around the room, picking out a desk strewn with papers, a computer, a calculator, two telephones. MacNeil glanced through some of the paperwork. Utility bills. A letter, which appeared to be in French, from a company called Omega 8, with an address in Sussex – there were several more with the same letterhead. A scientific paper of some sort, again in French.

There was a bookcase filled with leather-bound omnibus editions of classic English writers, a legacy of the original owner of the house, perhaps. A huge framed reproduction of a mediaeval map of London. There were more papers scattered across the floor as if discarded in anger. Two steps led down from a small half-landing outside the door to a bathroom at the top of the first flight of stairs. More stairs led up to a larger landing with two doors leading off to first-floor bedrooms. MacNeil leaned over the wooden bannister and looked into the well of the downstairs hall, light from the streetlamp outside broken into a thousand coloured fragments by the stained glass around the door and strewn across the parquet floor. And then he looked up to the attic landing twenty feet above, more doors leading to more bathrooms and more bedrooms. This was a big house for a family of three.

Choy's bedroom was at the back of the house on the first floor, half a flight up from the study. There was a narrow single bed pushed into one corner and a small desk under the window, a school satchel leaning against one of its legs. There was a homework jotter open on it, large, childish Chinese characters scrawled in coloured crayon. MacNeil shone the torch on it, and thought about all the bones he had seen laid out on the table at Lambeth Road. The tiny bones which had made up the little fingers that held the crayons to make these characters. How long ago had that been? Maybe only a matter of days. He looked around this sadly empty room. There were no pictures on the walls. No photographs, no drawings. No toys lying on the floor. He thought of the chaos that had been Sean's room, full to overflowing with the trappings of childhood.

Dr Castelli slid open the door of a built-in wardrobe. Choy's clothes hung in neat lines on wire hangers. Most of them seemed new. Blouses and skirts, a row of little shoes lined up beneath them. In a dresser they found a pile of charcoal grey jumpers, a school tie, knickers, socks. There were no T-shirts or jeans, no bright clothing to reflect a child's vibrant personality. Nothing playful in anything they found. What strange, spartan kind of existence had she lived here?

'Jeez, I've seen more fun in a kids' ward full of terminal cancer cases,' Dr Castelli said. She lifted one of the charcoal jumpers from its drawer and held it to her face. 'Poor kid.'

MacNeil looked at her. 'Isn't there a danger of infection?'

'The flu?' She shrugged. 'I doubt if I'll catch anything. I've been exposed to so many infectious diseases, Mr MacNeil. There are so many antibodies floating around my system, you could probably immunise the whole of London with a few pints of my blood.' She shook her head. 'I spent most of last year in Vietnam, chasing down cases of bird flu, trying to establish if there were any instances of human-to-human transmission. I didn't find any, but I came in contact with most of the victims. We decided to do blood tests on some of the relatives. And in a handful of cases we found that they had antibodies in their blood. It was like they'd had the flu, but without symptoms. Which gave us hope that maybe it wouldn't be the killer we all feared. We were wrong, of course. But then we tested my blood, and I had the antibodies too. Weird, huh?'

'You said you didn't find any cases of human-to-human transmission.'

'I didn't, no. But others did. The first widely accepted case was in Thailand. A family cluster in Kamphaeng Phet, about five hours north of Bangkok. They did some crude modelling on what would have happened if the transmission had been efficient. In the twenty-one days it took them to get up there, there would have been six hundred cases. Ten days after that, it would have been six thousand. That's why we were so worried, Mr MacNeil. With efficient transmission, and a mortality rate of seventy to eighty per cent, the death toll worldwide would have been unthinkable. You've heard of the Spanish Flu?'

MacNeil nodded.

'The worst pandemic in human history. Killed more than fifty million people in 1918. It had a mortality rate of less than two per cent.'

'I thought the Plague was worse than the Spanish Flu,' MacNeil said.

'It killed more people, certainly. But it took a few hundred years to do it. The Spanish Flu did its work in a matter of months.'

They left Choy's room and went into the front bedroom.

'The thing is,' she said, 'we were so sure that if the bird flu was going to be the source of the next pandemic, then it was going to start in south-east Asia and gradually spread to the rest of the world. That's why we concentrated all our efforts there. It would have reached London in the end, of course. But no one thought for a minute that this is where it would start.'

The front bedroom was a big room, with bay windows looking out on to the street. But blinds had been drawn to keep out the light, along with prying eyes. There was a large double bed which had not been made up since the last time it had been slept in. The pillow on the left side remained undisturbed, as if there had only been one occupant. In the drawers and cupboards, there were only men's clothes. No perfume or hairbrushes or make-up in the en-suite bathroom. If Mr Smith's wife had spent any time here at all, it was clear she had left some time ago.

Dr Castelli watched as MacNeil searched methodically through the room. 'The figures the government puts out,' she said. 'Crap! They're much worse.'

'How much worse?'

'Well, the population of Greater London's what, about seven million? Just do the math. A quarter of the population will get it. That's about 1.75 million. Around three-quarters of them will die. That's just over 1.3 million. Dead. No way back. Gone forever.'

MacNeil turned and looked at her in the ghostly yellow glow of the torch. It was clear that she thrived on statistics. 'Numbers aren't people, Dr Castelli. And people aren't numbers.' But he knew that's just what Sean had become. A number, another faceless victim, fodder for the furnace.

Something in his tone made her look at him quizzically. 'Was it someone very close?' she asked after a moment.

'My son.'

'I'm sorry.'

'Yeah.' He turned towards the door. 'Let's go downstairs.'

Most of the black and cream wall units in the kitchen were empty. A few cans, and several packets of dried food – noodles, spaghetti, sugar – was all MacNeil could find. The refrigerator contained a collection of half-used jars of sauce and olives and mayonnaise. There was an inch of milk left in a plastic bottle. MacNeil sniffed it and recoiled from its sour smell. He looked for the date. It was nearly two weeks beyond its use-by. A conservatory bay looked out from the kitchen on to the back garden. There was a small break-fast table in it, and two chairs. Perhaps Mr and Mrs Smith had not been in the habit of taking breakfast with their daughter. There were glass doors leading through to the main conservatory which was dominated by a large glass dining table with upholstered wrought-iron chairs. French windows opened into the living room.

'What are you looking for, Mr MacNeil?' Dr Castelli asked.

He shrugged. 'I don't know. What about you? What was it you thought you were going to find in here?'

'Oh, I imagine like you, I'll probably know when I see it. But anything that might give me an insight into where she caught her flu.'

MacNeil walked into the conservatory and she followed him through. He flashed light across the tabletop. It was littered with papers, documents and letters. All in French. A strip of paper fluttered to the floor as he lifted a letter to try to read it, but it was a long time since he had failed his French O level. It bore the Omega 8 letterhead, the same as the ones in the study.

Dr Castelli stooped to retrieve the strip of paper. 'You'd better have a look at this,' she said as she stood, and MacNeil turned to train his torch on it. It was a strip of passport photographs. There were three of them. The fourth had been cut off, presumably for use in a passport. In two of them, a little Chinese girl with a horribly disfigured upper lip was attempting to smile for the camera. Her hair looked as if it had been cut with pinking shears, and she wore an ugly pair of tortoiseshell-rimmed glasses. In the first, she was looking off, camera right, a perplexed expression on her face, saying something to someone just out of shot. So this was Choy. The bag of bones he had been called out to look at just nineteen hours ago on a building site near Westminster. This was the head that Amy had re-animated in her warehouse attic. And she had achieved a fair likeness.

'Is this her?' asked Dr Castelli.

'Probably.'

'Why can't you be certain?'

'There's nothing left of her but bones, Dr Castelli. She was stripped clean. Apart from a facial approximation made from her skull, we don't really know what she looked like.' He looked at the photographs again. The cleft lip was unmistakable. 'But it's a pretty good bet.'

He slipped the passport photographs into a plastic evidence bag and filed them away safely in an inside pocket, and they went back out into the hall.

A couple of days' mail lay on the floor beneath the letter box. A wad of unopened letters was piled untidily on the hall stand. Dr Castelli leafed through them. She made a grunting sound. 'Half of these are from me. He didn't even bother to open them. No wonder I didn't get any response.'

'Why were you writing?' MacNeil said. 'And what led you here in the first place?'

Dr Castelli let out a long, weary sigh of what sounded like resignation. 'I'm almost certain that the pandemic started at an outdoor activity centre for London schools in Kent. Back in October, during the mid-term break. Sprint Water Outdoor Centre. There were thousands of kids from London down there for the week, supervised by their teachers. It's a residential centre. You know the sort of thing. They have sailing and canoeing and rock-climbing. There are team-building events, and some of the students take part in the Duke of Edinburgh award scheme. They spend some of the time under canvas, they have campfires. The one thing all these kids have in common is that they're in each other's faces the whole time. Living in each other's pockets. In dor-mitories and dining halls and day-trips on buses. A perfect breeding ground for disease.'

She idly tore open one of her own letters and shook her head as she cast her eyes over it.

'All the families we managed to identify as the first to come down with the flu had kids at that outdoor centre in October. We might have got to this point quicker if we'd been faster off the mark. But it was several weeks before anyone realised what was happening. By that time the flu was out of control, and all we could do was wade back through the statistics. We've managed to trace all of the kids who were there, and rule them out as a source. We were looking for any connections with south-east Asia. And the best we've been able to come up with is Choy. We knew she was Chinese in origin, an adoptive child of French parents. But we've no idea how recently she came out of China, or whether she has any connection with the east at all. She might have been born in France for all we know. But she's the only one we haven't been able to get information on. Her parents haven't responded to letters or taken phone calls.'

She dropped her letter back on the hall stand and looked earnestly at MacNeil with darting little black eyes.

'By a process of elimination, Mr MacNeil, and in the absence of proof to the contrary, we have to make the assumption that Choy may well have been the source of the pandemic.'

CHAPTER TWENTY

The flat in Parfrey Street was opposite Charing Cross Hospital. Pinkie knew it had a reputation for amputations and sex changes – although not necessarily in that order. Before the pandemic, residents used to joke that they couldn't tell if someone coming out of the hospital was a man or a woman. The perfect place, Pinkie thought, for the couple he intended to visit.

Tom and Harry's flat at 13A was just above a florist's shop, which was also a café. Next door to the café was a twenty-four-hour general store that sold alcohol in blue plastic bags at all hours. Pre-pandemic there had been a regular traffic of pyjama'd patients, back and forth across the street. They went empty-handed, and returned with blue plastic bags.

Now most of the wards were filled with the dead and

dying. The hospital's regular trade had taken a back seat, and the twenty-four-hour shop was closed twenty-four-seven. As was the florist cum café, and the Pizza Express from which Tom and Harry used to feed themselves on the nights they couldn't be bothered cooking.

Pinkie cruised up a side street, away from the lights of the hospital and the comings and goings of the ambulances. You hardly ever heard them coming these days. A lack of traffic had made their sirens redundant. He found somewhere to park, and walked back to the door at number one. He drew a crowbar from inside his coat and levered it open. The wood cracked and splintered as the lock burst. The time for subtlety was over. He climbed the stairs quickly to 13A on the top floor and glanced at the nameplate. *Tom Bennet. Harry Schwartz.* He slipped the wedge-end of his crowbar between the door and the jamb and forced it open. More splintered wood. The noise of it reverberated around the landing, and the hall of the flat beyond. He pushed the door open, then quickly closed it behind him and stood listening in the dark. He heard the rustle of bed sheets, a groan, a sleepy voice. 'Jesus, Tom, is that you? What the hell are you doing?'

Pinkie turned and opened the bedroom door. He could see the prone figure of Harry wrapped in his duvet, half-raised on one elbow.

'I thought you were on all night.'

'I came home early,' Pinkie said. 'Because I wanted to put something in your mouth.'

Harry immediately reached for the bedside lamp. He turned it on, startled, and looked at Pinkie standing in the doorway. 'Who the fuck are you?'

Pinkie looked at Harry appraisingly. He could see what Tom saw in him. He was definitely the alfa male. Tall, well-built, a good head of thick, brown hair. He reminded Pinkie a little of George Clooney. Yes, he definitely had a touch of the film star about him. It was no wonder he was in such demand. Pinkie smiled and sat on the edge of the bed. 'A friend of Tom's,' he said. 'He told me you might be pleased to see me.' He glanced down at the duvet. 'I don't see any evidence of it yet.'

Harry sat upright and moved away from him. Pinkie didn't feel as though he was presenting that much of a threat. Why did Harry seem so scared? Time to introduce him to real fear. He drew his gun from beneath his jacket and levelled it at Harry's head. Harry's eyes opened wide.

'Jesus! Please don't.'

'Don't what? I'm not going to hurt you.' Pinkie moved the silencer to within an inch of Harry's mouth, and flicked it once. 'Come on. Open up. I told you I wanted to put something in your mouth.'

'Oh, my God,' Harry muttered, and with the parting of his lips, Pinkie pushed the silencer into his mouth and felt it clatter against his teeth. Harry froze, hardly daring to move or breathe.

'There,' Pinkie said soothingly. 'That wasn't so bad, was it?' He enjoyed their fear. Sometimes there wasn't time to dwell on it. Sometimes you just had to pull the trigger and be done. He remembered how it felt when the knife went down through the shoulder blades of his mother's attacker. It had glanced off bone, a sickening, jarring sensation that shot up his arm, before driving on into the heart. The man was dead, even before Pinkie rolled him off her. There had been no chance to register his fear and pain, that moment of realisation that death was upon him. So he liked to savour moments like this. But not for too long. Time was running out. 'I want you to do something for me, Harry. It will require me to remove the gun from your mouth. So I want you to be a good boy. Do you understand me?'

Harry nodded quickly.

CHAPTER TWENTY-ONE

I.

MacNeil shone his torch into the tiny bathroom beneath the stairs and saw that there was a door just inside it, on the right. He grabbed the handle and pushed it open into darkness. The beam of his torch picked out narrow wooden steps descending steeply into the cellar.

'You'd better wait here,' he said.

'I will not, Mr MacNeil,' Dr Castelli said firmly. 'Where you go, I follow.'

'Be careful, then. These steps are very steep.'

'Don't worry about me. I have my sensible shoes on. My housebreaking ones.'

He had to turn sideways to place his feet squarely on the

steps and ease his big frame down into the cold damp of the basement. It was a small room, divided in two by a brick wall. Faint yellow street light washed in from a narrow coal chute. A metal grille stopped animals from getting in. It was many years since the coalman had slid his last sack down this chute, but there was a pile of chopped pine beneath it, next to a small wood-burning stove. Low air pressure was forcing the smell of soot back down the black metal pipe that fed up into the chimney, sour like stale bacon. It was icy cold here, and MacNeil was unable to stop an involuntary shiver running through his upper body. He could feel the chill coming up through the floor, penetrating his shoes, wrapping itself around his feet and his ankles.

He ran the torch around bare walls. There was nothing much here. An empty wine rack, a damp cardboard box full of empty wine bottles. A rolled-up piece of carpet, an off-cut from one of the upstairs bedrooms. White, powdery damp oozed out through old brick. MacNeil had to duck as he passed through into the other half of the room. White-painted concrete beams supported a low ceiling. The walls were lined with empty wine racks.

'Someone must have been very thirsty,' Dr Castelli said, and her voice sounded strangely dead down here in this cold, claustrophobic space. On the back wall there was an old Belfast sink, a big white porcelain tub. In days gone by perhaps they had washed clothes down here. A single cold-water tap stuck out from the wall above it. Beneath it there was a large gas bottle, and an industrial-sized gas ring on a sturdy metal stand. A container the size of a small barrel stood next to it, covered with a towel. The centre of the room was taken up by a stout wooden table, like a giant butcher's block, which may well have been what it once was. It was chopped and scarred, and worn into a deep dent at one side, and bleached clean. MacNeil sniffed. He could smell it in the air.

So could Dr Castelli. 'Bleach,' she said.

He shone the torch around the room until it fell upon a rusted metal door set into the wall. It was about two feet high and one foot wide. MacNeil tried it, but it wouldn't move. It was either rusted solid, or locked.

'Maybe this'll open it.'

He turned to find the doctor holding up a big old iron key about six inches long. 'Where did you get that?'

'No big secret. It was hanging on the wall.' As he took it from her and turned to try it in the door, she said, 'What do you think it is? Some kind of safe?'

'It's probably an old silver safe. In a house like this the original owners would have been pretty wealthy. They'd have had silver cutlery, maybe a silver tea service. The servants would have locked it away in the silver safe after cleaning.'

The key groaned and complained as he twisted it clockwise. But it did turn, and the heavy steel door swung open, rusty hinges grating. There was a single wooden shelf set in the niche in the wall behind it. The beam of MacNeil's torch reflected back at them from an array of knives and choppers neatly arranged on the shelf. Not dissimilar to the cutting implements he had found in Flight's apartment.

He recoiled a little, as if the safe had breathed death in his face. This was no silver. This was stainless steel, lethally sharp, and he had no doubt that he'd found the instruments which had been used to strip the flesh from little Choy's bones. He lifted out a large butcher's knife and held it carefully between two gloved fingers. The blade was clean, reflecting shards of light around the walls from the glow of his torch, but as MacNeil held it up to look at it more closely, he saw that where the steel entered the wooden haft, there was a line of thick, dark matter dried in along the edge of the wood.

He handed the torch to Dr Castelli. 'Here, hold this for me.' And he took the knife to the table, laying it carefully on the wooden surface, before taking out his notebook and tearing out a clean page. He placed it on the table, and opened up a small penknife, scraping delicately along the joining edge between blade and haft. A dark, rusty brown dust crumbled on to the page of his notebook.

'Blood?' Dr Castelli said.

'It's a fair bet.'

'Choy's?'

He nodded grimly. 'I think this is almost certainly where it happened, doctor. I don't know if they killed her in here, but I think they very probably laid her body out on this very table and hacked the flesh from her bones. There must have been blood everywhere.'

'Then there'll be traces,' she said, 'no matter how fastidiously they cleaned up afterwards.'

MacNeil folded up the white paper to seal in the brown dust and slipped it into an evidence bag. 'Like this.'

'What do you think they did with the flesh and the organs?'

'Probably burned them. In that stove out there.' He nodded towards the outer half of the room. 'There should be traces in the ash.' He crossed to the sink and stooped to examine the gas ring beneath it. He pulled away the towel next to it to reveal a huge copper pot, two feet or more across. It had probably been used in happier days to make jam. 'I guess they must have boiled up the bones in this.' He knocked it with his knuckles and it rewarded him with a dull ring. He hoped that they had killed her quickly, mercifully. Because the horror of what had followed was unthinkable.

'You'll call in a forensics team, then,' the doctor said.

MacNeil stood up and sighed. 'I can't.'

'Why ever not?'

'Because we entered the house illegally. Any evidence we find here will be inadmissible in court.'

'That's ridiculous!'

'It's the law. Someone's going to have to come back with a warrant and search the place all over again. Legally this time. We were never here, doctor.'

'I was at home all night, Inspector.'

MacNeil managed a pale smile. 'You catch on quickly.'

'I was always fast. Made me very popular with the boys.'

MacNeil took back the torch and replaced the knife, locking the safe and returning the key to its nail on the wall. He looked around this grim little killing room and shivered. Only this time, it was not from the cold.

Back in the hall, coloured light rained in on them from the stained glass around the front door. MacNeil took out his mobile phone. The display blinked at him, telling him he still had one message waiting. He ignored it and dialled the FSS lab in Lambeth Road and asked for Dr Tom Bennet.

Tom sounded weary, as if perhaps he had been sleeping, slumped behind his desk with his door closed, willing away the hours of darkness and an end to the curfew, so that he could finally go home. 'Dr Bennet.'

'Tom, it's Jack MacNeil.'

There was a silence at the other end of the phone, and MacNeil could almost feel the hostility in it. 'Yes?' he said eventually, ice in his voice.

'Tom, I need a favour,' MacNeil said, without much hope now that he would get it. 'I have a sample of what I believe to be dried blood. I think it came from the little Chinese girl with the cleft palate. I need to compare it with DNA from the girl's bones.'

'That's hardly a favour, Detective Inspector. If you make an official request, then someone will do it. You don't even have to ask nicely.'

'I know that. But I need it to be off the record.'

More silence. Then, 'Why?'

MacNeil sighed. He had no time to be anything but honest. 'Because the sample was obtained illegally.'

'Then that would make me an accomplice to a crime.'

'I'm trying to catch a killer, Tom, and I'm running out of time.'

'Time to what? Be a hero?'

'I'm asking nicely.'

'Then why don't you ask your . . . *friend* . . . Amy? I'm sure she'd be happy to oblige.'

MacNeil understood immediately that he knew about him and Amy, and that the knowledge had filled him with poison and spite, just as Amy had always feared. She had known him too well. He heard another phone ringing somewhere in the background in Tom's office, and it gave the pathologist the perfect excuse to end their conversation.

'I'm sorry, I have another call. I have to go.' He didn't sound at all sorry, and he hung up abruptly.

II.

Harry sat fully dressed now on the side of his bed. His face was so pale it very nearly glowed in the dark. Pinkie sat close beside him, the barrel of his silencer pushed softly into Harry's neck. Harry held the phone to his ear with trembling fingers and listened as it rang at the other end. Then Tom's voice, crisp and businesslike, drove a sick feeling, like a sharpened wooden stake, deep into the pit of his partner's stomach. It might have been better for both of them if Tom had not been there.

'Dr Bennet.'

'Tom, it's Harry.'

Pinkie leaned in close to Harry's ear so that he could hear, too. And what he heard was Tom's pleasure.

'Hey, guy,' Tom said. 'Does this mean we're talking again?'

Pinkie nodded and Harry said, 'I guess.' He drew a deep, tremulous breath. 'Jesus Christ, Tom!'

Pinkie pushed the barrel hard into the soft flesh of Harry's neck and he squealed.

'What is it?' Tom sounded concerned now. 'Harry, are you alright?'

Pinkie took the phone from Harry. 'Harry's fine, Tom,' he said.

'Who the hell's this?'

'Doesn't matter,' Pinkie said soothingly. 'All you need to know is that if you do what I ask, then Harry is going to be just dandy. I won't harm a single hair on his pretty little head.'

III.

Amy had turned out all the lights, and sat now in the dark. She knew that the apartment was warm, but she was chilled through, her skin cold to the touch. She sat with a kitchen knife clutched tightly in her lap, watching the stairwell. Light from the landing below rose up and reflected in a distorted oblong on the pitched ceiling above it. If anyone came up the stairs, she would see his shadow immediately. She would have the advantage of surprise, and an elevated position, on her side. But in the hour or more since she had called MacNeil, there had been not a sound, not the faintest shadow of a movement.

That should, perhaps, have reassured her that whoever had cut Lyn's hair was long gone. But she found it hard to accept. She had been left so completely unnerved. It made no sense at all, and every time she thought of how he must have entered the house while she was so innocently naked and exposed in the shower, she wanted to curl up in a foetal ball and simply shut out the world. If only it was possible to pretend that none of this had happened, that in another moment she would turn over and wake up looking at the digital display on her bedside clock, daylight seeping in around the edges of her curtains.

But she knew that there was no such easy escape, and so she sat, rigid with tension and cold, and waited.

Across the room, the shorn head watched her in the dark, almost scornfully. Amy didn't know what fear was. Amy was still alive. Amy had hope, Amy had a future.

The telephone rang, and it so startled her that she nearly screamed. She grabbed the receiver. At last!

'Jack!'

'Sorry to disappoint. It's only Tom.' But she was disappointed. The momentary relief which had flooded her senses receded immediately, leaving her edgy and tense. And in spite of his attempt at flippancy, she detected something strangely off-key in Tom's tone.

'What do you want, Tom?' She hadn't meant to be so terse.

'I want you to come down to the lab,' he said evenly.

'Why?'

'I don't want to go into it on the phone. I just need you here now. As soon as possible.'

'Tom, have you any idea what time it is?'

'About three, I should think.'

'Well, what can you possibly want me there for at three in the morning?'

'I need you to bring the head and the skull.'

Amy's feeling of danger momentarily deserted her, to be replaced by consternation. 'I don't understand.'

'You don't have to understand, Amy.' Tom's self-control was deserting him. He sounded tetchy now. 'Just do it. Please.'

'Tom . . .'

'Amy!' he nearly shouted. 'Just do it.'

She almost recoiled from the phone. They'd had their rows over the years, but he had never spoken to her like this. And he seemed, immediately, to regret it.

'Amy, I'm sorry.' He was pleading now. 'I didn't mean to shout at you. It's just . . . this is really important. Just come. Please.' He paused. 'Trust me.'

Trust me. How could she not? They had been friends for so long, and he had been with her all the way to hell and back. They were the two words most guaranteed to invoke all the friendship and gratitude she owed him. *Trust me*. Of course she trusted him. And for all her misgivings, there was no way she could refuse him.

'It'll take me forty, maybe fifty minutes.'

The relief in his voice was nearly palpable. 'Thanks, Amy.'

The phone call had banished the sense of imminent danger in the apartment. And she began to wonder just

302

how much her imagination had played a role in it. She turned on the light again and wheeled across the room to lift the child's head from the table. She removed the wig before carefully wrapping the head in soft wadding and slipping it into an old hat box that she kept for transporting her heads. She dropped the wig in on top of it and replaced the lid.

As the stair lift droned slowly down to the first landing, her sense of acute vulnerability returned. She still clutched the kitchen knife on top of the hat box. But there was nobody there. Nobody in the bedroom or the bathroom, or in the coat cupboard when she retrieved the thick winter cape she used to drape over her shoulders.

The tiny hall at the foot of the final flight was deserted, cold and unadorned in the harsh yellow lamplight, and the smell of the skull rose up to greet her, through all its layers of plastic. A reminder, if she needed one, that the child was dead, and that they were still in the business of trying to find her killer.

She opened the door, and the night breathed its cold breath in her face. She pulled it shut behind her and motored down the ramp into the deserted square of granite cobbles. A tear opened up suddenly in the cloud overhead, and the briefest glimpse of silver light spilled across the courtyard, vanishing again in an instant. There was not a living soul to be seen, and Amy wondered if she had ever felt more alone. She turned her wheelchair and headed for Gainsford Street and the multi-storey car park.

CHAPTER TWENTY-TWO

I.

There were times when it was almost possible to believe that the millions of people who had once lived in this great city had simply packed up and left it. In this darkest of the small hours, when there were no vehicles on the road, no lights in any of the windows amongst the rows of silent houses they drove past, it felt abandoned. Lost.

Dr Castelli had left her car at Wandsworth, opting to stay with MacNeil, somewhere on the wrong side of the law. For his part he was glad of the company. The presence in the passenger seat beside him of this odd little lady, in her sensible housebreaking shoes and tweed suit, was comforting in a peculiar sort of way. Human contact. A voice to drown out the one in his head.

And she did like to talk. Perhaps it was nerves. A need to drive out her own demons.

She was talking now about H5N1. 'Of course, you've heard of antigenic shift?' she said, as if it might have been a topic of everyday conversation.

'No.'

'It's what we call an abrupt, major change in an influenza-A virus. Doesn't happen that often, but when it does, it creates a new influenza-A subtype, producing new hemagglutinin and neuraminidase proteins that infect humans. Most of us have little or no protection against them.'

'And H5N1 is an A virus?'

'It is. And it's probably been around for a very long time, in one form or another.'

'Before it shifted?'

'Exactly. And when it did that, it became lethal, not only to birds, but to humans as well. Of course, it still had to find an efficient way of transmitting itself from human to human, while retaining its remarkable propensity for killing us. They'll do that, you know, viruses. Real little bastards! Almost as though they're pre-programmed to find the best way of killing everything else. A virus only has one *raison d'être*, you know. To multiply exponentially. And once it starts, it's a hell of a hard thing to stop.'

'So what happened to make it transmit so efficiently from human to human?'

'Oh, recombination. Almost certainly.'

'Which is what?'

'Put simply, one virus meets another, they exchange genetic material, and effectively create a third virus. Pure chance whether or not it turns out to be something worse. A kind of little Frankenstein's monster of the virus world.'

'But that's what happened to the bird flu?'

'Oh, sure. On its travels, H5N1 probably encountered a human flu virus in one of its victims. They got together, swapped the worst, or best, of each of them, and created the nasty little SOB that's killing everyone now.'

They cruised past the flower market at the junction of Nine Elms Lane and Wandsworth Road, and MacNeil stared thoughtfully downriver towards the floodlit Houses of Parliament, and the unmistakable tower of Big Ben. 'Could something like that be done, you know, in a lab?'

'Well, of course.' Dr Castelli was warming to her subject. 'With genetic manipulation you could quite easily create an efficiently transmittable version of H5N1. Swap a human receptor binding domain from a human flu virus into an

H5 backbone and you'd improve transmission efficiency enormously. The last couple of years, they've been doing that in labs all over the world to try to anticipate what a human transmissible H5N1 would look like.'

'To create a vaccine.' MacNeil remembered the Stein-Francks doctor explaining it on television yesterday morning. Was that really only twenty-four hours ago? Less!

'Except that they all got it wrong, and had to start again from scratch when the real thing came along.' She sat silently for a moment, before turning towards him, a tiny frown playing around her eyes. 'What made you ask that?'

He said, 'A girl at the lab isolated a flu virus in marrow recovered from Choy's bones.'

He felt Dr Castelli watching him intently. 'And?'

'Well, it didn't mean much to me. But it seems like they were all excited because it wasn't H5N1. Or at least, not the version of it that we know. They said that it was artificial. That it had been man-made.'

II.

Pinkie drove across the square, past Westminster Hall and the Houses of Parliament. Westminster Abbey sat brooding in silent winter darkness, the branches of the trees in the park stark and leafless, brittle black skeletons standing witness to a plague sent, it seemed, from God to punish Man for his wickedness. For some reason they had sealed off Westminster Bridge, and so Pinkie was heading south to cross the river at Lambeth Bridge. Which, in any case, would bring him out almost opposite the laboratories.

Harry was gagged and masked and tied up in the back seat. At first he had struggled and whined, but he had long since given up, and Pinkie had not heard so much as a whimper from him in the last fifteen minutes.

Pinkie was feeling good. He liked it when he had to improvise. It tested his intelligence. It stretched him. It was a challenge. He had detected just a hint of hysteria buried somewhere deep in Mr Smith's voice. A rising panic that he was trying hard to hide. But Pinkie was still in control. It was what he was paid for. To get the job done. *Never start something you can't finish*, his mother had said. *If a job's worth doing, it's worth doing well.* Pinkie always finished the job. And he always did it well. He could hardly be held responsible for the shortcomings of others.

The fact that it was he who had introduced Kazinski to Mr Smith in the first place had niggled for a time. There was a chance that Mr Smith would blame Pinkie for Kazinski's failure. But Kazinski was gone, and Pinkie was back in charge. Whatever happened now, he would see it through to the end.

Victoria Tower Gardens separated them from the river to their left, St. John's concert hall just beyond Smith Square on their right. Pinkie could see Lambeth Bridge spanning the Thames ahead of them at the Millbank roundabout.

He slipped into third gear and slowed to make a left turn across the bridge. There was an army roadblock halfway across. A couple of trucks and half a dozen soldiers. Pinkie dropped another gear to slow his approach and give them plenty of time to check out his registration plate.

Roped hands suddenly looped over his head from behind, and he heard Harry grunt from the effort as he pulled back hard, pinning Pinkie to the headrest. The rough fibres of the rope burned Pinkie's skin, and he felt his windpipe being crushed. Involuntarily, his foot pushed down on the accelerator as he braced himself, and the car lurched forward at speed. Both his hands shot up to grab the rope and try to release the pressure on his throat. Harry head-butted him on the top of his head, and he felt a sickening pain like a vice closing around his skull. Light exploded behind his eyes. Harry was strong. He was not going to let go.

Pinkie could hear the soldiers shouting now, even above

the roar of the engine. Panic in their voices. But he was powerless to do anything about it. He could see them through the windscreen, rifles raised, pointed at the car, standing their ground and ready to fire. Harry was growling as he tightened his grip on Pinkie, sensing success in overcoming his abductor.

The first bullets hit the engine block. Pinkie knew that the soldiers were instructed to fire into the engine block of any vehicle that failed to stop. The next rounds would come through the windscreen. He knew he was going to die, and was powerless to do anything about it. But the second wave of bullets never came. He felt the car slewing sideways, saw pale, masked faces flashing past as soldiers scattered across the road. There was the sickening sound of metal tearing like paper, as the car struck one of the trucks and went spinning across the carriageway. Pinkie's foot was still pushed hard to the floor. The car was stuck in second gear, and the engine was screaming. He saw flames exploding out of the bonnet as Mr Smith's BMW struck the parapet, and Harry flew past him, narrowly missing Pinkie's head, and his face burst against the windscreen in a spray of red.

Pinkie smelled petrol, and then his whole world was engulfed by flames.

III.

MacNeil was approaching the roundabout at Lambeth Palace when they saw the explosion. Initial flames leapt twenty or thirty feet into the air. MacNeil jammed on his brakes and turned on to the bridge. They could see a vehicle half up on the parapet. It had demolished a lamp post, and all the lights had gone out. But the blaze lit the night sky and sent the shadows of running soldiers flitting across the roadway like fleeing rats.

'Sonofabitch!' Dr Castelli shouted. 'There's someone in the car. There's someone alive in that car!'

MacNeil could see an arm flapping behind the flames in the driver's seat, someone trying desperately to get out. He jumped out of the car and saw soldiers turn their rifles towards him. He waved his warrant card in the air and bellowed above the roar of the flames. 'Police. I've got a doctor with me. Is there anyone hurt?'

'Two guys in the car,' one of them shouted. 'But they're gone.'

But MacNeil could still see someone moving. He took off his coat and threw it over his head and ran at the car. The heat was intense. He could smell it burning his coat. He daren't breathe, or he knew he would damage his lungs. He wrapped his hand in the folds of the coat sleeve, felt for the door handle, found it and pulled. The door almost fell off. He could feel his trousers burning, his shoes, his hair. The figure behind the wheel half fell towards him, and he grasped the arm and pulled, dragging the man's dead weight free of the vehicle.

He could smell burned flesh now, and didn't know if it was his own. He fell in the roadway and rolled away from the choking, burning smoke, gasping for air, an agonising pain searing his hands and forearms. Two soldiers ran past him and dragged the other man clear of the blaze. 'Oh, Jesus!' he heard one of them gasp. 'Look at the state of this guy.'

Someone else threw a heavy coat over MacNeil and rolled him over several times, clouds of smoke rising from singeing clothes. Then he heard Dr Castelli, her voice full of urgency and concern. She was leaning over him, checking his face and arms and hands. 'You're mad, Mr MacNeil. Quite insane. And very lucky you only have first-degree burns.' She looked up and shouted, 'I need water fast. And clean dressings.' And then she said to MacNeil, 'How bad is it?'

'My hands,' he gasped. 'Hurt like hell.'

'Be thankful.' The little doctor grinned at him almost fondly. 'If it hurts it's not so bad.'

'That's easy for you to say.'

'The gentleman you pulled from the car, on the other hand, probably feels no pain.'

'Is he dead?'

'Not yet. But he will be. All that heroism, I'm afraid, Mr MacNeil, gone to waste.'

A soldier arrived with water in a jerry can, and a green first aid box. He looked at the doctor warily from behind his mask, and then moved away. MacNeil sat upright as the doctor poured water over his outstretched hands. There was instant relief from pain. But it returned again as soon as she stopped.

'More water!' she shouted. And then turned back to MacNeil. 'We really need to get these under running water to stop the burns doing any more damage.'

He glanced down at his hands. They were bright red. Then he looked across the road. Great clouds of white foam smothered the car as two soldiers blasted it with fire extinguishers. Several others were helping the man he had pulled from it to his feet. They half carried, half dragged him to the back of one of the trucks. A radio crackled somewhere in the night, a voice calling for an ambulance.

Dr Castelli was wrapping his forearms and hands in soft dry lint. 'Just to keep the burns infection-free,' she said. 'But you should have them treated properly.' She looked at his face by the flickering light of the almost burned-out car and shook her head. 'You even singed your eyelashes. You could have cooked, like your friend.'

MacNeil got to his feet. Shock was setting in now, and he felt his legs shaking. 'Let's take a look at him,' he said, and they crossed to the back of the truck.

Pinkie was lying on a canvas stretcher, bulbous eyes staring up at the roof, his breath rattling and gurgling in airways damaged beyond repair by the heat of the fire. The smell of burned meat, like a barbecue gone wrong, was almost overpowering. He presented such a grotesque vision MacNeil could barely bring himself to look. Much of his clothing had burned away, what was left sticking to charred flesh oozing red and amber fluids. The backs of his trousers and parts of his jacket remained, where they had been protected by the seat of the car. There were still portions of his shoes and socks visible in amongst the soot of burned flesh. The remnants of a collar clung to his neck.

His face was horrific, ears burned to shrivelled nubs, his nose, too, a dried, charred nubbin, the nasal ala pulled back like a bizarre parody of Michael Jackson in his last days.

The eyelids were gone, simply burned away, and his eyes wept. His mouth and cheeks were dreadfully distorted, lips contracted around his teeth towards the gums in a hellish grimace, almost as if he were smiling. His hair was reduced to a short, ginger stubble.

MacNeil felt sick. Perhaps it would have been kinder to have left him to die in the car. 'Can he see?' he asked the doctor.

'Probably, although his vision will be impaired. He might only see black and white.'

'But he doesn't feel any pain?'

'No.'

'How's that possible?' MacNeil said. 'My hands are still hurting like hell.'

Dr Castelli made a sad little shake of her head. 'Because he's been burned right down to the subcuticular fat,' she said. 'That's the layer of fat under the skin. Which is deeper than the pain receptors, which are located in the dermis – the layer just under the top layer. So he feels no pain. That golden amber colour you see, charred in crispy highlights like . . . like a crème brulée . . .'

'Jesus, doctor . . .'

'That's the exposed fat. And you can see those red rims around some of the less burned areas. That's the blood in the remaining skin getting pushed up by the drying out process. If they do anything at all, the surgeons will need to cut through some of the top burned layers to allow circulation in the deep tissues underneath. When the skin or the remnants cool and dry, they contract and choke off the underlying circulation. So the surgeons'll make deep, lengthwise cuts to allow the tissue to split open and relieve the pressure.' She took a deep breath. 'Debriding the burned areas is barbaric,' she said. 'The poor guy'll be unconscious, but the doctors get huge carving knives, and with a few assistants with electro-cautery at the ready, will literally carve off large patches of the burned tissue, down deep until they get to a layer of tissue that is healthy and bleeding. Then the assistants jump in and cauterise off the bleeding vessels. I had to assist in that once in med school.'

'But you said he wouldn't survive.'

'Not a chance. His body's losing fluid constantly. Let's face it, there's no skin left to regulate fluid loss through the pores. I mean, look at him. He's leaking serum all over the place.'

'So how long has he got?'

'With treatment, if he's lucky – or unlucky, depends how you look at it – maybe a day. Without, he'll be dead in a couple of hours.'

They walked slowly back towards their car. The blaze was over, the BMW a charred, burned-out skeleton. The remains of its second occupant could be seen, curled up foetally between the front seats. The Thames flowed calmly beneath their feet, reflecting the lights of the deserted city. The tide had turned, and was pushing upriver from the estuary.

'We need to get those burns of yours treated,' the doctor said.

'I'm not going to a hospital,' MacNeil told her. 'You never know what you might catch.'

'Where, then?'

'Drive me back to the police station. It's only a few minutes away. We've got first aid stuff there.'

IV.

Pinkie lay in the back of the truck, every word the doctor had spoken reverberating around his head. Why did doctors always talk about you in your presence as if you weren't there? Perhaps she had simply dismissed him as dead already. But she was right. He felt no pain. Although she was wrong about his vision. He saw quite well. It just felt strange not being able to blink.

In fact, all things considered, he felt not too bad. His breathing was the worst thing. That was difficult, and painful. He tried moving his arms and legs in turn, and found that they responded quite well. He had to fight against the stiffness caused by muscles contracted in the heat. But he could do it. He had no intention of letting the surgeons – what was it the doctor had called it? – debride his burns. The idea of them wielding large knives to slice away his flesh was more than he could contemplate.

And, besides, he had not yet finished what he had started.

The soldier at the back of the truck who had radioed for the ambulance came forward to see how he was. The young man crouched over him, and Pinkie was glad that his mask hid his horror. He reached up towards the soldier and the trooper reflexively recoiled. Pinkie gurgled and whispered, trying to form words that the boy could hear. The soldier leaned forward, trying to catch what he said, and Pinkie found enough flexibility in his fingers to slip the knife from the sheath strapped to the young man's belt.

He gurgled again, and the soldier leaned in closer, and Pinkie enjoyed the way the shock and surprise registered in the boy's eyes as his own blade slid neatly between his ribs.

When his comrades in arms returned to the truck they would find him dead, his SA80 rifle missing, and Pinkie gone without a trace, except for a few charred footprints on the road.

CHAPTER TWENTY-THREE

I.

She had held his hands and arms under running water for nearly fifteen minutes, breaking every five minutes to ask how he felt, and whether or not his hands were numb. 'We don't want you going numb,' she said, 'because that can damage the surrounding tissue.' The pain had eased considerably, to a level MacNeil felt he could bear without being constantly distracted by it.

Now Dr Castelli carefully bandaged his forearm with a fresh dressing, and wrapped fine lint around individual fingers so that he would still have the use of them. 'A pair of gloves to protect the dressing,' she said, 'and you'll be right as rain.'

His gloved hands felt thick and clumsy, but at least now he no longer felt incapacitated by the burns. From his locker he retrieved jeans and a donkey jacket that he kept for undercover work, and a pair of Doc Martens. Dr Castelli looked at him appraisingly. 'Well,' she said, 'if you were going to a fancy dress party as an undercover cop, you'd probably win first prize.' Which made him smile, in spite of everything.

DS Dawson said, 'A fine way to spend your last night, Jack. Were you *trying* to get yourself killed?'

'Just thought I'd save them the trouble of paying out on my police pension,' MacNeil said. Then, 'See if you can find out who it was I pulled from that car, Ruf. Just out of interest. The army must have to make some kind of report on it.'

'Sure.' He picked up a phone, then paused. 'By the way, that property in Routh Road. It's owned by a company called Omega 8. The letting agents are based at Clapham. They say they are not currently letting the property. The owners told them it was being used to accommodate company employees.'

'Omega 8,' Dr Castelli said. 'Wasn't that the name on those letterheads at the house?'

'You've been at the house?' Dawson said, surprised.

'You didn't hear that, Rufus,' MacNeil told him.

'Been meaning to get my ears syringed for weeks,' Dawson said, and he started dialling.

The detectives' office was almost empty. A couple of clerks were chattering away on keyboards at the far end. The overhead strip lights had been turned off, and desk lamps cast pools of bright white light only at desks where people were still working. A feeble orange glow cast itself across the office from the street lights outside.

'Have you a computer I could use?' the doctor asked.

'Sure.'

'I can probably find out who Omega 8 are.'

'Help yourself.' He waved his hand vaguely towards any of half a dozen terminals, and she sat herself down at the nearest.

MacNeil retrieved the strip of photographs from his fire-damaged jacket. The plastic of the evidence bag had shrivelled from the heat, but the photographs were still intact. He carefully drew them out and laid the strip on his desk, under the glare of his desk lamp. Choy stared back at him through her heavy-rimmed glasses, a strained half-smile betraying her unease. His eyes were drawn to her mouth. Why hadn't her adoptive parents done something about it? He was certain that in this day and age plastic surgery could have done much to improve it. He felt inestimably saddened by her wistful gaze, almost as if she were appealing for help. Someone, somewhere, someday, surely, would see this picture and know that she needed rescuing. And it had fallen to MacNeil to see it. But it was already too late.

He was about to put the photographs away in a drawer, when something caught his eye and he looked again. It was the first in the series of pictures, the one where she was looking towards someone off-camera. Asking a question, maybe. Or replying to one. In the curve of the lenses was the reflection of that someone. One in each lens. Silhouetted against the light behind it.

MacNeil held the photograph up to the light to try to get a better look. But the image was just too small. He glanced around. 'Anyone got a magnifying glass?' he called. No one had.

Dawson hung up and came across. 'No report filed by the army yet,' he said. 'What do you want a magnifying glass for?'

MacNeil showed him the picture. 'Shit,' Dawson said. 'Is that the little girl you found in the park?'

MacNeil nodded. 'See how there's someone reflected in the lens of her glasses?' he said. 'That could be our Mr Smith. Could be our killer.'

Dawson looked at the photograph thoughtfully. 'Why don't we scan it into the computer? We've got some pretty sophisticated photographic software in there. We could blow it up, enhance it.'

'You know how to use that stuff?'

'Sure.'

MacNeil looked at him. 'You see, that's why you'll never make DI, Rufus. You're far too smart.'

The scanner hummed, bright light seeped out from around the edges of its lid, and then a jpeg file appeared on the computer screen. Dawson flicked his mouse towards the applications folder and opened up the photographic software. When the programme had booted, he pulled down the File menu and opened up the jpeg on the desktop.

Suddenly the photograph of Choy's sad little face filled most of the screen. It had scanned at full resolution, and was remarkably sharp. Dawson manipulated the cursor to make a box of flashing dots around the right-hand lens of her glasses, and hit the return key. Now it was just the lens that filled the screen. The definition was seriously reduced, but the image of the man leaning in towards little Choy was hugely enlarged. It was not, however, clear enough to identify his features. Dawson selected just his image, and enlarged it again. Now they had the shape of his head. But the pixels were so large and spaced that it was just a blur. Dawson reduced the brightness and increased the contrast, and features began to emerge. They could see now that he was also wearing glasses. His hair seemed blond, or silver, and was cropped very short.

Dawson pulled down another menu and selected the 'enhance' option. Now the software filled in the gaps by cloning the nearest pixels, and suddenly there was a face looking back at them. The face that Choy had seen in that very moment, on the day they had her passport photographs taken. The man looked to be in his forties. He had large, dark eyes, beneath thick black eyebrows. His blond hair was crew-cut, and his spectacles had silver-rimmed oval lenses. MacNeil looked at him with a jarring sense of recognition. And yet he had no idea who he was.

'Look familiar to you?' Dawson asked.

'Yeah.'

'Me, too. Don't know where from, though.'

'Me neither.'

Both men stared at it. Dawson said, 'Damn, I *know* that face.'

'You should. It's been on television every other day.' Both men were startled by Dr Castelli's unexpected intervention. She stood behind them, and between them, looking

326

at the screen. 'Although the mask was a convenient way of keeping it relatively anonymous.'

'Who is it?' MacNeil said.

'Dr Roger Blume. He heads up Stein-Francks' FluKill Pandemic Task Force.'

MacNeil looked at the face again and cursed softly. That's why it was so familiar. He had watched him speak at that televised press conference just yesterday morning. He turned back to Dr Castelli. 'You know him?'

'Oh, yes. I've met him a few times over the years. Very smooth, very charming, and a real little shit. He comes about second in the pecking order at Stein-Francks.'

MacNeil sat trying to come to terms with the implications. Blume was Mr Smith. Blume was Choy's adoptive father. Blume was a senior executive of a pharmaceutical company which stood to make billions from the pandemic. 'Oh, my God,' he whispered.

'It gets worse,' said Dr Castelli. 'Or better. Depends how you look at it. Omega 8 is a small pharmaceutical services laboratory in Sussex. It was privately owned until last year when it was bought over by Stein-Francks.'

MacNeil stood up and said to Dawson, 'Can you print me off a copy of that?' He flicked a thumb at the image of Blume on the screen.

'As many as you like, Jack.'

'If we can get the neighbour at Routh Road to make a positive ID . . .' He turned to Dr Castelli. 'And if you're prepared to go before a magistrate and tell him you think Choy is the source of the pandemic, then we can get a warrant to tear that house apart stone by stone.'

II.

Amy turned left at the roundabout at Lambeth Palace, into Lambeth Road. She could see that there was activity on the bridge. Military vehicles and a gathering of soldiers next to what looked like a burned-out car half up on the parapet. There was an ambulance, medics standing around idly, and an orange light flashing on a camouflaged jeep.

But she was preoccupied. Still focused on her troubled night, random thoughts rattling around inside her head: the genetically modified virus that Zoe had found in the bone marrow; Sam's sudden abandonment of their online conversation; the intruder who had cut the hair on Lyn's head; the call from Tom, his strange insistence that she bring head and skull back to the lab. And MacNeil. Where *was* he? Why had he not answered her call?

She passed the visitors' entrance to Fairley House School, and the Archbishop Davidson centre next to the alleyway that led into Archbishop's Park. She turned right into Pratt Walk and drew up opposite the steps to the lab at 109 Lambeth Road. There were only a handful of lights burning in windows in the four-storey complex. It took several minutes to get herself out of the car and cross the street to the double ramps they had installed especially for her. Glass doors slid open into the foyer. The lobby hummed under the glare of fluorescent lights and was strangely empty. There was no one at the security desk. Amy crossed to the lift, pressed the button and manoeuvred herself into it. It was not until she had turned, and pressed the button for the third floor, that she saw the legs of the security guard poking out from behind the desk. There was blood smeared all over the tiles. She could see his hand lying motionless at the end of an arm extended through a pool of red. Quickly she hit the button to stop the lift, but too late. The doors closed, and with a jerk, it began its rattling ascent.

Amy went rigid with fear, her breath coming in short, sharp bursts. Her throat swelled up, trying to choke her. What to do? She considered hitting the alarm, but the thought of being trapped in the lift between floors for God knew how long was more than she could bear. So she waited, for what seemed like an eternity, until the lift reached the third floor. The doors slid open, and she could see down the length of the darkened corridor. Light fell out here and there in geometric slabs from open doors to labs and offices.

The whine of the electric motor in her wheelchair seemed deafening as she propelled herself out of the lift and into the corridor. She nearly jumped out of her skin when the doors slid shut behind her, leaving the corridor even darker than before. She sat for a minute, maybe two, just listening. But there was nothing save the hums and murmurs and burrs of heating and ventilation and lights, the sounds a building always makes, but that you never hear.

'Hello,' she called out, and her voice seemed feeble in the dark. 'Is there anyone there?'

As she moved forward a shadowy smudge on the floor caught her attention. She leaned over to take a closer look. It was the smear of a bloody footprint. Her mouth was completely dry. She could barely keep her tongue from sticking to the roof of it. Her hands trembled on the controller as she made herself go forward.

The door of Tom's office stood wide open. But it was empty. She rolled past a couple of other doors, both closed, before she reached the lab. A light shone through a glass panel in the door. But it was too high for Amy to see in. She pushed it open and propelled herself forward. Tom was standing at a workbench not twenty feet away. She had never seen him so pale. And it was hard to define the expression on his face. Somewhere between abject terror and unbearable guilt. He stood absolutely motionless.

'Tom, what's wrong?'

He glanced beyond her, and Amy half-turned as Zoe was pushed into the nearest bench, letting out a yelp as she slipped and fell heavily to the floor.

A movement in her peripheral vision made Amy turn further, and in quite the most involuntary reaction she had ever experienced, a scream tore itself from her throat and reverberated around the lab.

The figure that presented itself to her was like something out of a nightmare. She had seen burn victims before. But this bad, they were usually dead on a slab. Protruding eyes stared at her, lips stretched back in a hellish imitation of a smile. Burned, exposed, subcutaneous fat wept constantly, dripping on the floor. The smell reached her now, of charred meat, sickening, almost overpowering. He was holding a British Army-issue SA80 rifle, and moving with difficulty as the scorched muscles in his arms and legs contracted further. He was freshly burned, she could tell that much, and there was a chance that he was still cooking.

His breath came in short, rasping bursts. He stepped forward and checked that she had the head and the skull, and she pressed herself back in her chair, gripped by revulsion. He stopped, his face close to hers, and stared deeply into her eyes. It was hard to believe that he was human.

He straightened up and turned towards Tom, waving his rifle at the door. Tom lifted the plastic bin bags which Pinkie had forced him to fill with the child's bones and all the samples they had taken and tests they had made.

Zoe got to her feet and gasped twice before sneezing violently, charred dust in the air inflaming the sensors in her nose. Pinkie turned and shot her three times in the chest. Amy recoiled from each shot, as from a blow, and stared in disbelief as the girl slid to the floor. There was no question that she was dead.

'I hate people who sneeze,' Pinkie said. 'Didn't her mother ever tell her to cover her mouth?' But all that Amy and Tom heard was a strange gurgling that issued from somewhere deep in the back of his throat.

III.

Sara Castelli's car was parked where she had left it at the top of Routh Road. MacNeil pulled in behind it, and they got out and walked down to the neighbour's house. Le Saux had continued to leave his security lights off as MacNeil had advised, and they approached his front door by the light falling in fragments through the trees from the streetlamps beyond. MacNeil pressed the bell push several times and a buzzer sounded somewhere inside the house. He stepped back into the visual field of the CCTV camera above the porch. Le Saux's annoyance was clear in a voice thick with sleep.

'What is it now?'

MacNeil held up the print-off that DS Dawson had given him. 'Can you see that alright?'

'Yes, I can see it.'

'Is that Mr Smith, your neighbour?'

Le Saux came back without hesitation. 'Yes, that's him.'

'Thank you, Mr Le Saux.' MacNeil folded the photograph into his pocket and strode back down the path to the front gate. Dr Castelli hurried after him.

'So what now, Mr MacNeil?'

'We go and wake up a magistrate, and you tell him all about Choy.'

'You know where all this is leading, don't you?'

'I don't even want to think about it, doctor.'

'Scotland the Brave' rang out along Routh Road. MacNeil fumbled for his phone. It was Dawson.

'Jack. Thought you'd want to know straight away. That car. The one you pulled the guy from on Lambeth Bridge . . . It's officially registered to Stein-Francks. Designated driver, one Dr Roger Blume.'

MacNeil came to a halt in the middle of the road, staring straight into nowhere, as if he had caught a glimpse of some other world, something beyond the one we know and feel and see. Dr Castelli stopped abruptly beside him. 'Are you okay?'

MacNeil said to Dawson, 'That wasn't Blume I pulled from the car.'

'I don't know who it was. And neither do they. Apparently after you'd gone, he killed one of the soldiers and disappeared with his rifle.'

'Jesus,' MacNeil whispered. It was hard to imagine that the creature they had seen lying in the back of the truck might even be capable of such a thing. But a Stein-Francks car? It didn't seem possible. 'What about the other person in the vehicle? Have they any idea who that was?'

'Not a clue.'

When they finished their call, MacNeil stared at the road, thrown into confusion. Was Blume the other occupant of the car? What in God's name was it doing there? And what strange quirk of fate had brought MacNeil to Lambeth Bridge just at that moment?

Dr Castelli was still badgering him for information. But he hardly knew where to begin. He glanced at the display on his mobile phone, still lit from his call with Dawson. It reminded him that there was a message. He had forgotten all about it.

He raised a hand to silence the doctor. 'Just a minute.' And he dialled his voicemail.

A pre-recorded female voice said, 'You have one new message. At two-oh-five a-m today.' A beep, and then Amy's voice. Abnormally strained and quivering with fear. *'Jack, there's someone here in the house. Please, come quickly. I'm scared.'*

CHAPTER TWENTY-FOUR

I.

MacNeil drove like a man possessed. Reflected street lights floated across their windscreen like a stream of disembodied yellow heads. They passed Kennington Oval and headed north-east along Kennington Park Road. MacNeil was trying Amy's number every few minutes. Each time it rang out. He reached for the phone again, but this time Dr Castelli got to it first. 'I can do that,' she said quickly. 'It's not beyond me. And it's better than winding up wrapped around a lamp post.'

She made the call and let it ring for thirty seconds or more. Then she shook her head and hung up.

MacNeil had a horrible vision of Amy lying dead on the

floor of her apartment. He knew that these people were utterly ruthless. Why wouldn't they go after Amy, too? She had the skull, after all, and she'd rebuilt the head of the murdered girl. Why in the name of God had he not picked up her message earlier? He knew he could never forgive himself if anything had happened to her. This whole investigation had been about him. About his obsession. About his need to close his mind off from the death of his son. It had made him blind to everything else.

There was an army roadblock at Elephant and Castle. It wasn't enough to slow down to let them check his number. After the incident on Lambeth Bridge, all checkpoints were under orders to stop every vehicle. A senior officer checked their papers, and took his time about it. MacNeil knew it was pointless to try to hurry him. He gripped the steering wheel with still burning hands and clenched his jaw. The tension in him was greater than his pain. He felt like an elastic band stretched to breaking point. The edges were fraying. It was only a matter of time before he would snap.

Finally the officer stood back and waved them on. MacNeil left rubber and smoke in his wake as he accelerated along New Kent Road to the junction with Tower Bridge Road and turned north. Straight ahead, in the distance, they could see the lights of Tower Bridge itself, and the Tower of

London beyond on the far side of the river. MacNeil swung the wheel sharp right, and they careened across the junction into Tooley Street.

In Gainsford Street, he abandoned his car and ran. Dr Castelli chased gamely after him. He punched in the entry code at the gate to Butlers and Colonial and sprinted across the cobbles to Amy's door. He fumbled infuriatingly with clumsy, bandaged fingers to get his key in the lock. The door flew open, and he immediately saw the stair lift at the foot of the staircase.

He stood looking at it with a mixture of relief and confusion. Dr Castelli caught up with him in the doorway, gasping for breath. 'I haven't run that fast since I came in second at the egg-and-spoon race,' she said. He looked at her, and she said, 'I know, I'm sorry. I'm renowned for saying the most inappropriate things at the most inopportune moments.' She looked at the stair lift. 'So she's out, huh?'

'If the lift's at the foot of the stairs, that's usually what it means. And her wheelchair's gone.' But he wasn't taking it as read. He ran up the stairs two at a time to the first landing. The other stair lift was there, silently waiting at the foot of the next flight. He searched her bedroom, the bathroom, the coat closet, flicking on lights as he went, and then ran up to the attic. He switched on all the lights at the top of the steps and flooded the roof space with hard, bright light.

'Amy!' He called her name, but knew she wouldn't answer. She wasn't here. He checked the little metal balcony, but the French windows were locked, and he could see that there was no one out there. And then he noticed that the head of the child had gone. All that was left on the table were clippings from the black wig. As Dr Castelli reached the top landing MacNeil said to her, 'Wait here.'

'Don't worry,' she called after him. 'It'll take me half an hour to get my breath back.'

He was gone less than five minutes, and when he returned he looked troubled. 'Her car's gone,' he said. 'She has a place in the multi-storey next door. It's gone.' He looked at the doctor, who had recovered her breath by now, although her face was still pink. She was sitting at Amy's computer. 'Where would she have gone in the middle of the night?'

'Maybe you should take a look at this,' Dr Castelli said, and he crossed the room to stand behind her and look at the computer screen. It was Amy's instant message dialogue window. 'Who's Sam?'

'Sam's Amy's mentor in an organisation that specialises in identifying human remains.' He read the final exchange.

Amy – *Here's something strange – Zoe said it wasn't H5N1. At least, not the version that's caused the pandemic.*

Sam – *How does she know that?*

Amy – *She said she'd recovered the virus, and the RNA coding. It's all a bit beyond me, Sam. Something to do with restriction sites and code words that shouldn't be there. Anyway, she said this virus was genetically engineered.*

Amy – *Hello, Sam, are you still there?*

Sam – *I'm still here, Amy.*

Amy – *So what do you think?*

Sam – *I think that changes everything.*

And then clearly Sam had left the conversation without explanation. There was a sense of confusion and hurt in Amy's plaintive *Sam, are you still there? Hello? Sam? Talk to me!*

Dr Castelli said, 'Seems to me like Sam was taking just a little too much interest in your investigation. And Amy was doing just a little too much talking.'

MacNeil leaned over her shoulder to take the mouse and scroll back through a day's worth of dialogue. Sam had come back to Amy repeatedly, asking how the investigation was going. Were there any new developments? Had DI MacNeil picked up any new leads? Questions about the head, about the recovery of the bone marrow. Discussions about toxicology, the request for DNA, the discovery of the flu virus.

'She told him everything,' MacNeil said, and a red mist of depression and anger descended on him. 'Every little detail.' Sam had been able to follow his investigation every step of the way. Every time MacNeil had phoned Amy, she had talked to Sam. There wasn't anything he had done that Sam hadn't known about. Amy had been an unwitting conduit, an unknowing spy in his camp. She had trusted Sam with everything. MacNeil had to choke off his anger and think rationally. Why shouldn't she? Amy and Sam had a history. They discussed stuff all the time. They were on the same side. Weren't they?

Thoughts crowded MacNeil's head like a flock of startled pigeons. So who the hell *was* Sam? This name in the ether who had been looking over his shoulder all day. Watching him all night. He spotted Amy's address book on the dock at the foot of the screen.

'Let me in,' he said to Dr Castelli, and she vacated the seat. He clicked on the address book and its window opened up on the screen in front of him. It didn't occur to him to wonder why it was Tom Bennet's address that came up first – the last address to be searched for. He was in too much of a hurry to consider why Amy would need to look it up. He typed *Sam* in the search window, and the software immediately pulled Sam's name and address out of its database. *Dr Samantha Looker, 42A Consort House, St. Davids Square, Island Gardens, Isle of Dogs.* He swore softly.

Dr Castelli peered at the screen. 'So Sam's a woman,' she said.

More startled pigeons in MacNeil's head. He desperately tried to focus on a single one, like a hunter with a gun attempting to bring one down. But he kept missing. Nothing made any sense. How could this Dr Samantha Looker possibly be involved? And yet somehow she was.

Almost as if she had read his mind, Dr Castelli said, 'I guess you're going to have to ask her.'

MacNeil lifted Amy's phone from beside the computer and dialled Sam's number from the address book. He waited a long time before hanging up on the unanswered call. He shook his head. 'Looks like we'll never know.'

'Maybe she's just not answering the phone. We can always go to her house.'

'She lives on the Isle of Dogs.'

'So?'

'They haven't been allowed to report it in the press, but it's a no-go area. Sealed off from the rest of the city. A little island of flu-free London that the people who live there want to keep that way.'

'But you're a police officer.'

'I could be the Queen and it wouldn't make any difference. If we try to get on to the Isle of Dogs they'll shoot us.'

'Sounds more like the Wild West than the East End of London,' the doctor said. She frowned for a moment, and then her face lit up. 'I know how we might be able to get on.'

'*You're* not going anywhere,' MacNeil said. 'Especially anywhere near the Isle of Dogs.'

Dr Castelli shrugged. 'Then you can find your own way.' He gave her a dangerous look, but she only smiled. 'Trust me,' she said. 'I'm a doctor.'

But MacNeil wasn't smiling. Samantha Looker was a doctor, too. Amy had trusted her, and now she'd disappeared. And MacNeil couldn't think of any other way of finding out what had happened to her. He turned to Dr Castelli. 'Okay. Tell me.'

II.

In the narrative poem 'Tam O'Shanter', by the Scots bard Robert Burns, the eponymous hero sees a young woman

343

clad only in a cut-down shift, dancing to the Devil's tune in a haunted churchyard. He cries out, quite involuntarily, 'Weel done, Cutty-sark!', thereby attracting the unwanted attention of witches and warlocks. And providing the name for the most famous tea clipper ever to ply its trade across the world's oceans. The Cutty Sark, lovingly restored to its former glory, was visited each year by millions. It sat now in the brooding darkness of its dry dock at Greenwich, five hundred miles from its birthplace at Dumbarton on the River Clyde.

MacNeil left his car in Greenwich Church Street, and he and Dr Castelli hurried past the towering masts of the clipper, across the huge open concourse that led to Greenwich pier and the distinctive red-brick rotunda above the entrance to the Greenwich Foot Tunnel. Just four hundred yards to the north, the lights of the Isle of Dogs reflected across the sluggish waters of the Thames. They could see the apartment blocks lining the embankment on the far side, the street lights in St. Davids Square. They were so close. Almost within touching distance. And yet it seemed to MacNeil that the gap was an impossible one to bridge. He knew that snipers kept watch from the rooftops. He knew, too, that although no one had yet been shot in this stand-off, the risk of it was real enough. And he didn't want to be the first.

The domed roof of the rotunda was glazed like a conservatory, and in the daylight hours let in light to illuminate the lift shaft and the spiral staircase that led down to the tunnel below. Tonight, the hundreds of panes of glass reflected what little light there was back at the sky, and the interior was mired in the deepest gloom. There were two entrances side by side. One was completely closed off by a heavy, black-painted steel door. The way through the other was barred by a steel gate with a row of tall spikes along the top. There was a gap of about three feet between the spikes and the lintel.

MacNeil surveyed it warily. 'Supposing I manage to scale the gate and get inside without wrecking my manhood, what guarantee is there we'd be able to get out at the other side?'

'Because it's exactly the same,' said the doctor. 'They're like peas in a pod. Twin rotundas. The Victorians were pretty anal about their need for symmetry.' She paused. 'Although strictly speaking, I should say Edwardians. Because the tunnel didn't open until the year after Victoria died. But it was conceived and mostly built during her reign, so I think we could safely say it *was* Victorian.'

MacNeil regarded her with a mixture of awe and irritation. 'How the hell do you know all this?'

'Oh, you know, when I first came to London, I had to do all the tourist stuff. The Greenwich Foot Tunnel was just one of the items on the itinerary.'

'I suppose you probably know how long it is.'

'Twelve hundred feet,' she said without hesitation. 'It's nine feet high, and lined with more than two hundred thousand tiles. Ask me another.'

'I'd ask you to shut up, but I'm too polite.'

MacNeil held the torch and helped the doctor up to a foothold at the bottom of the spikes. She had to draw up her tweed skirt, revealing muscular little legs, in order to straddle the spikes and get a foothold on the other side. 'No peeking,' she said.

She dropped down to safety and MacNeil handed the torch through the bars. He pulled himself up and swung himself easily over the top of the spikes to jump down beside her and take back the torch. A white, tiled wall led away to their right, towards the doors of the lift which stood silent and dark behind its glass-panelled shaft. To their left, steel-studded steps spiralled down into blackness. The beam of the torch barely penetrated the thick, damp air, moisture hanging in it like smoke.

A smell of damp earth and rust rose to greet them as they made their way down, the staircase curving around the exterior of the lift shaft. It felt like a very long descent. The air got colder as they went, their breath billowing in white clouds in front of them. Finally, at the foot of the stairs, they turned left into the tunnel itself, reinforced as it dipped beneath the river by huge bolted sections of curved steel. The tunnel stretched away into impenetrable darkness, yellowed white tiles arching around and above them to the rusted trunking that ran overhead carrying power cables for lights that had been extinguished weeks ago.

They could feel the gentle downward slope of the tunnel underfoot as it tilted below the riverbed. Water dripped from the roof and lay in puddles all along the concrete floor. Their footsteps and their breath echoed back at them like the spirits of all those who had gone this way before. The cold was intense now, and the sense of claustrophobia almost unbearable.

'Jeez,' Dr Castelli whispered, 'it wasn't like this when we did it with the tour guide.'

MacNeil barely heard her. Something about the dark and the cold, and the sense of the river bearing down on them from above, increased his sense of frustration. Somehow everything had got out of control. He was no longer running an investigation. He was being swept along by events.

Events he could neither predict nor manage. And his sense of frustration increased his sense of urgency. He broke into a run.

'What are you doing?' the doctor called after him.

'I can't afford the time to walk,' he called over his shoulder. 'If you can't keep up, go back.'

'I'll never get out on my own,' she shouted, and he heard her sensible shoes clatter across the concrete as she chased after him. The fact that he still had her torch was probably an added incentive.

By the time he reached the lift shaft at the far end of the tunnel, he was breathing heavily. Dr Castelli had fallen a good bit behind, but he could hear her still running after him in the dark, and he didn't have the heart to leave her. Her face swam into the beam of the torch, pink and per-spiring, something close to distress in her darting little coal-black eyes.

'You're *trying* to lose me, aren't you?' she gasped. She leaned over, her hands on her knees.

'Not doing a very good job of it, am I?' He started up the stairs. 'Come on.' He heard her groan as she straightened up and drew breath to chase wearily after him.

As they neared the top of the stairs, light from street-lamps along the perimeter of Island Gardens park bled through the gate and down into the dark. MacNeil approached it cautiously and peered out into the park. Twenty yards away across the grass, there was a light in the Island Gardens Café. It was a tiny little brick building next to the fence. In the summer, patrons would sit out on its terrace and sip coffee and cold drinks and gaze out across the Thames towards the Old Royal Naval College at Greenwich. Now the terrace was deserted, and through the window MacNeil could see the figure of a man slumped in a chair. The blue light of a television screen flickered in the dark. He could see the barrel of a rifle pointed towards the ceiling, the weapon wedged through the arm of the man's seat. Clearly, he was there to guard the entrance to the foot tunnel. And he must have thought it a sinecure. For who would want to try to get on to the island through the tunnel? And why? MacNeil put his finger to his lips to warn the doctor to silence, and he watched for several minutes. The man wasn't moving. There was a good chance he was asleep, but there was no way of telling until they climbed the gate and moved into the open. By which time it would be too late. But MacNeil couldn't see any alternative, and he tried to gauge how quickly he could cover the distance between the rotunda and the café if the guard became alerted to their presence. Not fast enough, he thought. But if the guard really was sleeping, then he would be groggy, and the few seconds it took him to become fully alert might just be enough to allow MacNeil to reach him. Only one way to find out. He slipped the torch in his pocket and climbed quickly up and over the gate. He dropped down silently on the far side and pressed himself into the shadows, looking anxiously towards the café. Still no sign of movement. He nodded to Dr Castelli, and she struggled to pull herself up to the spikes. There she hesitated.

'I don't know if I can make it,' she whispered.

He sighed and looked to the heavens. Why on earth had he let her talk him into bringing her along? He moved into the lamplight and reached up towards her. 'Come on, grab my hand.'

She grasped it, and he winced from the pressure on his burns. She used his strength to steady herself as she strad-dled the spikes, and then she lost her balance, toppling forward, the sound of her skirt tearing behind her. She cried out as MacNeil caught her and cushioned her fall. It was a small sound she made, little more than a gasp. But it seemed to ring around the silence of the park. MacNeil let go of her, and she sprawled on her knees. He spun around in time to see the guard getting to his feet.

'Shit!' No time to think. Nowhere to run. MacNeil

sprinted towards the café as fast as his legs would carry him, fists punching the air like pistons. He could see the startled look on the man's face, bleary and not fully awake, as MacNeil came hurtling towards him. There was incomprehension there, too. And those moments of confusion were enough to allow MacNeil to cover the distance. He stepped sideways to smash through the door and propel himself, full weight, into the bewildered guard. Both men crashed to the floor. The portable television went spinning away across the room in a splintering of glass, and sound and vision went dead.

He heard the man grunt as he landed on top of him, all the air expelled from his lungs in a single, debilitating breath. His rifle clattered to the floor beside them. MacNeil grabbed his collar and turned him on to his back and punched him twice, big fists like Belfast hams. The first one split the man's lip. The second one rendered him unconscious.

MacNeil remained crouching over the prone figure, fighting to recapture his breath, hands hurting almost as badly as when he had first burned them. He looked around as he heard Dr Castelli approach. She stood in the broken doorway looking at him.

'Ruined my goddamned skirt,' she said. He glared at her,

and she added, 'You certainly seem to make a habit of sitting on people, Mr MacNeil.'

They pulled off the guard's shirt and trousers and tore them into lengths to bind and gag him. MacNeil lifted his rifle, and they set off across the park into Saunders Ness Road. The street was deserted, overlooked by semi-detached houses and blocks of flats, and MacNeil felt very exposed out here in the full glare of the street lights. But there was no movement anywhere, no light in any of the houses. He wondered if the people who lived here slept better knowing that men with guns were out there keeping them safe from the flu.

At the end of the street they passed the Poplar Rowing Club and turned into Ferry Street.

III.

From St. Davids Square, they could see back across the river from where they had come. The masts and rigging of the *Cutty Sark*, the Old Royal Naval College, the cranes lined up along the opposite shore brought in to build new luxury apartments, but idle since the declaration of the emergency. On the mud banks below the quay, the carcasses of three bicycles lay rusting, half-buried in the sludge.

They found Consort House at the south-east corner of the square and took the stairs to the top floor. Just as Pinkie had done nearly twenty-four hours before, they found number 42A at the end of the corridor, next to a window looking out over the river. Her name was on the door plate. *Dr Samantha Looker*. MacNeil tested the door with his fingertips, and it swung open. Someone had left it on the latch. The hall beyond was in darkness. MacNeil indicated to Dr Castelli that she should remain where she was. He held the rifle across his chest and moved cautiously into the apartment. He had been good on the ranges, consistently hitting the target as often as nineteen times out of twenty. But he had never fired a weapon in anger, and never pointed one at another human being. Ahead, he could see street lights laying the shape of windows across the carpet of the living room. He passed an open door to a bedroom. He looked in. The bed was empty. It hadn't been slept in. On his left, the bathroom door, and then a door to the kitchen. The apartment was warm, but there was no sense of occupation. He did not, by now, expect to find anyone in the living room at the end of the hall. But still, he proceeded with caution.

As he stepped into the room, something moved under his feet, and a screeching filled the air.

'Jesus!' he said, and he jumped back and saw the fleeting

shape of something small and black streaking away across the carpet. He fumbled for the light switch, and as cold yellow light flooded the room, he turned quickly into it swinging his rifle through a ninety-degree arc.

Dr Samantha Looker lay face first in her own blood, where Pinkie had left her. Her computer was still on, its screen saver taking it on an endlessly repeating journey to the planets of the solar system. A small black cat with white bib and socks glared at MacNeil from across the room. He had stood on its tail or its paw, and it was watching him warily.

He turned sharply as Dr Castelli came into the room. 'Oh, good God,' she said when she saw the body on the floor, and she immediately knelt at Sam's side to feel for a pulse. She looked up and shook her head. 'Stone cold.' She felt the muscles of the arms. 'Rigor mortis is fully developed. So she's been dead at least twelve hours.' She looked back down at the corpse. MacNeil supposed there was probably not a great age difference between the two doctors. They were similar, too, in build, and both had short-cut grey hair. Perhaps all of those things gave Dr Castelli a greater sense of her own mortality. She seemed shaken. For once there were no wisecracks. 'I suppose this is Sam,' she said.

'I suppose it must be.'

'So who was Amy talking to all day?'

But MacNeil just shook his head. It could have been anyone. Text on a screen. How could you ever know? He stepped over the body and moved the computer mouse to clear away the screen saver. And there, on the screen, was the same dialogue box he had seen on Amy's computer. Dr Castelli got to her feet and looked at it.

'It must have been like a three-way chat,' she said. 'A conference call. Only, Amy never knew there was a third party.' She took the mouse from MacNeil and clicked to see the participants. 'It only shows Sam and Amy. So the other person must also have been logged in as Sam, from another computer somewhere else. Amy had no idea she wasn't talking to her mentor.'

The cursor was blinking steadily at the end of Amy's last message. *Sam, are you still there? Hello? Sam? Talk to me!*

It was a dead end. Literally. 'So there's no way of ever knowing for sure who it was she was talking to,' MacNeil said.

'Unless he's still there.'

He looked at her. 'What do you mean?'

'Well, the chat's still open. Maybe our phantom "Sam" is still online.'

'How can we tell?'

'Ask him.' The doctor looked at MacNeil, one eyebrow raised, and he realised what she meant. He pulled up the chair and sat down at the keyboard, and then realised that his banana fingers were never going to type anything very accurately.

'Here, you'd better do it,' he said, and stood up to let her in.

'What'll I say?'

MacNeil thought about it. Who *had* Amy been talking to? Logic said it could only have been Smith. And they knew now that Smith was Roger Blume. 'Hello, Dr Blume,' he said.

Dr Castelli looked at him, and then nodded, understanding why. Her fingers rattled across the keyboard.

– *Hello, Dr Blume.*

The cursor blinked silently for a long time. 'He's not there,' MacNeil said. Then a *wwwooo-oop* sound alerted them to an incoming message.

– *Mr MacNeil, I presume.*

MacNeil carefully peeled off his gloves and nudged the doctor aside. He needed direct contact, no matter how painful. He typed carefully.

– *Yes.*

– *What took you so long?*

– *You're not an easy man to find.*

– *And now that you've found me?*

– *Where's Amy?*

– *Ah, straight to the point.*

– *It's over, Blume.*

– *Not until the fat lady sings.*

– *We have blood from the house in Routh Road. We have a photograph of you from a reflection in Choy's glasses in one of her passport pics. We know that Stein-Francks owns the house. And you have been identified by one of your neighbours.*

– *And I have everything else, Mr MacNeil. The bones, the head, the marrow, all the samples and tests. Without which you have nothing.*

MacNeil sat staring at the screen. If that was true, then Blume was right. They did have nothing. With no body, there was no murder. No way to prove anything. And any evidence they did have had been obtained illegally.

'Smug bastard!' Dr Castelli muttered at the computer.

– *What's wrong, MacNeil? Cat got your tongue?*

MacNeil looked at the cat still watching them from across the room. Had they been face to face, he might have found words to throw back at Blume. But the keyboard defeated him.

– *Oh, and one other thing. I also have Tom. And Amy. So perhaps we can trade.*

– *Trade what?*

– *Whatever residual evidence you might have, in exchange for your girlfriend.*

'Don't believe a word of it,' Dr Castelli said. 'He's a lying little shit.'

MacNeil thought for a moment before typing.

– *Where and when?*

– *The London Eye. But you'd better be quick, Mr MacNeil. It's after five, and it would be best to have business completed before the curfew is lifted, and you become just another private citizen.*

CHAPTER TWENTY-FIVE

I.

The London Eye was a Ferris wheel for grown-ups on the South Bank of the Thames. Like the wheel of a giant's bicycle, it stood one hundred and thirty-five metres high, comprising seventeen thousand tonnes of steel and cable, and had been built in an age of optimism to celebrate the millennium. More than thirty glass capsules turned around its outside edge on circular mounting rings as it revolved. The unrestricted views of London from its highest point were unparalleled. Before the emergency, fifteen thousand tourists a day flocked to fill its capsules. But since the arrival of the flu, it had stood silent and still, a constant daily reminder to the people of London that things had changed. Perhaps irrevocably.

Pinkie sat in the wooden control hut, amongst the broken glass, and surveyed the command panel with its green and red push lights. It was all quite simple, really. No great mystique. It was the sort of thing you dreamt of as a child, to have that kind of power at your fingertips. Press this button to make it go, press that button to make it stop. This one opens the door, this one locks it again, each pod individually controlled.

He looked across the landing and departure deck and saw Tom and Amy locked away in their glass pod. He had made Tom carry her in and prop her up on the slatted oval bench at its centre. Now it was a prison without bars. Just glass. Could there be any worse kind of prison than one from which you could always see out? One from which freedom was ever visible, a constant reminder of your own lack of it?

Pinkie knew he could not have survived in prison. Of course, they had never charged him. He had killed a man to protect his mother, and the authorities had deemed in any case that he was too young to accept any legal responsibility for his actions. But later, when he had started doing it for pleasure, and money, he knew that should he ever be caught he would have to take his own life, too. He could never be shut away in a confined space like that for days, weeks, years, the door locked – as it always had been in the cupboard under the stairs. The breathlessness would have crushed him.

He wasn't feeling so good now. Fluid was gathering around him on the floor. He felt nauseous and weak. His muscles were seizing up. He knew that the computer screen was casting light on his face, and that if he turned to his right he would see his reflection in the window which looked out on to the queuing area. But he did not want to see what he looked like. He wanted to remember himself as he had been the last time he looked in the mirror. He knew he wasn't handsome – he had never harboured such illusions – but he'd had good, strong features. He couldn't bear to see himself as he was now.

The gurgling in his chest was getting worse. It was becoming harder to breathe. Where was Mr Smith? He should have been here long ago as arranged in their exchange of texts on the dead soldier's phone. Pinkie looked out of the window. All the floodlit towers and spires of the Houses of Parliament pierced the black sky on the far side of the river, reflecting in the slow, steady flow of black water. A noise to his left made him turn, and there was Mr Smith, finally, standing in the doorway looking at him open-mouthed, eyes wide with horror. And Pinkie was reminded again of how he looked to others.

'Who – who the hell are you?' Mr Smith said uncertainly.

Pinkie tried very hard to make what was left of his mouth form his name. 'Ssssphhh . . . phinkie,' he said.

Mr Smith gaped at him in disbelief. 'Pinkie?' Pinkie nodded. 'Holy Mother of God,' Mr Smith whispered. 'What happened?'

'Chhh . . . car crash.'

'Jesus!'

Pinkie could see in his eyes that Mr Smith knew he was going to die. But he was here, wasn't he? He was going to finish the job. He had never started anything he couldn't finish. He reached over to swing the black bin bag across the control room to his employer, and Mr Smith looked inside. Pinkie saw him flinch from the smell. The bones were still ripe.

'Is that everything?' Mr Smith asked.

Pinkie nodded.

'Good. Can you still walk?'

Pinkie nodded again.

'I want you to go with the girl up to the top. MacNeil is on his way. As long as she is up there out of his reach, I've got something to bargain with. Are you up to it?'

Amy sat silently on the slatted wooden bench, staring bleakly out at the Thames. It was hard to believe that the burned man was still alive. She knew that he could not survive for very much longer. He was losing so much fluid it was amazing he could still stand. She wondered what could possibly drive him to do what he was doing. Surely he knew that he was going to die?

A tense silence had settled between her and Tom. He had made that phone call to her knowing full well that she was being lured into a trap. *Trust me*, he had said. And she had. Only to be rewarded with deceit and betrayal.

'I had no choice,' he'd told her. 'It was you or Harry.'

'So you chose me.'

He'd turned away then, guilt in the very way he held himself. And there had been nothing more to say.

There was a *phssss* of pneumatic pistons, and the end of the pod split open as the doors at the landing stage side disengaged and slid apart. Tom stood up. 'There's two of them now,' he said.

Amy could see the silhouettes of two men approaching the pod. The burned man could barely walk, but he was still carrying his SA80. He stepped up into the pod, followed by a man who looked vaguely familiar. He wasn't tall. He had cropped fair hair and unusually dark eyebrows. Silver-rimmed oval glasses. His face looked drained of blood, and he was clearly tense.

'What's going on?' Tom asked, and Amy could hear fear crack his voice.

The man with the glasses ignored him. He looked at Amy, and then turned to the burned man. 'Where's the other one?'

'Yes,' Tom said. 'Where's Harry? You promised he would be safe.'

If Pinkie could have smiled, he would. 'Dead,' he said, and he didn't need lips to form the word. It came out of his mouth as clear as day.

There was just a moment of silence before a dreadful, feral howl escaped Tom's lips. He lunged across the pod at Pinkie. A short, deafening burst of fire from the semi-automatic rifle spat half a dozen bullets deep into the pathologist's chest, nearly lifting him off his feet. Blood spattered all over the glass, and Tom hit the floor with a shuddering finality. Amy screamed. She could not believe what she was seeing. He might have betrayed her, but she still loved him. You didn't just wipe out twelve years with a single phone call. And yet suddenly he was dead. There was no going back. No saying sorry. No fixing things. The burned man had killed him in a moment. He was gone forever. Life might be hard. But death was so frighteningly easy.

PETER MAY

The man with the glasses held his head in his hands, fingers pressed to his temples.

'For God's sake, Pinkie! You nearly burst my ear drums!' And then he glanced anxiously across the Thames, wondering perhaps if the gunfire had been audible at any of the checkpoints on the north bank. But most of the sound of it had been contained within the capsule.

'What do you want?' Amy screamed at him.

The man turned towards her. 'I want you to shut up,' he said tersely. 'Pinkie's going to take you up top. I need you as a bargaining chip in my discussions with Mr MacNeil. And I want you well out of his reach. Any trouble, and Pinkie will push you out.'

Amy closed her eyes. The nightmare had just got worse. If that was possible. She would be trapped in this pod 443 feet above London with a horribly burned psychopath whose remit was to push her out if negotiations on the ground went badly. And there was nothing she could do about it. The only faint ray of hope was that MacNeil knew she was here, and that he was on his way.

She said to the man, 'What are you going to trade me for?'

'Any remaining evidence that might implicate me in the death of little Choy.'

It was the first time that Amy had heard her name. She had got so used to thinking of her as Lyn, it came as a shock to hear her real name. 'Choy,' she said. '*You* killed her?' The man said nothing, and Amy said, 'MacNeil will never agree.'

'Then I'll kill him, too.'

'You wouldn't have the guts to kill a serving police officer.'

'If I can kill a ten-year-old child and strip the flesh from her bones, I can kill a policeman.'

Amy shook her head, trying to stop the tremor in her voice, trying to appear calm and defiant when fear had turned her insides to mush. 'There's one big difference.'

'What's that?'

'Ten-year-old girls can't fight back.' She hoped she had managed to convey the contempt she felt.

He turned away, stepping over Tom's body and out on to the landing stage. He paused, then, and turned back to Pinkie. 'The green button on the right?'

Pinkie nodded, and the man walked away to the control hut. After a moment, there was a slight judder, and then slowly they began to move. Amy clutched the edge of her seat and looked up through the roof of the pod. She could see the huge spokes start to turn, and a strange sense of weightlessness as their capsule moved forward, lifting as it went, starting its long, gradual ascent to the top of the wheel.

CHAPTER TWENTY-SIX

There were voices calling in the night. They could hear the sound of running feet. The beams of torches crossed and criss-crossed in the dark. There was no way back.

Several vehicles were pulled up outside the park in Saunders Ness Road, motors running, headlights blazing, turning night into day. Somehow the man guarding the foot tunnel had got free, or someone had come to relieve him and found him bound and gagged. The alarm had been raised. Someone had got on to the island. Someone who might be carrying the flu. MacNeil knew, now, they would be shot on sight. Panic was a great dissipater of the rational.

He grabbed Dr Castelli's wrist, and they ran back along Ferry Road. Her sensible shoes clattered resoundingly in the night. Excitement raised voices behind them. A motor gunned, and they heard the squeal of tyres.

'Get rid of the shoes!' MacNeil told her, and half-hopping, half-running, she plucked the shoes from her feet, each in turn, and threw them away across the road. He dragged her off the street, down an alleyway between brick bungalows with shallow pitched roofs. He saw a street sign. Livingstone Place. Lights were going on in houses everywhere. Someone was screaming, 'Intruders! Intruders!'

MacNeil was starting to panic. They ran past neat little gardens behind well-trimmed hedges, more light falling on to manicured lawns.

Someone shouted, 'There they are!' A shot rang out. MacNeil heard the bullet ricocheting off brick somewhere very close by.

Someone else shouted, 'Don't shoot, for Chrissake! We'll be shooting each other.' There were more feet running now out in the street behind them.

They reached the end of the alley and turned into a river-front walkway. It was about a hundred yards long. And blocked at each end. They were trapped.

'Excuse my French,' Dr Castelli said. 'But oh, fuck!'

MacNeil peered over the wall, down to the river. The tide

was washing in against a couple of yards of mud flat and rock, breaking fluorescent all along the river's edge.

Dr Castelli looked at him. 'No,' she said.

'No choice,' MacNeil told her. 'If they catch us, they'll shoot us.'

She dropped down first and landed ankle-deep in the mud. He landed beside her and fell to his knees. Mud sucked at his feet as he staggered upright and grabbed her arm, pulling her in flat against the wall.

Voices and torches streamed out along the top of the wall above them. Beams of cold white light panned across the mud inches in front of them and then vanished. 'They're not here!' someone called, and the footsteps immediately receded, running back up the alley towards the road. 'Search the gardens!'

'Now,' MacNeil whispered, and still holding Dr Castelli's wrist, pulled her after him along the edge of the wall. It was heavy going, through mud reluctant to let each footstep go. And then they reached a rocky outcrop and it became easier. The wall curved away to their right, apartments overhanging the retaining wall above them. There were dozens of lights now, shining out from windows across the water. It seemed as if everyone on this southern tip of the Isle of Dogs was awake. And looking for them. They clambered over rocks and boulders and the jetsam washed up by the tides, the refuse of a society careless with its world, until ahead of them they saw the dark shape of the old Felstead Wharf extending into the water.

They reached the safety of the deep shadow it cast along the riverbank, and found steps leading up. On the wharf itself, they felt exposed again. They could hear voices somewhere beyond the apartment blocks. Windows everywhere were filled with light. On the far side of the wharf, more steps led down to a small jetty. An ancient, tiny, two-person speed boat was tied up there, rising and falling gently on the swell. MacNeil knew it was their only chance of getting off the island.

Dr Castelli ran after him down the steps, and MacNeil jumped into the boat, sending it rocking dangerously. He ripped off the dash and looked at the bewildering spaghetti of coloured wiring that he had exposed. This was something he ought to know how to do. But he'd always been on the right side of the law. There had to be a logic to it, though, and he tried following the wires back to the ignition lock.

Dr Castelli pushed him out of the way. 'Here,' she said. 'Let me. Where I came from we used to steal cars for fun on a Saturday night.'

She quickly established the circuit logic and ripped out

a green and then a red wire, exposing their frayed, silver ends. She touched them together and the motor coughed and died. 'Shit,' she said. It wouldn't take many failed attempts to attract the whole of the island to the wharf.

MacNeil reached across her and pulled out the choke. 'Try again,' he said.

This time the engine fired and caught. She twisted the ends of the wires expertly together, establishing permanent contact, and then let him in behind the wheel. The motor was sluggish, and MacNeil pushed the choke in a touch, before gunning it hard. Diesel smoke and the smell of it filled the air.

'Untie her!' he shouted, and the doctor leaned over to slip the loop of tethering rope over the top of its wooden capstan. MacNeil engaged the gear, grabbed the wheel and pulled back on the throttle. The front of the boat lifted dramatically as the water behind them churned white, and they slewed out from the shadow of the wharf into the main drag of the river.

Behind them, they heard voices raised in anger, and then several shots. MacNeil ducked instinctively, and saw tiny plumes of white raised from the Thames by bullets aimed in their direction. He wondered why they were bothering. If he and the doctor had brought the flu with them, then it was too late now anyway.

He sent the boat weaving towards the far bank, out of range of the rifles on the island, and turned and called back to the doctor, 'We'll be quicker to take the boat all the way. There's a pier at the Eye.' She nodded, and as they reached the South Bank, he turned north to traverse the loop of the river, keeping his distance from the Isle of Dogs which was waking up in fear across the water.

CHAPTER TWENTY-SEVEN

I.

The lights of the city spread out below them, an irregular hotchpotch of jumbled boroughs crowding one on top of the other around the serpentining eastward progress of the Thames. The Houses of Parliament, the controversial Portcullis House, the concrete iceberg that was the Ministry of Defence – two-thirds of it hidden underground. Away to their right, the lights of St. Thomas' Hospital, and beyond it the building site in Archbishop's Park, where Choy's bones had been uncovered just twenty-four hours earlier, setting in train the unpredictable sequence of events which had led inexorably to this. Work had begun again after a short over-night break, and workers moved around like tiny orange ants beneath the arc lights. Too far away to help. Even if they were to look up towards the wheel, it was unlit, and moving too slowly to attract attention.

Amy watched as the capsule which had been above them throughout their ascent reached its apex and started dipping away beneath them. Their pod sat proud now on the very top of this giant wheel, cold pre-dawn air whipping around its open doors. It whistled through all the spokes, whining amongst the cables, almost as if it were alive and giving voice to her fear.

With a slight jerk, the wheel came to a standstill, and the pod rocked gently upon its axis. They were as high as they could go. Amy couldn't look directly down. It made her giddy and turned her stomach. She glanced across the pod towards Pinkie. He was sitting on the floor with his back against the glass, and seemed semi-comatose. If there had been a moment when an able-bodied person might have overpowered him, it would have been now. But Amy was powerless to do anything. And as the pod came to a stop, Pinkie seemed to revive. He got back to his feet with difficulty, leaving a pool of serum on the floor, and shuffled across the pod to the door. He leaned out and looked down, and she heard his breath crackling in his ruined airways as he sucked in the cold air. He turned back and leaned his gun against the wall, and then with great difficulty began dragging Tom towards the opening.

It took Amy a moment to realise what it was he was going to do. 'Don't!' she called. 'Please. He's dead. He deserves better than that.'

Pinkie looked up and held her eye for a moment. They seemed strangely sad, his eyes, full of a watery melancholy. And then he returned to his task, dragging the body to the very lip of the door. He stood up, fighting for breath, and tipped the body over with his foot. Tom fell silently out into the night, striking the superstructure of the wheel, before spinning off out of sight into darkness.

Pinkie retrieved his gun and straightened himself against the glass wall to the left of the door. Amy looked at him with hate and revulsion in her heart. 'I hope you rot in hell.'

Pinkie tried to speak. But nothing would come, except for a bubbling noise in his throat. He was fading fast.

II

They were approaching Tower Bridge, St. Katharine's Dock and the hideous concrete monstrosity that was the Thistle Tower Hotel off to their right. On their left were the converted warehouses of Butler's Wharf. Not far beyond them lay Amy's apartment, dark and empty. The wind was strong, blowing upriver from the estuary, and the flow of the tide helped their progress. Their wake glowed green behind them, like some luminous jet stream reflecting in the water.

MacNeil kept his concentration on the river that lay ahead. The old entry to the Traitor's Gate in the Tower of London was all bricked up. And there was no sign of life aboard HMS *Belfast* as they cruised past her mooring. A thousand years of history crowded the banks of the river all around them. The *Golden Hind*, the Globe Theatre, St. Paul's Cathedral, and bridge after bridge spanning the waters of a river which had borne witness to everything from the beheading of kings to the Great Fire of London and the German Blitz. All that human endeavour, inspiration and wickedness, genius and evil, brought to this sad end. People cowering in their homes, frightened to walk the streets, reduced to a life of fear and loathing by a single, deadly organism.

He turned to Dr Castelli. Perhaps now it was time to confront the truth. 'So what do you think happened?' he said. 'With Choy and Blume.'

She shook her head. 'Who knows? Stein-Francks were

chasing down a vaccine. Trying to get ahead of the game. But there were plenty of others doing the same. After all, whoever could produce an effective vaccine would make billions. You know, the EU alone has over a billion euros set aside annually to buy in vaccines and antivirals in the event of a pandemic.' She gazed off across the water. 'But they could only produce a vaccine ahead of the game by artificially creating a version of the virus that would transmit easily from person to person. Somehow the genie got out of the bottle. Choy must have got infected. God knows how. She went with her school to Sprint Water during the October break and passed it on unwittingly to hundreds of others.'

Dr Castelli sucked in a deep breath. 'The thing about kids is, they're just about the most effective incubators you can get. And they're great at passing on infection. Most adults are infectious from just before the onset of symptoms, and then for four or five days afterwards. Kids shed virus from six days before symptoms, until as long as twenty-one days after. They are walking time bombs. They have no idea they have it, but they're passing it on to everyone they meet – when they talk, cough, sneeze. You touch stuff they've touched, and you're infected. Incubation is usually one to three days, and the average person will infect one-point-four people. Kids'll do better than that, and in closed communities they spread the virus like wildfire.'

'So a school camp with a couple of thousand other kids is just about the worst place to send an infected child?' MacNeil said.

'If you were a bioterrorist, you could hardly have picked a better scenario.'

'But Stein-Francks aren't bioterrorists.'

'No, they're just trying to make money. But this time they made a bigger killing than they expected. Millions of people are going to die because somehow, somewhere along the way, they screwed up. And Choy would have been the living proof of it. Destroy her, you destroy the evidence.'

MacNeil forced himself to focus on what Dr Castelli was saying, to try to follow her logic. 'I don't understand. Surely she has the same virus as everyone else, so that wouldn't prove anything.'

'No. Her virus is different, Mr MacNeil. You told me yourself that the lab said Choy's version of H5N1 had been genetically engineered.'

'That's right.'

'So it's different from the one that infected everyone else.'

'How's that possible?'

'Because it mutated.' Dr Castelli shrugged her shoulders as if it were the most natural thing in the world. Which it was. 'The flu virus does it all the time – antigenic shift, reassortment, recombination. That's why the vaccine that Stein-Francks produced didn't work. Of course, they'd have known the virus was bound to mutate, but not as much as it did. And we had no idea that the virus that's killing everyone had evolved from something man-made.' She waggled a finger at him. 'But here's the thing. We know that Choy was at the epicentre of the pandemic, and if we'd been able to compare her virus with the one used to produce the Stein-Francks vaccine, we'd have known straight away where it came from. As good as a fingerprint. Don't you see? That's why they had to get rid of her.'

They were motoring up King's Reach now, Waterloo Bridge ahead of them, the South Bank Centre to their left. Already they could see the Eye dwarfing the buildings on the south side of the river, dark, silent and still, reflecting city lights against a black sky. There was no way MacNeil could have known that Amy was a prisoner in the topmost capsule, held there by the man he had pulled from a burning car on Lambeth Bridge two hours earlier. What he did know was that once they had passed the Royal Festival Hall, and gone under the Hungerford Bridge, they would be visible to anyone watching the river from the Eye. But Blume would not be expecting them to arrive by boat. He would be on the far side of the wheel watching the road. If they cut their motor, and made a silent approach to the pier, then they might be able to catch him, and any accomplice, unawares.

As the boat passed beneath the new footbridges suspended from either side of the rail bridge carrying trains into Charing Cross, he pulled Dr Castelli's wires apart and the motor died. They emerged silently into the short stretch of water leading down to the pier immediately opposite the Ministry of Defence.

Two girdered walkways led out from either side of the base of the wheel to the Eye's landing stage. A large pleasure cruiser was tied up there, bobbing gently on the rise and fall. MacNeil looked up at the vast structure soaring above them. It was only when you got this close that the full scale of it made its impact. He could see a light in the control hut at the far side of the boarding and disembarkation area, but there was no sign of life.

He steered the boat gently into the pier and jumped out to tie its lanyard to the white railing that ran along its length. The little boat bumped and scraped along the edge of the pier. He knelt down beside it. Dr Castelli thought he was going to give her a hand out, but instead he whispered, 'I want you to stay here.' She was going to protest, but he cut her off. 'These people are killers,' he said. 'No messing.'

She seemed resigned and leaned back into the boat to retrieve the rifle they had taken from the guard on the Isle of Dogs. 'You'll need this, then.'

But he just shook his head. 'You keep it. If anyone comes near you, shoot them.'

'What if it's you?'

He gave her a look. 'Make an exception.'

'Okay.'

He swung himself over the rail and trotted up a covered ramp to the walkway at the south end of the pier. There, he stopped and peered towards the base of the wheel. The four huge red motors, whose rubber wheels worked like cogs to make the big wheel turn, were still. Apart from the light glowing in the control hut, there was still no sign of life. MacNeil emerged from the shadow of the ramp and felt vulnerable beneath the clear Perspex of the walkway as he covered the thirty or so yards to the embankment at a gentle run. As he passed beneath it, he glanced up at a spiral staircase climbing into darkness overhead, mainte-nance access to the vast motors suspended above. Ahead, a tubular gate barred his further progress. It rattled as he climbed it and dropped down on the other side. The ramps that zigzagged up to the boarding platform – where thousands had once queued daily to experience the thrill of the ride – seemed oddly haunted in their emptiness. He heard the wind as it sang through the taut spokes of the wheel, and rattled the naked branches of trees on the open concourse. Massive cables, the thickness of a man's leg, swooped overhead to anchor the structure firmly in concrete. There were a couple of circular booths, all closed up. A café terrace, long deserted; beyond, a playpark sadly forlorn in the absence of the children's voices which had once animated it.

Blume was standing by a statue raised to the memory of the International Brigade, who had volunteered to help the Spanish people in their fight against fascism. Fists raised in the air, faces turned to heaven. A quarter of them had died. He turned, caught completely off-guard by the sound of MacNeil's voice. 'You've got thirty seconds to tell me what you've done with her before I break your neck.'

His tension gave way to a smile, almost of relief. 'Well, that would be very foolish of you, Mr MacNeil. Because she'll break a lot more than her neck if anything happens to me.'

'Where is she?' MacNeil was disturbed. He had made certain that Blume was completely alone before making his approach. And yet, why would Blume have exposed himself like this, on his own and unprotected, unless he felt confident that he had an edge on MacNeil?

Blume tipped his head back and looked up into the sky. 'She's up there,' he said. And for a moment MacNeil didn't understand, until he turned and followed Blume's eyeline and realised he was talking about the wheel. Blume smiled at MacNeil's confusion. 'Right at the very top,' he said. 'Best seat in the house, absolutely free of charge. But it's a long way down – if *you're* a bad boy.'

MacNeil stared at him, every fibre of his being urging him to do this man physical damage. It took a supreme effort of will to control himself. 'What do you want?'

'I want to know what you know, and who else knows it.'

MacNeil's eye fell on the inscription engraved in the black marble plinth of the statue. *They went because their open eyes could see no other way.* He said, 'I know there was some kind of accident. That Choy got infected with the flu virus you were working on. That this whole pandemic is happening because you people got careless.'

Blume rolled his eyes and shook his head. 'Is that what you think?' he said. 'Is it really? How charitable.'

'What do you mean?'

'I mean, it wasn't an accident, Mr MacNeil. We infected

poor little Choy quite deliberately. And we sent her to Sprint Water knowing – no, hoping – that she was going to trigger a pandemic.'

Whatever MacNeil might have expected to hear, it hadn't been this. Blume's simple confession was breathtaking in its scale. To the extent that MacNeil couldn't think of anything to say, except, 'Why?'

Blume sighed. 'It's a long and painful story, Mr MacNeil. Stein-Francks was on the verge of ruin. A catastrophic collapse. And it had all been going so well. A certain amount of money had, shall we say, changed hands. Certain officials at the World Health Organization had declared FluKill as the drug of choice against the bird flu pandemic that everyone was predicting.' He smiled wistfully. 'Which didn't please our competitors at Roche. Basically, we put Tamiflu out of business.' He folded his arms across his chest and leaned against the International Brigade. 'All the major Western countries were putting in orders. And I'm talking billions. Of course, you have to speculate to accumulate. And so we invested hugely in production. We had to increase output to meet demand. We started building a new production facility in France. We put all our eggs in the one basket – or in this case, the one nest. But it seemed like such a sure thing. Everyone wanted FluKill. And then . . . well, then, the

Vietnamese and the Cambodians and the Chinese started killing millions of birds. Millions! The economic damage was unthinkable. But they did it. And in the course of a season, the threat began to fade. The bird flu was passing, the scare stories started disappearing from the columns of the press. Even the WHO became distracted by other issues. And governments all over the world suddenly decided that they had other priorities for the money they had earmarked for FluKill. Orders were cancelled. Others never materialised. Stein-Francks was all but finished, Mr MacNeil. Oh, we still had plenty of money. The trouble is, it was in all the wrong places. Mostly in a product nobody wanted to buy any more.'

Understanding dawned on MacNeil, like mist clearing on an autumn morning. 'So in the absence of a market for your drug, you decided to create one.'

Blume nodded slowly. 'That pretty much sums it up. We knew we were playing with fire, but we really did think we could control it. Produce a version of H5N1 that would spread easily amongst humans, and then produce the vaccine that would prevent them from getting it. Not, of course, before all those orders for FluKill had been fulfilled. Naturally, we knew the virus would mutate. But we figured it would almost certainly still come within the compass of the vaccine. That, I'm afraid, was where it all went wrong.'

He looked at MacNeil, and the big Scotsman saw regret in his eyes. But MacNeil knew that it wasn't regret for all those lost lives. Blume was only sorry that it 'all went wrong' for the same simple commercial reasons that had motivated him in the first place. 'Millions of people are going to die,' MacNeil said. 'Millions already have.'

Blume breathed his exasperation. 'What difference does it make? One life, a million, ten million. It's just a matter of scale.'

'You're right,' MacNeil said. 'But only because each individual life is important. And when it's you, or someone close to you, then it's personal.'

'Exactly.'

'Like losing a son.'

Blume looked at him, and for the first time his self-confidence visibly wavered. 'I'm sorry about that,' he said.

'No, you're not. You killed him. As surely as if you'd taken a gun and put a bullet in his head. As surely as you killed that little Chinese girl and stripped the flesh from her bones. Your own daughter!'

Blume blew air through contemptuous lips. 'She wasn't my daughter. Not even my adopted daughter. Her paperwork will tell you that she was adopted by Mr and Mrs Walter Smith, whoever they might be. In fact we bought her. In the international marketplace. It's amazing how cheaply people can be bought these days. Literally. And children with such disfigurement, well, they cost pennies.'

MacNeil pictured the head that Amy had fashioned from the child's skull, and wondered what miseries she had known. Discarded by her natural parents, bought and sold, smuggled across borders. God only knew what kind of treatment she had suffered at the hands of the men and women who had so ruthlessly exploited her. And then, suddenly, to have found herself living in an affluent London suburb, attending the local school, being sent on a holiday to Sprint Water. She must have thought she had died and gone to heaven. Only to be infected by a deadly flu, and when it failed to kill her, murdered by the very people she had probably come to trust.

'She was supposed to die from the flu,' Blume said, 'and be cremated with all the rest. How could any of us have predicted that she would survive it? We couldn't afford to have her around, living proof of what we'd done. Especially with that woman from the Health Protection Agency poking around.'

'You're not human,' MacNeil said. He took a step towards

him, and Blume pulled a small handgun from his coat pocket. He pointed it unsteadily at the policeman.

'That's close enough,' he said. 'There's not going to be any negotiating with you, Mr MacNeil, is there?'

MacNeil felt his own lips trembling with anger. 'No. There's not.'

'Then I'm just going to have to kill you.'

'Aye, I guess you are.' A movement in his peripheral vision made him glance to his right as the tiny figure of Dr Castelli stepped determinedly out from behind the statue and swung the butt-end of her rifle at Blume's head. It caught him a bruising blow just above the temple and sent him sprawling to the ground. His gun rattled away across the cobblestones.

'You despicable little shit!' she said. 'You killed all these people for money! I can't believe you did that. You . . . you sent that child amongst us, to infect us with your abomination, like some poor little angel of death. You . . . you . . .' She had no more words to express her anger, and instead she wrestled the rifle to her shoulder and fought to point it clumsily at Blume. He dragged himself up on to one elbow and raised a hand as if that might protect him from the bullet. 'No, don't,' he shouted.

But MacNeil stepped in and pushed the barrel of the rifle

up in the air and took it away from her. 'Don't you want to kill him?' Dr Castelli raged. It was hard to imagine such anger and indignation seething within such a small frame. 'He killed your boy.'

But MacNeil just shook his head. 'I don't want revenge,' he said. 'I want justice. I want him to face the consequences of his actions. I want him to face a jury of his peers, the verdict of humanity. I want him to spend the rest of his life rotting in a prison somewhere, with every single hour of every single day to reflect on his lack of it.'

Dr Castelli sucked in a deep breath and pulled a face. 'I couldn't get the goddamned thing to fire anyway.'

MacNeil said, 'It helps if you take off the safety.'

A single shot rang out, and MacNeil heard Dr Castelli gasp. He whipped around to see Blume still on the ground. But he had retrieved his gun and fired it. Now he turned it towards MacNeil and pulled the trigger again. Nothing happened. He tried once more. Still nothing. He threw it away and staggered to his feet and began sprinting towards the wheel.

Dr Castelli fell back against the statue and sat down heavily. Her right hand was flung across the left side of her chest, and there was blood oozing through her fingers. 'I'm shot,' she said, shocked that it should have happened so simply.

MacNeil knelt down beside her. 'What can I do?'

'Go after him.'

'I can't leave you like this.'

'It missed my heart or I'd be dead,' she said. 'And I'm still breathing, so I figure it missed my lung, too. Go!'

MacNeil did not need a further invitation. He turned and ran after Blume. After all, he still had Amy. And presumably she wasn't up there in that capsule on her own.

But as he approached the wheel he realised he'd lost sight of Blume. He ran up the ramp to the control room. It was empty. And then the clatter of feet on metal drew his eyes up to the twin spiral staircases that flanked the huge motor on the north-east side of the Eye. Blume was running up the left-hand spiral, up towards the outer rim of the wheel, forced to take small, awkward steps. MacNeil went after him. But by the time he was on the spiral itself, Blume had already transferred to the circular ladder which ran around the outside contour of the wheel. MacNeil stared up at him incredulously. The man was insane. Evidently he thought he could climb all the way up to the top of the wheel to get to the pod where Amy was being held. MacNeil was left with no choice but to go after him, whether he liked it or not.

At the top of the spiral he looked back down and saw Dr Castelli on the ramp below. She was supporting herself on the rail and gazing up at him. 'See if you can start this thing!' he shouted, and he turned and swung himself on to the inside curve of the ladder. He tipped his head back and looked up. Blume was eighty feet or more above him, scrambling from rung to rung like a man possessed. MacNeil started to climb, and his hands stung from the burns beneath his bandages.

He knew there was no point in trying to take it too fast. He had to go steady, one rung at a time, one step after another. Don't look down. And as soon as the thought entered his head, he looked down. He seemed to have come an incredibly long way in a very short time. His heart filled his chest so that he thought he was going to choke. He missed his footing and almost fell. His fear was debilitating. Look up, he told himself. And as he did, he saw Blume transfer from the inside of the ladder to the outside, so that he would be above it as it curved around the top of the wheel. MacNeil pressed on.

The wind was tugging fiercely now at his donkey jacket, whistling amongst the spokes all around him. For all the pain that burned them, he felt his hands start to go numb with the cold. The ladder was beginning to tip him backwards. Time to transfer. He swung around and caught an outside rung and fumbled for a foothold with his ungainly Doc Martens. He was so scared there was hardly any strength left in his arms. And for several moments he simply clung to the very outside edge of the wheel, the city canted at an odd angle below him. He could see the four chimneys belching out their human waste at the old Battersea Power Station. *I Think, Therefore I Can. Welcome to the Ideas Generation.* It seemed so long ago that he had driven past those hoardings in search of a man called Kazinski.

Away to his left, beyond St. Thomas' Hospital, was the building site where it had all begun. This time yesterday morning he had been dreaming about playing truant from work, asleep in a single bed in Islington, too short for his six-foot-four frame. This time yesterday morning, Sean had still been alive. How easy it would be just to let go. Just to drift away into the night, and put an end to all this. How much easier life would be in death. It was a seductive notion. It caressed him, tempted him. Until he thought of Amy.

He gritted his teeth and started to climb again, up and up, following the outer curve of the wheel as it arced towards its apex. By now, he was crouched on top of it, holding on for dear life as the wind did its best to yank him free. He looked up and saw the topmost pod almost directly above him. He could see two figures moving about inside, and the merest whisper of a shadow somewhere at its centre.

It might have been Amy, but he wasn't sure. What he was sure of was that Blume was safely inside, and that he was out here, horribly exposed to the night, four hundred feet above the icy cold waters of the Thames. Another few rungs, and he was directly beneath the pod, where they couldn't see him. He clung on to the tubular superstructure and craned to see a way up. The doors of the pod split in two and slid out to either side. He could swing himself up on the left-hand door and get on to the narrow ledge they used for boarding and disembarking.

He crouched there in the shadow of the capsule, buffeted by the wind, eyes closed, summoning the courage. If he failed, then he failed. He thought of the inscription on the statue below. *They went because their open eyes could see no other way.* He opened his eyes. It was time to go.

At almost the same moment that he swung himself up to grab the pneumatic bar that controlled the door, the whole wheel juddered and began to move. Dr Castelli had figured out the controls. But it was enough to force a misjudgement, and MacNeil missed the bar. His bandaged hand grasped fresh air and he felt himself tipping impossibly backwards. The city tilted below him and he saw the river turn through ninety degrees.

His elbows struck the boarding platform, and he found

himself hanging from it, his face at floor level, looking into the pod. All the time slipping, losing his grip, legs kicking the air beneath him, knowing he was going to fall.

He barely heard Amy screaming.

III.

Pinkie had been astonished to see Mr Smith clambering across the top of the wheel and reaching out for a hand up into the pod. He had always known that Mr Smith was a man possessed, by who knew what demons, but this seemed like an extraordinary feat, even for him.

And then MacNeil had appeared, and they had all seen him. His jacket billowing out in the wind, his upturned face pale and frightened. He had seemed very fragile, somehow, for such a big, strong man.

But for Pinkie none of it mattered any more. Job done. It was just about time for him to check out. He felt weak and faint, slightly delirious. And he was amazed to see MacNeil's big frame suddenly swing across the opening to the pod, and then fall away, only to clatter on to the little ledge outside, hands fighting for something to grasp, and failing to find it.

He heard Mr Smith shout his derision and saw him step forward to the door. He kicked MacNeil in the face and then stood on his bandaged hands. Pinkie looked at those hands, ragged bandages wrapped around painful burns. And it came to him for the first time that it had been MacNeil who had come charging through the flames to drag Pinkie from the burning car.

'Don't do that,' he told Mr Smith. But the only sound that came was some whispered, strangulated breath. 'It's not fair,' he said. But Mr Smith wasn't listening. 'Stop!' he roared. A fearsome gurgle. Mr Smith heard that alright. He turned as Pinkie raised his SA80 rifle.

'Pinkie, what are you doing?'

The remaining bullets in the magazine propelled Mr Smith right out of the door, and he soared like one of his own angels of death into the night.

MacNeil was going. He couldn't hold on any longer. Pinkie heard Amy's sobs of frustration and impotence. Such a shame, he thought. He dropped the rifle and staggered to the door. He met MacNeil's eye. He saw his fear. And he felt his own life slipping away. He dropped to his knees. 'I'm sorry,' he whispered, and meant it. But knew that nobody would ever hear him.

MacNeil was gone when Pinkie caught him. And Pinkie

held him now, his life literally in Pinkie's hands. Perhaps they should go together. Or would a life saved by this dead man's hand give his own life, finally, the meaning it had always lacked?

MacNeil closed his eyes. He didn't understand any of this. But there were no questions he could think of that were worth asking when you were going to die. He knew this was the man he had pulled from the burning car on Lambeth Bridge. And he had no reason to be grateful to MacNeil, condemned as he had been to what must have been several hours of living hell. He hung there at the end of an arm of charred and weeping flesh, and as he looked into the man's eyes, it was like staring into the abyss. A huge void, empty of anything. Another hand grabbed his collar and pulled. A superhuman effort. Legs braced against each edge of the door. A deep rasping sigh issuing from burned-out lungs. MacNeil got a handhold on the edge of the door, and then a knee on the ledge, and he fell inside, sprawling on the floor, utterly spent.

He rolled over to look up at his saviour. But there was no one there. He had gone, somewhere into the abyss that was his own soul.

MacNeil turned and saw poor Amy, tears streaming down

her face, and managed to pull himself up on to legs like jelly. He slumped beside her on the bench and took her in his arms.

In the distance, the first glimmer of light in the winter sky reflected all the way upriver from the east, and MacNeil felt the first tickle at the back of his nose, and the first roughness at the back of his throat.

End

ACKNOWLEDGEMENTS

I would like to offer my grateful thanks to all those who gave so generously of their time and expertise during my researches for *Lockdown*. In particular, I'd like to express my gratitude to pathologist Steven C. Campman, MD, Medical Examiner, San Diego, California; Professor Joe Cummins, Emeritus of Genetics, University of Western Ontario; Dr A.W. (Freddy) Martin (CRFP), Past President of the British Association of Forensic Odontologists; Detective Sergeant George Murray, Northern Constabulary; Graham and Fiona Kane for letting me plagiarise their home; and Alison Campbell Jensen for her cinnamon and cloves.